ONDELLE OF GRIOTH

Danika Dinsmore

D0047997

Hydra House ❖ Seattle, Washington

Library of Congress Cataloging-in-Publication Data

Dinsmore, Danika.
  Ondelle of Grioth / by Danika Dinsmore.
    pages cm. -- (Faerie tales of the White Forest ; book 3)
  ISBN 978-0-9890828-3-9
  I. Title.
  PZ7.D619On 2014
  [Fic]--dc23
                                    2014001035

ISBN: 978-0-9890828-3-9

First printing.

Cover art by Julie Fain
www.juliefain.com

Illustrations by Alison Woodward
alisonannwoodward.blogspot.com

Cover design by Christian Fink-Jensen
finkjensen.com

Interior design by Tod McCoy
www.todmccoy.com

Copyediting by Shannon Page

Published by:
Hydra House
1122 E Pike St. #1451
Seattle, WA 98122
www.hydrahousebooks.com

Printed through CreateSpace.

To all the Connies, in all the CoZi cafes,
who feed the hungry writers.

I would also like to thank my focus group readers
for their assistance in getting this story into shape:
Kate Fink-Jensen, Kelly and Karyn Hoskins, Natalie
Smith, and Jeremy Zimmerman.

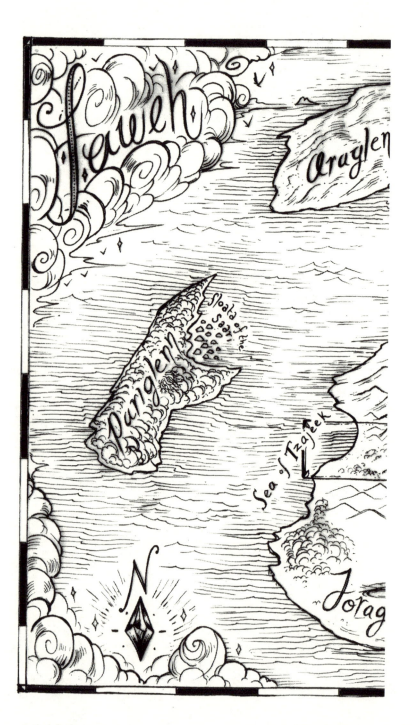

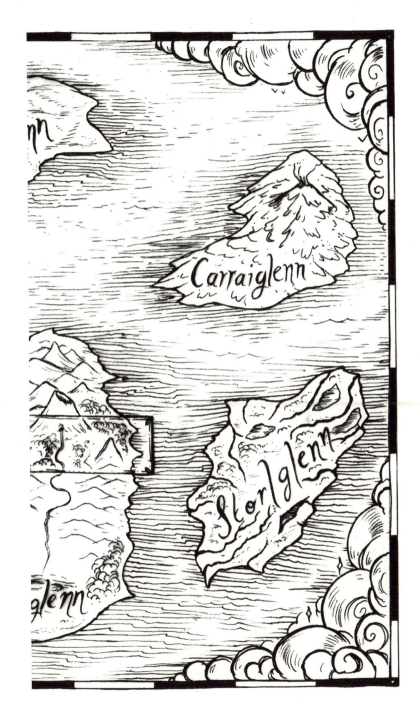

Dead Mountain

To Pariglenn

THE Standing Stones

White Forest

Forever Beach

Sea of Tzajeek

The Dark Fo[rest]

North Central Foraglenn

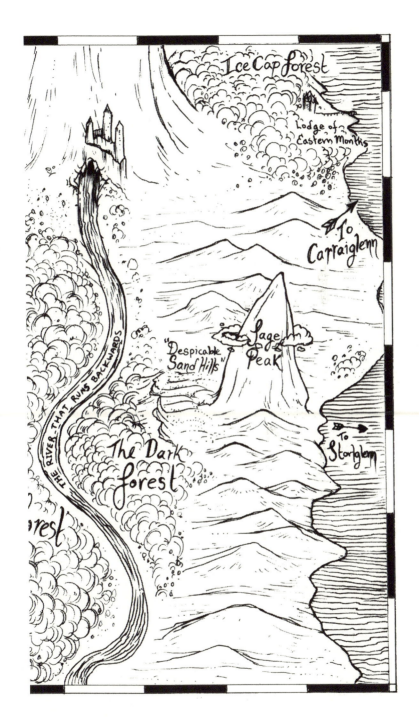

Chapter One

Ondelle and Hrathgar poked through the brush, giggling while they pulled branches away to spy on Cam, a sun-kissed and muscular Air Faerie Perimeter Guard. Cam stood before The Shift as the rocky river crumbled over itself in an infinite loop around the White Forest. He picked up a stick and tossed it into the protective field, which rippled with the impact before the stick continued out the other side. He listened for a moment, then nodded to no one, and leapt into the air to finish his rounds.

When he was a speck in the distance, Ondelle pulled herself out of the dense foliage and gazed after him. As she wiped herself off, Hrathgar fluttered out of the bush toward The Shift. At the final tree before the dirt moat began, she paused to pluck a broodnut from its branches.

"What are you doing?" asked Ondelle, red wings quivering.

Hrathgar didn't answer, only pulled her arm back and catapulted the nut into The Shift. It skipped once on a rock before flipping through the field.

"Come on, Gar." Ondelle flitted over to her friend, who hovered in the air as she stared after the nut. "We should get back. Auntie Parmaline will wonder where we've gotten off to."

"One of these days . . ." Hrathgar murmured toward the Dark Forest, then turned to face Ondelle, tears stippling the corners of her green eyes. "I'm going through that field."

Before Ondelle could respond, another faerie streamed out of the brush toward them.

"Hrathgar, no!" she cried. It was young Fernatta of Gyllenhale. The fresh Earth Elder glyphs on her laurel wings appeared wet in the warm sunlight.

"Oh, for the Dragon, Ferna," scolded Hrathgar, dropping to the ground and placing her hands on her hips. "What are you doing out this far on your own?"

"I'm not on my own," Fernatta pointed out, stepping past the edge of the forest as Hrathgar slowly drifted away, riding along on the immense rocky river. "I followed the two of you."

"That was unwise," said Ondelle from above them.

Hrathgar and Fernatta regarded each other and then burst out laughing.

"That was unwise," Hrathgar repeated, imitating Ondelle's serious tone. She leapt back up into the air. "You're not even an Apprentice yet and you sound just like Earth Elder Grish Ba."

"You said you were going to leave the forest!" said Fernatta. "You mustn't! There are horrible beasts out there just waiting to rip off your wings."

"Fernatta's right," said Ondelle. "It's unthinkable." She turned to escort the younger faerie back into the forest as Hrathgar stewed over The Shift.

"Do you know what's unthinkable?" asked Hrathgar, catching up with Ondelle and grabbing her arm. "That I won't be an Apprentice for ages. That I'll be wasting my time collecting eggshells for Auntie Parmaline's festival masks. That

I'll have one wing in the ethers by the time I'm an Elder."

"You don't know that," said Ondelle.

"You were marked first," Hrathgar pointed out. "You'll be the next Fire Apprentice even though we were born only a few seasons apart."

"Just because I was born in Grioth doesn't mean I'll apprentice with a Fire Elder," Ondelle responded. "I could just as easily become an Air Apprentice."

"Fozk of Fhorsa is already marked for Air Eldership, Ondelle," said Hrathgar, anger rising in her voice. "You know that perfectly well."

She let go of Ondelle's arm and looked intently into her black moon eyes. "And let's just say that you live a long and healthy life—which I wish for you because you're my friend—but as I do, I'm wishing for my own pointless existence."

"Unless Ondelle becomes High Priestess," Fernatta interjected. "Then you would take her place as Fire Elder on the council."

"I would never presume such a thing," said Ondelle.

"Exactly," said Hrathgar, "so we must assume you will remain an Elder, which means I will not become an Elder until you disperse."

"And you can't wait that long?" Ondelle half-heartedly teased.

"It's not that." Hrathgar twisted in the air to face the Dark Forest. "I'm afraid that a part of me will always hope something bad happens to you. I don't want to live being pulled in two directions like that, always fighting off some resentment." She gestured across The Shift. "I'd rather take my chances out there. At least I could have my own adventure."

Tears sprung to Hrathgar's eyes once more and Ondelle wrapped an arm around her friend. As she searched herself for words of comfort, the clouds above The Shift rippled, then drifted open. She dropped her arm and stared up at them.

"What's wrong?" asked Fernatta, turning to glance at the sky.

"Ondelle?" asked Hrathgar. "Are you all right?"

Overhead, a flock of bright flecks spun through the opening in the clouds like tiny luminescent birds. Bewildered, Ondelle pointed toward the strange, sparkling swarm.

"What are those?" she asked.

"What are what?" Hrathgar squinted up at the clouds.

"You can't see them?"

"No, do you see anything, Ferna?"

Fernatta shook her head and shrugged.

"They're . . . so beautiful . . . and . . . " Ondelle felt a tug from somewhere deep within her heart, and she shivered as the flecks twisted into a funnel, spinning faster and faster until, all at once, they bolted into the trees.

"Freena!" Brigitta cried out and leapt to her feet.

Around her, Air Faeries paused in their relay practice and hovered over the flying fields, staring at her poised on the edge of the plateau.

"Uh," Jarlath stood up next to her, "Brigitta?"

She spun around to face him, taking a moment to recall where she was. The Air Faeries remained curious until a momentary glare from Jarlath sent them back to their practice relays.

He stepped closer to Brigitta so as not to be heard. "Another vision?" he whispered.

Brigitta tried to shake the images away, but they were now a part of her, as if she had lived those moments herself. It was always the same.

"They're not visions, Jarlath," she snapped back, then collected her emotions as she reminded herself she was speaking to one of the few faeries she truly trusted. "They're memories. Ondelle's memories. And they're getting worse."

"Or getting better," Jarlath offered, trying to make light of the situation.

Brigitta groaned and turned back to watch the Air Faeries flying in and out of an intricate loop system made from connected tree branches. Higher up, three faeries were experimenting with a wind-winder, a new contraption created by an Air Faerie Inventor, a large bubble-shaped net that could hold pockets of conjured air.

The memories, as Brigitta insisted they be called, had started as vague whispers. Snippets of waking dreams. Brief lapses ending in dull headaches Auntie Ferna had treated with warm ceunias compresses and lyllium tea.

Over time, the headaches had subsided, but the memories had grown sharper and more elaborate.

"Auntie Ferna," Brigitta murmured.

"You need to see your Auntie?" asked Jarlath.

"No." Brigitta stared into his starry eyes. "The memory was of Ondelle with Auntie Ferna and Hrathgar. Before she left the forest." She dropped her voice to a whisper. "And something else."

"You cried out," said Jarlath. "What's Freena?"

"Not what," said Brigitta. "Who. Freena was High Priestess a long time ago. When she dispersed, Grish Ba became High Priest." She paused, sorting through her new knowledge. "But why would Ondelle feel so intensely for Freena? She was too young to have mentored with her. She wasn't even an Apprentice yet. She mentored with Fire Elder Oka Kan . . ."

"You've lost me," said Jarlath, easing her back down to the rock she had been sitting on before her outburst.

"The lineage doesn't matter," said Brigitta, "but what I saw, I mean, what I *remembered* was seeing the Ethereal energy coming to disperse Freena's spirit." She grabbed onto Jarlath's arm. "Ondelle saw the Ethereal energy, but Hrathgar and Auntie Ferna couldn't. She saw the energy and knew it had come for Freena's spirit."

Jarlath glanced down to where Brigitta gripped his bicep, and a slight pink bloomed on his cheeks. His muscle tensed and warmed beneath her fingers. She pulled her hand away and gestured to the air fields.

"We should finish up here."

"Are you sure?" asked Jarlath, sitting down beside her.

"The sooner the better," she said. "They don't like me being here."

She gestured for Jarlath to continue his observations. He had the task of making recommendations to the Elders and the Master of the Perimeter Guard, having served on Mabbe's guard for several seasons, as well as having first-hand knowledge of what went on in the outside world. For the first time in the history of the White Forest, the Elders were stepping up their security.

All around them the Air Faeries completed their relays, flying up and over and through the obstacle course of tall grasses, formed branches, and sculpted rocks, shooting nervous glances at Brigitta and Jarlath as they observed their movements. Blown off course, the wind-winder had climbed higher into the air where the three Air Faeries struggled to keep the net in its optimum globe shape. An older Air Faerie buzzed up to help them, hands slightly apart, palms facing each other, brewing up thick patches of air.

"What use is that thing if it takes four faeries to control it?" Jarlath laughed and crossed his arms.

"Poppa's Inventor friend says it's meant to help weaker flyers go higher," responded Brigitta skeptically. She wondered about the maximum height one could travel within it. Could a faerie drift through the clouds? Disappear from sight?

A part of Brigitta dearly wanted to escape from view and hide among the clouds, yet another part of her yearned to embrace the Air Faeries as her new kin. Ever since Ondelle had gifted her with her Air element, there was something inside Brigitta longing to express itself. That part wanted to join in the relays, plummet from the trees, listen to her ancestors on the wind. But the Elders had postponed her Air element lessons "until further notice," and none of the Air Faeries showed any interest in helping her develop her new talents because they were afraid of her.

At least that was her assumption. It's not like she had empathed them for this information. She wouldn't even practice mind-misting around anyone anymore. She didn't want to do anything that would make her seem suspicious. It was bad enough that her body mysteriously housed the Air energy of a dead High Priestess, continually reminding them of their loss. What had saved her in the Valley of

Noe, she now tucked back as much as possible. But it took so much effort to restrain it that it exhausted Brigitta, and she found herself crawling into bed each night.

She rubbed at her temples as she contemplated the group of candidates before them. Jarlath stood next to her, scrunching up his mouth and drumming on the end of his chin with his fingers.

"What do you think?" she asked him. "Have you decided?"

"Yeah." He nodded. "I've got about a dozen candidates."

He watched the relays for another moonsbreath and then snapped his fingers in front of Brigitta's face. "Race you back to the Center Realm!"

He sprung up from the Flying Field plateau before she could even answer and hovered in the air wearing a mischievous grin. She managed a laugh and flew after him, feeling the stares of the Air Faeries behind them.

"Please, please!" called High Priest Fozk into the crowded chamber. "If you cannot find a seat, just try to get comfortable."

"These meetings are drawing more and more faeries each time," said Water Elder Dervia, tapping her fingers against the armrest of her Elder chair, which had been pushed back to make room for everyone.

At the carved wooden table sat twelve Village-Nest Caretakers, including Orl Featherkind from Tiragarrow. Four more Caretakers sat on wooden chests lining the wall. Reykia of Rivenbow, the tall Master of the Air Faerie Perimeter Guards, stood on one side of the door with her bold purple wings at attention, as if ready to act at a moment's notice. Gaowen of Thachreek, the Guard who had caught the whisper light Brigitta and Ondelle brought to the Valley of Noe, stood on the other. He was Reykia's Lead Guard.

The First Apprentices were forced to sit on the ground, and they grumbled as they lowered themselves onto the woven mats that the Wisings—Kiera, Lalam, and Bastian, the newest Wising—brought in for them. Seated on the floor next to Dervia's chair, Brigitta was the only Second Apprentice present, and Jarlath, the only White Forest outsider among them, stood behind her protectively. She leaned into his legs for support, moral and otherwise, exhausted from digesting Ondelle's memory that morning and aching from holding back her Air energy all day. She was not in the mood for this gathering of anxious faeries.

"The lack of accommodation in this room should indicate that what we are doing is counter to the Ancients' intentions," muttered Adaire.

"Or," Fozk looked sternly at her, "that the Ancients did not prepare us for all possibilities."

The room quickly hushed. If it had not been High Priest Fozk speaking, Brigitta thought someone would have surely called him out on such blasphemy.

"Now that I have your attention," said Fozk, sitting down in his chair, "Elder Adaire?" He gestured to the sturdy Earth Faerie on his left.

Elder Adaire stood and addressed the Village-Nest Caretakers. "Thank you all for being here in these questionable times. As you may have heard, we are assigning Air Faerie Guards to each village-nest."

A collective grumbling issued from the assembled faeries.

"As there are not enough faeries destiny-marked for such a task," continued Adaire, raising her voice over their murmurs, "we have taken volunteers, who have been participating in relays for our training team: Reykia, Gaowen, and Jarlath of Noe—"

"Pardon, Elder Adaire," spoke Bailen, Caretaker of Ithcommon, "but isn't he a bit young?"

Brigitta felt Jarlath's body stiffen behind her, poised to defend himself, and she bristled as well.

"And not even from the White Forest," added Plinth of Erriondower, avoiding Jarlath's eyes. "How can—"

Adaire put her hand up to interrupt Plinth before Jarlath, or Brigitta, could interject. "If any of you have more experience dealing with the threats of the outside world, you are welcome to replace him," she said, scanning the room for any takers.

"What outside threats?" asked Bailen. He turned to the Air Faerie Perimeter Guards at the door. "Has something entered the forest again? What is it? What have you seen?"

The faeries buzzed excitedly until Fozk could quiet them again. He nodded to Reykia.

"Nothing has entered the forest that we know of," she said carefully, "but the beasts do seem to be braving The Shift more often."

"And it's only a matter of time before Croilus makes himself known," added Jarlath.

"You don't know that," countered Plinth. "You don't even know if he's alive, let alone what his intensions are. You've said so yourself."

"My kin," Fozk's soothing voice encircled the room, "we are merely taking precautions while we contemplate our long-term objectives."

"Long-term objectives?" piped up Violetta, Caretaker of Dmvyle. "Like what to do with all the destinyless children? We'll have a nursery full in Dmvyle before long."

Several other Caretakers nodded in response.

"Just make them all Perimeter Guards," grumbled Bailen.

"There'll be nothing to guard if the Hourglass isn't turned," said Plinth. He turned to address Fozk. "The scepter needs to be taken to the Eternal Dragon."

"If we haven't lost touch with It as well," added Caretaker Violetta softly.

All of the faeries exploded in new conversation until Fozk stood, clapped his hands twice, and the cacophony of sound was swept up in a blanket of wind and hung above them, muffling the din.

"How do you expect me to take such a journey if I cannot rely on you to manage yourselves while I'm away?" he asked, his voice on edge.

As Fozk waited for the faeries to settle down, Brigitta examined his face. In the season she had been home from her journey to Noe, his skin had paled, his hair thinned, and deep circles now haunted his eyes. She did not envy High Priest Fozk's position, although she had trouble sympathizing with him since he had disallowed her to resume her lessons. Plus, as much as she hated to admit it, she agreed with Plinth. The Eternal Dragon was their connection to Blue Spell, which was required to turn the Hourglass and renew the protective field around their forest.

He clapped his hands again, the blanket of air dropped, and the voices dissipated in the room.

"Now," he continued, sitting back down and motioning to Adaire.

"If you have questions," she said, "please raise your hand and I'll—"

Nine Caretaker hands, two First Apprentice hands, and Reykia's hand all shot into the air. Adaire pointed to Orl Featherkind, whose dark russet hair was streaked with more gray than Brigitta remembered, and looked as if it had not been combed in many moons.

"What if something *does* get into the forest?" he asked, yellow eyes darting to each Elder's face. "What then?"

"That is why we have Jarlath working with the perimeter team," answered Adaire. "He can prepare us for that event. As can Brigitta . . . when she is ready." The Elder glanced quickly in Brigitta's direction.

"I'm ready now!" she burst out, and then cringed as an assortment of unnerved faces turned to stare at her. Only Earth Wising Lalam of Ithcommon, with his shaggy brown hair and ruddy boyish cheeks, cast a smile of encouragement her way.

"Yes, Reykia?" asked Adaire, redirecting everyone's attention.

Reykia pulled down her hand. "What about Gola?"

"What do you mean what about Gola?" shot Brigitta again before she could stop herself.

"Please, Brigitta," said Water Elder Dervia, placing a hand on her shoulder.

"Well," continued Reykia, "how do we know we can trust her? She's from the outside, and she knows Dark Forest magic."

"I can vouch for Gola's intentions," put in Jarlath. "I've been working closely with her since I arrived."

"She's quite unsocial," said Caretaker Grindel of Grioth. "She never attends Fire Realm festivities and barely visits the marketplace any more." He gestured to Jarlath. "She sends him or that Minq beast instead."

The rest of the Fire Faerie Caretakers nodded their heads.

"That's because she's an old Drutan," explained Brigitta. "She's practically rooted to the earth."

Grindel addressed Fire Elder Hammus. "You're not going to let her root in the Fire Realm, are you? Who knows what effect that will have on our forest."

"Let's save that for a later discussion," replied Hammus. "Right now we need to—"

Brigitta fluttered to her feet. "For a later discussion?!"

"Sit down, Apprentice Brigitta," said Adaire. "We need to stay focused."

Brigitta turned to Grindel, ignoring Elder Adaire's request. "How can you even say such a thing!" She turned the rest of the faeries. "There wouldn't even be a Fire Realm, let alone a White Forest, if it weren't for Gola!"

"Brigitta, I will not ask again," warned Adaire, hands on hips and gray hair springing loose from the wiry bun on her head.

Jarlath reached for Brigitta's arm, but she shook him off, overcome by her anger and frustration. "Gola's place in this forest would never have been questioned by Ondelle!"

"That is enough," said Water Elder Dervia, rising to meet her. "You cannot presume what our departed High Priestess would say or do at a time like this."

"Yes, I can!" cried Brigitta, fatigue overtaking all caution. Tears sprung to her eyes without warning.

"I can!" she cried again. "I can, I can. I carry her here." Brigitta pounded on her chest. She burst into sobs and Dervia wrapped her arms around her, pulling her into her bosom.

As Brigitta wept, she relinquished the insufferable hold she had on her Air energy, and it radiated forth, whipping the hair and tunics of every faerie in the room.

It grew frighteningly still; the only sound was Fozk's deep inhale before he spoke.

"Second Apprentice Brigitta," he said, his own typically steady voice wavering as he rose, "please follow me into the corridor."

Dervia handed a teary Brigitta off to Wising Lalam, who had appeared with an herbal compress, which he applied to the back of her neck. Jarlath stepped forth to assist him, but Dervia shook her head.

Before she knew it, Brigitta was alone in the cool and quiet corridor. The comforting compress was still at her neck, but Lalam had slipped back into the room, quiet as a shadowfly, before she could thank him.

"Ondelle was a wise leader," Fozk said gently from behind her.

She turned to catch his watery eyes of sky as he approached.

"We all miss her dearly," he continued, folding his hands together, "but she may have done a disservice to you, and for that, I am truly sorry."

He took a long, steadying breath and Brigitta found herself taking a breath and exhaling along with him. "I believe that your experience in Noe and this transference of energy have distressed you beyond our original assessment."

Brigitta simply sniffed and nodded, too upset to speak.

"It is with deep regret," said Fozk, looking very regretful indeed, "and due to no wrongdoing on your behalf, that I must relieve you of all Apprentice and Center Realm duties for the time being."

"But—"

He placed a hand on her shoulder. "You will return to Tiragarrow until further notice."

Chapter Two

Ondelle sucked at her thumb as she scooted further into the cupboard. It was her favorite place to hide. It smelled of earth and wood. Wood from her Momma's leftover carvings. Half-done, or half-undone, depending upon how one looked at it. Ondelle could sense the livingness of the uncarved wood. The wanting of it to be something new to the world. She wished she knew how to carve. Perhaps then, she could make her Momma happy.

She could hear voices in the gathering room. Her Poppa's hushed and calming. Her Momma's strained, tired, afraid.

"You weren't there, Sade," her Momma said, all color dropping from her words.

"Yes, Runida," he said, soothing as ever, "I was lying right next to you."

"Asleep."

Ondelle's Poppa sighed and then she could sense him pacing the room. Could picture the way he scrunched his thin, dark eyebrows in concern. "Perhaps if you started carving again? We've had many requests for—"

"It won't help," said Runida.

"You could try," Sade responded. "Just try for my sake. For our sake. It will give you something to occupy yourself while I'm away."

"Please don't leave me alone with her."

"I'll only be gone for a few suns, five at most. Our team must finish the Moonsrise Amphitheater before the Ithcommon faeries lose their patience."

Runida was quiet as the rocking chair creaked beneath her.

"Others are talking," said Sade. "You're making them nervous."

"They should be nervous."

"Runida . . ."

The creaking chair halted. "What reason is there for her to have both Air and Fire?"

"It's not impossible," said Sade. "It's a wonder, yes, but not impossible. We must have Air ancestors somewhere along—"

"She's not mine."

"She is our child!" Sade yelled, and Ondelle's foot slipped, startled by her Poppa's sudden outburst, and knocked over a block of wood with a dull thud.

A moment later and the cupboard door opened. Light streamed in and Ondelle blinked. Her Poppa didn't look angry, as she had expected; he looked very sad as he pushed aside the blocks of uncarved wood and reached in for his daughter. He pulled her out and looked deep into her eyes with his own large, black ones. He always said she had his eyes, and that should mean something.

He pulled her to him and she dropped her chin onto his shoulder, absorbing the warmth of him. As he lifted her up, she could see her Momma in her worn wooden rocking chair, staring into the fire. She never looked at Ondelle anymore. She never spoke to Ondelle anymore. She never left the cottage.

Brigitta sobbed in Gola's barky arms. Ondelle's memory had come upon her so suddenly and painfully that she had dropped to the ground as soon as she had reached the old Drutan's door. She had awoken in Gola's bed and quickly related everything that had happened that day, relieved to tell someone who understood.

"They don't believe me about Ondelle's memories," murmured Brigitta as Gola rocked her back and forth.

The sorrow she felt had as much to do with her dismissal from the Center Realm as it had to do with the memory of Ondelle's mother. That feeling of rejection had settled in Brigitta, and Ondelle's heartbreak had melded with her own. So pervasive was it that she was having trouble remembering that her own mother loved her very much.

She shifted in Gola's lap as she tried to conjure images of her mother's kindly face. Gola's body wasn't the most comfortable place to lay oneself, but at the moment, Brigitta didn't care. She had done nothing wrong; Fozk had said so himself.

"Several faeries at the gathering even questioned your right to be here," she said.

Gola sat quietly for a moment as she stroked Brigitta's hair. "It is not my forest; it is not my place to disagree."

Brigitta pulled back in surprise to gaze at the blind tree woman. "But that's so unfair! You helped save our forest. And, and . . . you're old! You wouldn't survive being thrown back into the Dark Forest."

Gola's familiar throaty chuckle tickled the air, and her only remaining pair of winged Eyes gazed at Brigitta from their perch on the back of her chair. "My child, I am not going to survive anywhere for much longer. Not even in the protected realm."

She eased Brigitta off her lap and onto the floor, stood and stretched, and then shuffled to her small kitchen to fetch Brigitta a cup of tingermint tea. The Eyes reluctantly leapt from the chair and puttered after her.

"If I'm quick about it," Gola said as she ladled the brew into a mug, "maybe I can root myself in your forest before they drive me away."

"How can you even joke like that?"

The old Drutan returned, handed the mug to Brigitta, and settled back into her chair, Eyes dropping down onto her shoulder and tucking in their leathery wings. She hefted her feet onto the worn pillows beneath her, the ones she used to keep herself from rooting right there in her cottage.

"So, the memories have grown stronger," she said.

Brigitta held the warm mug between her hands and studied the thick little fibers growing from the bottoms of Gola's feet. A few of them quivered and twisted in the air, as if searching for a place to bury themselves.

"It's not little jolts of images and emotions any longer," she said, looking away from the growing tendrils and staring down into her drink. "I see more detail now. And when I look out onto the world from her eyes, I feel just as she felt." She traced the rim of her mug with a finger, then dipped it into her tea. She pulled it out and tasted it: a perfect combination of warmth and mint, with just a hint of earthiness. Gola had done it; she had mastered a faultless brew.

"Ondelle could sense things others couldn't," Brigitta continued. "Even when she was young. It made her different and lonely, and now I carry her loneliness inside of me."

"And it's too much of a burden in addition to your own?"

"Maybe. I don't know . . . I'm just wondering why she saw these things? Was it her deodyte nature? Am I going to start seeing things, too?"

"I imagine it is more about the original owner of the energies than the dual nature of them."

"Original owner?" Brigitta looked up from her cup. "What are you talking about?"

"Where do you believe the elemental energies originally came from?" asked Gola.

"Gifted by the Ancients," Brigitta recited dutifully.

"Yes, gifted by the Ancients," agreed Gola, "from their own energies. The Ancients were bound by all four of your elements, plus the fifth element, which bound them to the ethers."

Brigitta stared at Gola, incredulous. "You mean our elements, the elements of all the White Forest faeries, were originally bound to the Ancients themselves?"

"I do."

"Save for Ether, they divided their own elemental energies up among us, and we've been carrying them over and over through generations?"

"Yes."

A little storm of water and air brewed in Brigitta's veins. It grew until her heart and head pounded with it. "Why do you always do that!" she exclaimed, slamming her mug of tea down on the floor, steamy liquid sloshing over the side. "No wonder the other faeries don't trust you. You hold onto information about us, keep it a secret until . . . until . . . you decide when it's right for us to know!"

"It is not a decision I make," said Gola. "It is information that surfaces when the time for the question to be answered arrives."

"Hagspit!" Brigitta swore as she stood, wings flung wide.

"I have told you before," said Gola, her own voice on edge, "it is not my place—"

"You know things that could help me understand what's happening to me!" Brigitta's voice echoed through the small tree-home. "You know things that could help save our forest! And you're just going to hold onto it all until I ask the exact right questions at the exact right time?"

Brigitta glared down at Gola, breath heavy. The Drutan's mouth grew stern. Her barky eyebrows knit and the winged Eyes imitated her expression from her shoulder. "Are you quite finished with your tantrum?" she asked.

"Our forest is in danger and you don't care!" Brigitta continued and kicked her cup across the floor, splattering the tea about the room. "You could help yourself and help us, and you don't care!"

"Are you now presuming to know what I feel?"

"Maybe all your secrets are what drove Hrathgar mad!" spat Brigitta, immediately wishing she could withdraw her comment. She had gone too far. The air grew thick around her accusation.

"I am beginning to think High Priest Fozk's decision was a wise one," Gola said slowly. "At least until you can sort through your emotions."

Furious, Brigitta tore from Gola's tree-home without looking back. She sped toward Tiragarrow, paying no attention to the hard smacks of branches against her skin and wings. She could not believe how Gola picked and chose the knowledge she shared, while Brigitta struggled and their forest sat on the brink of danger. She had trusted Gola with all of her own secrets. How could the old Drutan she loved so dearly not return that trust?

Since Brigitta had been cast out of the Center Realm, and she wasn't in the mood to visit with any of her Noe friends, she was forced to return to her family's cottage for the night. She dreaded having to explain to them what had happened, though the news had probably spread to her village-nest already, since Orl Featherkind, Tiragarrow's Caretaker, had been at the gathering when she was banished.

Not banished, Brigitta reminded herself, *relieved of duty until you are sufficiently recovered.*

She ignored the furtive looks that followed her as she criss-crossed through Tiragarrow and landed on her parents' porch. As soon as she had done so, the door opened and Minq's pointy face poked out, the ends of his long ears clasped together like two worrying hands.

"Heard news," he said, shaking his head.

Her foul mood had subsided into a dull ache along the journey home, and she allowed her dear friend to wrap himself around her in a heartfelt embrace. When he looked up at her with his sad rodent-like eyes, she nearly burst into tears again. But she was not going to cry. It seemed all she could manage these days was anger or sadness, with nothing in between.

"Your Momma and Poppa away," said Minq.

She patted him on the head and entered the cottage to

wait for Pippet and Mousha.

Himalette was entertaining Roane in the gathering room, working on a song that she had suspended in the air. As she pointed to each of eight variously colored pebblenotes, a different glassy sound vibrated, and she and Roane hummed along with the melody.

As Brigitta fluttered into the room, Roane squealed and tackled her with a hug.

"Brigitta!" he called, cheeks flush with excitement. He leapt back over to her sister before she could even return the hug. "Listen to what Himalette can do now."

"It's called a song flight." Himalette turned to demonstrate her new talent. She collected the pebblenotes from the air and, one by one, hummed a note into each, releasing them back into the air where they hovered and vibrated harmoniously.

"Song Master Helvine loaned me her pebblenotes," Himalette admitted. "I can't make any myself yet, but isn't it beautiful?"

"Yeah, great," Brigitta mumbled and fell into a cushiony mushroom chair. "When Croilus attacks we can song flight him out of the forest."

The little pebblenotes dropped to the floor, tinkling as they scattered in all directions, and Himalette crossed her arms. "Just because I can't be one of your precious Village Guards doesn't mean you have to be such a mossbottom to me."

"Mossbottom?" Brigitta snorted. "You've been hanging around Thistle too much."

Himalette stuck her tongue out at her sister as she Roane gathered the notes. Then she grabbed Roane's hand and stomped off to her room.

Brigitta sank into the chair. "I can't seem to do anything right anymore. I can't even open my mouth without offending someone. And now, other than Hrathgar, I'm the only faerie who has ever been banned from her apprenticeship."

"Many hardship in Noe," Minq responded. "Need time to heal."

"Not you, too!" said Brigitta, sitting up in the chair. "You know, I would be perfectly fine if everyone would just listen to me."

"I listen," Minq said, perking up his long ears. "That my specialty."

Brigitta closed her eyes and released the Air energy she had been suppressing since the incident in the Hive. It relieved her head of so much tension she was surprised she didn't spark the room again. She breathed in and out, allowing her Water and Air energies to mingle, like a morning fog on Green Lake.

Her eyes were still closed when Minq spoke. "You want me leave you alone?"

"No, no," murmured Brigitta, "just give me a moonsbreath."

Relaxing into her breathing, her body began to calm itself. The fact that she had refrained from any empathing or mind mist practice for so long might have something to do with her unsteady emotions. On the other hand, she'd been in no condition for concentrated mind work. That kind of skill took balance, and she had been neither balanced nor relaxed since Ondelle's memories started.

That was what she found so frustrating. Everyone thought she was reeling from the loss of Ondelle, when she was truly plagued by her increasing presence, which they interpreted as her inability to let go.

How does one let go of something that is a part of her? Could any faerie let go of her sight or hearing?

Brigitta continued to breathe and relax, breathe and relax, until she could conjure a light mind mist. A few moments later, she felt balanced enough, more balanced than she had felt in moons, and misted her mind out, touching the familiar energies of the objects in her old home. Her mist meandered through the hall and into her old bedroom, and she was slightly charmed to find that the room felt the same. She wondered if her parents had changed it at all.

Feeling stronger, she drifted to the wall to see how well she could identify the objects in the room and found that she could almost make out an old thunderbug symphony vine that was strung across her walls. It was easier to mind mist at home than it had been in Noe, and she impressed herself when the soft woven blankets that occupied her bed popped into view. And then a reed painting on her dresser that Himalette had made for her seasons ago.

More and more distinct images appeared as she roamed her room before misting to the window and coming to a halt. Outside, it felt pitch dark, which she knew to be impossible. Curious, she misted closer to the window, and then she moved through.

Chapter Three

Ondelle stood on the edge of a dense forest before a wide expanse of sand, cold wind stinging her arms and face. It was daytime, yet the sky was dark and thick with slate green clouds. Along the beach, little whirlwinds of sand spun crazily in and out of each other like mad dance partners. Past the beach, a dark sea stretched into the distance, strangely calm. Rhythmic waves lapped the pebbly sand, pulling shells and rocks with them as they receded.

Wind snipped at her tunic as she scanned the edge of the forest. To the north, the enormous dark plateau she had skirted to get to the beach. To the south, wind-bedraggled trees stretched into the sand. And submerged a few wingbeats ahead of her was a large solitary rock. She flitted toward it, pausing only to shield her face when the sands stormed up around her.

What had first appeared as one stone was in fact two long, flat stones that came together at the top of the beach and opened up to the sea in an immense V. Between the stones, where they met at the apex of the V, was just enough room for a few fingers. Ondelle removed a cloth bundle from her back and unraveled the scepter within. She gripped it in both hands, stepped back, and in one swift motion lifted the scepter up and slammed the bottom end into the sand between the rocks.

She pulled away and waited, hugging herself against the chill.

The stones began to shake, loosening themselves from the sand and knocking Ondelle backward. She scrambled down the beach to the edge of the water as the stones rose and expanded, stretching up and out, extending into the sea, with her imprisoned between them. Up the beach, her scepter was now a mere speck in the apex of the V.

When she was certain the stones had grown to their full size, she flew back to where the rocks met and hefted her scepter out of the sand, lighting it with a concentrated breath. With her other hand she held onto her hourglass necklace and returned her gaze to the great sea, only then becoming conscious of the silenced winds.

"Stay sharp, Ondelle," she cautioned herself.

She fluttered to the shoreline, cliffs looming above her malevolently, and dipped her scepter into the water. The glowing orb atop it shattered, scattering its brilliance into the dark sea like a school of frightened fish.

She pulled back and waited, watching the thick green clouds accumulate around the tops of the cliffs, enclosing her within. When she turned her attention back to the sea, she caught a glimpse of silver in the distance. A moment later, a series of sharp silver fins arced up and over so gracefully they could have been mistaken for a trick of light on the waves. She waited, transfixed, as the silvery movement swirled and arced and then finally surfaced.

A long neck rose from the darkness, glistening as if fashioned from the Great Moon's beams. Atop the neck was a slender earless head that ended in a black snout into which its eyes perfectly slanted. When its eyes opened, Ondelle gasped, for they didn't bulge outward as one would expect, but fell inward, pulling her into their abyss.

The Eternal Dragon.

Ondelle was afraid, not of the dragon itself, but of the feeling of complete insignificance in an eternity of eternities. The dragon's head stretched toward her. It inhaled through its great nostrils and then blew, a bubble breezing forth from its mouth enveloping Ondelle before she could move. The feeling of falling into a void ceased as she was cocooned inside. The dragon's head dropped back down into the water.

"Wait!" Ondelle cried, reaching forward only to be confronted by the thick, mucousy bubble-wall.

A moonsbreath later, and the bubble was inhaled by the sea itself, and Ondelle along with it. She panicked and tried to resist, but it was no use. As she was dragged into the ocean, she closed her eyes and braced herself for the icy impact.

But there was no impact. She was encased safely in the dragon's breath bubble as it was drawn farther and farther down the ocean floor. Dark and murky green, it was impossible to see where she was headed. Her hand flew to her scepter, having forgotten that the orb was now gone. When the bubble jolted to a halt, she stood, heart pounding, on the bottom of the sea.

The dragon sped past in a silver streak and the water cleared. In front of her was another bubble, just like her own, and a young faerie was trapped inside.

"Brigitta?" a faraway voice called to her, "Iola?" A warm hand settled on her cheek.

"Minq, what happened?" another voice asked. A familiar voice. Anxious.

Brigitta blinked open her eyes. She was lying on the floor with her parents, Minq, Himalette, and Roane gathered around her.

"Oh, thank the Dragon," her mother Pippet cooed, helping Brigitta to sit up.

"The Dragon . . ." Brigitta looked around at her family as if they were the vision. She grabbed her mother's arm, startling her. "I have to get back!"

"Get back where?" Pippet asked, concern etched on her rosy face. "You haven't been anywhere."

"You under meditation," Minq said. "Me wait and you cry out. Fall to floor. Not know what to do."

"We were in discussion with Orl Featherkind," said Mousha carefully, placing his hand on Brigitta's back to steady her.

Pippet hushed him with a look. "We can talk about that later." She turned to her younger daughter. "Himalette, please go fetch a ceunias compress from the marketplace."

"Aw, Momma," Himalette pouted, pink wings quivering, "I have to practice for the Masquerade."

"It's not a suggestion, Himalette."

"I'll do it," said Roane.

"No," Brigitta said, getting to her feet. She wobbled and Mousha caught her. Pain shot through her skull and she grimaced. "Don't bother; I'm fine. I just need some water."

Pippet and Mousha looked skeptically at Brigitta as she tried her best to appear "fine." She did not want Himmy or Roane talking about her at the Dionsdale marketplace, not after what had happened in the Hive that morning. There would be enough gossip around the Water Faerie Realm.

"I can get water," Himalette said and headed toward the kitchen before her mother could argue. As Himalette disappeared around the corner she called over her shoulder, "Even though you were a stinky bog bug earlier."

"Himalette!" Pippet scolded her.

Brigitta forced a laugh. "It's all right, Momma, I was a stinky bog bug earlier."

"And a mossbottom!" Himalette shouted from the kitchen.

Roane giggled, and Brigitta reached down to tickle his sides. He fell into her lap in a fit of laughter.

"Let's at least get you something warm to eat," said Pippet. "That will help."

Food, Brigitta thought, tussling Roane's hair, her Momma's answer to everything.

It was not easy to hide how unnerved she was by Ondelle's memory, but after a light snack, Brigitta managed to convince her momma that a trip to the lyllium field with Minq would be the best thing for her. Outside of their cottage, she grabbed Roucho, her Poppa's featherless delivery bird, from his roost, hastily scratched a message into a broodnut, and sent the bird to find Jarlath. As it flutter-wobbled into the trees, she thought of Gola, and supposed she should send a message of apology when Roucho returned. First things first, though. She needed to figure out a way back to Ondelle's memory of the Eternal Dragon.

She and Minq settled quietly in the lyllium field to wait for Jarlath. Removing her booties, she stretched her feet into the flowers and it did actually calm her, as it always had. It had been ages since she had lain in the field, soaking up the warmth. They lay there side by side in the hazy Gray Season sun, and she assured Minq she was all right.

"I just need to figure some things out," she said, picking one of the small white flowers from above her head and chewing on the end of its sweet stem.

"What figure?" Minq asked.

"Well, for one thing, how to purposely connect with Ondelle's memories. I don't know exactly how they're triggered or have any control over which ones I see."

"Why need control?"

"Because I need to remember something." Brigitta rolled onto her side and leaned up on her elbow, facing Minq. "I saw the Eternal Dragon."

Her stomach plummeted with the mention of Its name. As if the memory were her own, she could recall the eternity in Its eyes, the feeling of falling forward into an abyss.

A whistling noise escaped from Minq's whiskered mouth.

"It took Ondelle to see a girl, an Ancient faerie, I'm sure of it. She was trapped at the bottom of the sea. And when I looked at her through Ondelle's eyes . . ." Brigitta paused. Not having an element, she wasn't sure Minq would understand. "I felt me."

"Felt you?" Minq scratched his back where his wings were attached when he wore them.

"My Water energy. This Ancient faerie girl had my energy."

"You sure this not dream?"

"I know the difference between dreaming and a

memory, Minq." She flopped onto her back, cushioned by the mass of flowers beneath her. She watched the innocent clouds as they dawdled over the forest, forming and reforming in a slow orchestra of light and shadow.

"You remember when we met, right?"

"How I forget?" Minq said. "Almost eaten by giant caterpillar."

"Right. It's just like remembering that, only mixed up with these other things now. I remember Hrathgar as a child, but then I remember her at Dead Mountain with us. I also remember High Priestess Freena and Elder Grish Ba and others who died before I was even born."

Minq thought about this while Brigitta thumped on the ground with her fists. "I need to figure out how to control the memories so I can get to that specific one," she finally said. "I need to go back to that faerie."

They settled back into the flowers and had nearly dozed off when Jarlath buzzed into the lyllium field on his shimmering wings. Himalette always called them "sunbrown," because they resembled light glancing off of wet late-season leaves. His crystal blue eyes were bright with mischief.

"I'm meant to be back at the Air Fields, but they can wait."

Brigitta and Minq sat up as he landed and plopped himself down in front of them.

"I'm sorry, Brigitta," he said, eyes turning serious. "It's really unfair. And I would've come earlier, but the Elders—"

"No," she said quickly, "you need to stay in their good graces. We can't both get released from our duties. Promise me you won't cause trouble over this."

Jarlath nodded grimly.

Brigitta recounted her visit with Gola, and how she'd learned that all the White Forest faeries had been carrying the energies of the Ancients all these seasons. Then she related the memory of the Ancient girl under the sea with her own Water energy, who she intended to reach again. She wanted Minq to stand guard, which he did grumbling, and Jarlath to help her stay focused.

"I'll try," he said. "You know I'm not good at this kind of thing. I have no element to work with."

"You used your connection to the Ancients to help me in Noe."

"Yeah, it's just . . ." He paused and shook his head. "Never mind, let's concentrate on you."

Brigitta looked at him quizzically as he sat up straighter. "Well?" he asked and held out his hand as if he were asking her to dance. "Shall we?"

She laughed and took his hand, which had lost much of its roughness since moving to the White Forest and didn't startle her with buzzing voices anymore. Not since she had contacted the Ancients through him in Noe. Comforted by his willingness, she closed her eyes. She appreciated him more than anything at that moment, the way he never dismissed her ideas as absurd.

Focusing on the image of the Ancient faerie girl on the bottom of the sea, she let her mind mist out across the field, tickling the tops of the flowers. It was tricky accessing her emotions about the girl without upsetting her own balance. She allowed Jarlath to be an anchor for her, an extension, losing the distinction between her hand and his.

Slowly and carefully, she misted around the perimeter

of the field, pausing at Minq's nervous energy, and then she misted up and up, over the tops of the trees to the clouds and back down again, but nothing triggered the memory. And what was left of it was already growing vague, as memories did after time had muddled them.

Finally, she dropped Jarlath's hand. "It's no use," she said.

"Maybe you're trying too hard?" he suggested. "Or maybe you're not meant to control them?"

"What's the point of Ondelle giving me her memories if I can't use them when I want to!" Brigitta picked up a small rock and chucked it across the field, disturbing a flock of shadowflies.

From the edge of the meadow, Minq turned his immense ears toward them. Brigitta waved to indicate that she was fine, and then turned to stare after the shadowflies flitting and weaving over the field.

"What if," Jarlath said after a few moments, "it's not time to have them yet?"

One by one, the shadowflies disappeared into the trees. Brigitta gazed after them until she could no longer see their flutterings.

"Wait," she swung around to meet Jarlath's eyes, "what did you just say?"

"That maybe you're not supposed to have all the memories yet? Maybe they only come when you're ready for them?"

She stared past him to where Minq stood, ears stretched to capacity. "It's not a decision I make . . ." she said slowly. "It's information that surfaces when the time for the question arrives."

"Uh, sure."

"No, that's what Gola said!" Brigitta's thoughts raced. Had Gola meant that she literally could not give Brigitta any information before it was time? Was she under some kind of spell that only allowed this information to surface when the time was right? And if so, why hadn't she just told her so? Or was that part of the spell, too?

"Brigitta?"

What if Ondelle's memories were triggered, like clues, specifically when she needed them? What if they were leading her to something or somewhere?

An idea struck her. A terrible idea. An *unthinkable* one.

"I have to go there myself," she said.

"Go where?" asked Jarlath.

"To visit the Eternal Dragon."

Minq's ears, and then the rest of him, were quickly beside Brigitta. "Now you talk nonsense," he said, hands on hips, standing above her.

He shook his head as Brigitta explained that it made perfect sense. And the more she thought about it, the more positive she was that she was meant to go. The Elders didn't believe her, Fozk had postponed the ritual journey each High Priest or Priestess took to Forever Beach, and in the meantime, the White Forest was probably losing its only connection to the Ancients. She was sure that the memory of this girl was triggered to help her, just like Gola's information was always triggered to assist her in some way.

Gola . . . she had behaved horribly to the Drutan. What she had said about her driving Hrathgar mad was cruel. Gola had shared what she could with Hrathgar, and her heart had been broken. Now Brigitta was shattering it all over again.

She shook herself into the present. She would make

things right with Gola before she left. But for now, she had to think about the leaving part.

"The Festival of the Moons is approaching. Everyone will be preoccupied with the Masquerade. It's the perfect time to go."

"I'm coming with you," said Jarlath emphatically.

"I was hoping you'd say that," said Brigitta, taking his hand again and giving it a squeeze.

"Bad idea," said Minq. "You been outside. Very dangerous place."

"Yes, I've been outside twice, and Jarlath lived most of his life in Noe. We're the most qualified faeries to make the trip if you ask me."

"Trip based on mind tricks?" asked Minq. "No like idea at all."

"You don't have to, Minq," said Jarlath. "I believe Brigitta. If she says we have to go to this Eternal Dragon, I'm going. I owe my life to her. And so do you."

"Yes," said Minq sadly. "I yours. Still no good idea, but I yours."

Brigitta scratched him behind his ear. "The most difficult part will be getting into the Elder chambers on Masquerade night."

"What for?" asked Jarlath. "I can get anything you need from your Apprentice room."

"It's not my possessions I'm after," said Brigitta, standing up and brushing herself off. "It's Fozk's scepter. We have to take it with us."

Silence descended upon the lyllium field as if the flowers themselves had hushed the beasts around them. Both Minq and Jarlath stared at Brigitta like she was completely deranged, but she insisted she needed the scepter to call the Dragon and get to the girl. They followed her over the field as she explained.

"I saw it in Ondelle's memory," she said. "Besides, it's useless to them right now. It's empty of power. Maybe I can get it recharged? Then Fozk doesn't even need to go!"

"Steal from Elders and mess with destiny," lamented Minq, fluttering behind her.

"Destiny has already been messed with," said Jarlath. "I don't think it cares."

"Still, big trouble!"

"How much more trouble could I get into?" asked Brigitta. "And anyway, I think you're wrong. I think destiny is calling to us right now."

They definitely needed a plan, but Brigitta wanted to mull it over, so they decided to meet up at Moonsrise Ridge the next morning. No one was to be told what they were up to.

"Not Granae nor Thistle nor even Gola," Brigitta said. "At least not yet."

Jarlath agreed, but Minq shook his head. "What if something go wrong?" he asked. "Need help, protection, spell?"

"That's why you'll stay here in the White Forest, Minq," said Brigitta as they landed in the village-nest. She lowered her voice. "Somebody has to know where we are. Just in case."

"Just in case maybe too late," he said.

She shushed him as three Tiragarrow faeries flitted past. "We'll talk about it tomorrow."

"See you then," said Jarlath, saluting her as he took off.

Inside her parents' cottage, the air was tinged with tension. Brigitta moved into the dining nook to discover High Priest Fozk sitting across the table from her parents. They all looked up as she entered.

Fozk stood and smiled. With his characteristic whites and pale blues, it was like having the sky and clouds inside one's cottage. She was astonished that she'd never realized how tall he was before. His presence dominated the nook.

"Hello, Brigitta. I stopped by to make sure your parents understood the Elders' concerns and to see if they had any questions." His eyes showed sympathy, but Brigitta couldn't help her suspicion. A personal visit from a High Priest was pretty unusual. "How are you feeling?"

"Um, okay," Brigitta managed, glancing at her parents. "I've been relaxing in the lyllium field with Minq." She waved at Minq standing behind her in the doorway. He flashed a nervous grin before waving good-bye with an ear and retreating from the room.

"Your parents tell me you've had another episode?"

Brigitta glanced at them as Pippet fidgeted with the hem of her tunic and Mousha tapped his wings together. She took a deep breath to contain her emotions.

"I did," she answered, sitting down next to Pippet as casually as she could manage, "but the lylliums comforted me."

"I'm glad. I find mind mist meditation beneficial when I'm unsettled." Fozk sat down across from Brigitta and placed a hand on her forearm. His watery eyes urged trust. "I know you will adjust, in time, with the support of your family and friends."

Brigitta nodded. Adjust? Did he mean that she didn't fit in any longer in the White Forest? Or did he mean she would grow used to being a deodyte?

"You are a fine Second Apprentice, Brigitta, both inquisitive and quick to learn. But, it was irresponsible of us to overlook how the events in Noe and the death of Ondelle might have significant and lasting effects on you.

"As well, we are aware of some prejudice against you. We need to ease the minds of other White Forest faeries for your own peace of mind."

"They think I'll turn out like Hrathgar," she blurted out.

"Oh, no, lola," cooed Pippet, reaching over to give Brigitta's shoulders a squeeze. "Of course they don't."

Her Poppa grunted in agreement, but Fozk, Brigitta noted, did not comment. She gazed into his bright sky eyes. There was wisdom there, and an inviting sincerity. It reminded her of when Mabbe forced her to tell the truth with her sincerity spell. She removed her arm from his grasp and stood up.

"Let me fetch you some tea," she said. "Momma's is the best in Tiragarrow."

"Possibly in all the forest," he chuckled and held up an empty mug. "I've already enjoyed one cup while waiting for your return."

Brigitta cocked her head. There was something he wasn't telling her. "You didn't come just to check on me, did you?"

Both of her parents glanced around the room and Mousha's wing taps halted.

"You see?" Fozk said, tapping a finger on his temple. "Perceptive."

Brigitta sat back down with a dreadful knot in her stomach.

"Yes, there is one more thing." He gestured toward her necklace. "As Ondelle has now passed, so her hourglass needs passing."

"What do you mean?"

"He means," said Pippet gently, "that you need to return it to the Elders."

Brigitta's hand automatically went to her necklace. "But it was a gift from Ondelle!"

"I don't think she meant for you to keep it forever."

"She said I was Protector of the Forest," insisted Brigitta, a little less emphatically.

"That was just an honorary title, dear," said Mousha, frowning at the hourglass necklace as if he would miss it, too. "There's no such thing."

"Actually . . ." all eyes flew to Fozk as he spoke, "before I could request the necklace be returned, I had to do some research on the matter. We never take the actions of a High Priest or Priestess lightly and Ondelle knew this of course."

"Are you saying there was more to it?" asked Mousha.

"According to the first Chronicler, Chevalde of Grobjahar, the 'Protector of the Forest' is appointed in case a High Priest or Priestess is incapacitated beyond the ability to perform his or her duties."

"You—you mean," stammered Brigitta, "if Ondelle had been badly injured I would have become the High Priestess?"

"Not exactly," said Fozk. "You would have stood in for her until a new High Priest or Priestess was revealed via his or her destiny markings."

"I've never heard of such a thing!" said Pippet.

"Neither had I," Fozk admitted, "nor had any of the Elders."

"Well," Pippet put a strong arm protectively around her daughter, "I'm sure she never intended such a thing. What a ridiculous idea!"

"I must say," added Mousha, "it does seem irrational."

"Ondelle never did anything without intention."

Brigitta's mother bent close to her daughter's face. "Brigitta, you must give it back," she said earnestly.

Brigitta held the hourglass in her hands, twisting her fingers around it.

"I do realize it has served you well, and you it," said Fozk, "but there are only five necklaces, one for each Elder and one for the High Priest or Priestess."

It was completely selfish of her, she knew, but all she could think about was how it had saved her life in Noe. She had not expected to leave the White Forest without it, but she certainly couldn't use that as a reason to keep it. Really, there was no reason she could give.

"While she was High Priestess, it was her prerogative. Perhaps in her prescience she had known something was going to happen to her in Noe and was preparing us for this emergency. But, we are a full council again, and it must be returned to us or we will not be able to function effectively."

Everyone looked at Brigitta expectantly. What could she do? If she refused his request, it might test the limits of the Elders' patience. What would her punishment be for such a thing? Would it jeopardize her plan to leave the forest?

"Brigitta," said Mousha, "we know how much Ondelle meant to you. We understand the necklace is a comfort. But you must do the right thing, no matter how painful it may be."

She closed her eyes against a storm of tears and pulled the chain over her head. There was a slight bluish crackle in the air as the ownership spell Ondelle had cast was dissolved, the one that allowed only Brigitta to remove it, which she hadn't done since it was first gifted to her almost two season cycles ago.

Immediately, a coldness took over where it had lain, and she felt naked in the room. As she handed the necklace to Fozk, he patted her shoulder.

"Thank you," Fozk's bright sky eyes bore into her, "Brigitta of the White Forest."

He was wise enough not to attempt to console her with words, simply slipping the necklace into his tunic pocket and leaving the table. As Pippet and Mousha escorted him from the cottage, Brigitta burst into tears, flew to her bedroom, and slammed the door.

Chapter Four

Ondelle stepped into Pippet and Mousha's gathering room, and Mousha brushed off his best mushroom chair so she could sit down. The young couple's eyes were bright and curious as Ondelle looked around the room. If she stretched out her enormous fiery wings, she would probably knock the pottery from the shelves. It was a cozy room.

Mousha fidgeted behind Pippet, who eased her very pregnant body down onto a wide pillowed bench across from Ondelle.

"To what do we owe this pleasant surprise?" asked Pippet.

"I was at the Gyllenhale marketplace today and took lunch with Fernatta, who mentioned that you were due soon with a child."

Pippet laughed, her round cheeks rosy with motherhood. "It doesn't take any special kind of insight to know that, does it?"

"I am fond of visiting expectant families. Each birth is a celebration, and I enjoy welcoming new kin into our forest."

"That is very kind of you," beamed Pippet.

Ondelle slipped from her chair, kneeled before a startled Pippet and Mousha, and held up her hands. "Do you mind?" she asked.

Pippet gestured to her overlarge belly, and Ondelle placed her hands on either side of it, while Mousha peered down from behind Pippet's shoulder.

"Oh, silly me," said Pippet, "our manners! Mousha, some honeyroll and pipberry tea for the High Priestess."

As Mousha buzzed to the kitchen, Ondelle looked up from Pippet's belly. "Would you like to know anything about it?" she asked.

The mother-to-be shook her head. "Oh, no. I'm happy not knowing. I want to experience everything as it happens. It's all so new."

A crash sounded from the kitchen and Pippet cringed.

"Mousha?" she called, craning her neck to peer down the hall. "Is everything all right, dear?"

"Fine, fine!" he yelled, and then stuck his head around the corner. "Just be a moonsbreath."

They exchanged smiles as he pulled back into the kitchen. While Pippet was momentarily distracted, Ondelle grabbed her hourglass necklace with her free hand, and with a practiced pull from the depths of the secret corners of her body, she drew the hidden Water energy out and propelled it forth, down her arm, through the palm of her hand, and into Pippet.

Pippet gave a little cry and spun back around. "Did you do that?"

"Do what?" Ondelle got up off the floor, swiped her hands, and sat back down in the chair with a smile.

"I can feel her Water energy!" cried Pippet. "I couldn't feel it before, but now there it is. It's—it's—it's extraordinary!" She felt her own belly with her hands, tears of joy springing to her eyes. "Mousha! Come quick!"

"I have never been a mother," said Ondelle. "I do not know what it feels like to sense a child's energy for the first time. But I can sense it, too."

"What is it?" Mousha rushed in from the kitchen with a slice of honeyroll on a plate and a cup of steamy brew, dropping them on a stool. The cup toppled into the plate, soaking the bread, and dripping down the stool onto the floor.

"Oh, dear," said Ondelle through a laugh.

Ignoring the mess, Pippet took his hand and placed it on her belly. He smiled a wide, proud poppa-to-be smile as he placed his other hand over hers.

Distracted by the miracle, and by their love, Pippet and Mousha did not see Ondelle take hold of her necklace with both hands, close her eyes, and send a delicate mind mist out in search of the child.

Brigitta's hands shook as she packed a lunch of roasted gundlebeans and ripe pipberries. She grabbed a knife and sliced into a fresh honeyroll. When Pippet stepped into the kitchen with an armful of lyllium roots, Brigitta was staring at the slice as it sat on the counter.

"Lola?" Pippet asked as she set the roots down next to a large bowl on her prep table. "Are you all right?"

"Did Ondelle visit you just before I was born?"

Pippet considered her daughter for a moment and then picked up the first lyllium root. "Of course; she was fond of visiting new families." She stripped the skin off the root and set the exposed portion in a large bowl of water.

"I never knew her to do that," responded Brigitta,

wrapping the honeyroll slice in a cloth napkin.

"Well, she probably got so busy she had to stop," Pippet said and picked up the next root.

"Do you know of anyone else she visited who was pregnant? Did she come when you were pregnant with Himalette?"

Pippet stopped shucking her root and frowned at Brigitta. "What are you getting at, lola? That Ondelle knew you were special before you were born? I wouldn't be surprised if she'd known you'd be marked as an Elder, she was quite—"

"No, no," Brigitta shook her head. "I wasn't special, that's my point. Ondelle *made* me special. Ondelle gave me my Water energy. Maybe even my destiny."

Going back to her lyllium roots, Pippet laughed. "Brigitta, there was no possibility of you being any other element. Both your Poppa and I are Water Faeries and so were my parents and Mousha's father . . . I suppose you might have inherited his mother's Earth element, but I can't think of a case where that has happened. It must be rare."

Brigitta shoved her lunch into her pack. "Ondelle was Fire and Air and both her parents were only Air."

Pippet's eyes drifted off in search of this bit of history. "Hmmm. You might be right about that. I never knew her parents."

"High Priestess Freena gave Ondelle her elements when Runida was pregnant. And when you were pregnant with me, Ondelle moved her Water Energy into me, just like she did in Noe when she gave me her Air."

"Ondelle didn't have any Water energy, of that much I'm sure."

"She had it," Brigitta said stubbornly as she threw her pack on her back, "and she gave it to you. You didn't see it happen because Poppa distracted you from the kitchen."

Pippet dropped the root in her hand and turned to her daughter. "Did Mousha tell you this?"

"I saw it in Ondelle's memory. She gave me my Water. That was the moment you felt it for the first time, wasn't it?"

"I don't recall, Brigitta, it was a long time ago."

"After she became High Priestess she went to visit the Eternal Dragon. When she was there—" Brigitta stopped before she gave too much away. That faerie in the memory had Brigitta's Water. She must have given it to Ondelle, and then Ondelle had given it to Brigitta. Did that mean Ondelle's Fire and Air had belonged to this Ancient faerie as well?

And there was something else about that underwater faerie. Something she had kept to herself. Something she hadn't even told Jarlath.

Pippet wiped her hands on a cloth and took Brigitta's shoulders. "Lola, you must stop with this obsession. It won't do you any good, and it could prolong your suspension from the Center Realm."

"You knew." Brigitta looked into Pippet's hazel eyes. "Deep down, when it happened, you knew, and you won't admit it! Ondelle gave me her Water energy!"

"It was time for the energy to appear," said Pippet. "There was nothing unusual about it."

"Ondelle made me this way!" Brigitta insisted, choking back her tears. "She asked me to forgive her in Noe and I didn't understand! Now I do. She chose me and she made me . . . and then she left me!"

Pippet attempted to pull Brigitta into her arms, but

her daughter spun away from her. If her mother held her now, she would surely burst open like a raincloud and give everything away.

"You are in mourning, Brigitta," Pippet said. "You are trying to make connections where there are none. You must let go or else—"

Brigitta sped out of the cottage before her mother could tell her what that imagined "or else" could be.

She flew as hard and fast as she could for Moonsrise Ridge, northwest of Gyllenhale, charging each wingstroke with her sadness and pain. She took the bird's route, as the faeries say, cutting straight through the forest rather than following the river or drawing west and gliding over Green Lake.

Minq was waiting for her at the southern tail of the crescent-shaped ridge on a path that rose up from the forest. He sensed her mood, but simply patted her arm with an ear in greeting before they headed up the trail.

The ridge was open, exposed, a way of hiding in plain sight as anyone approaching would be spotted far before reaching them. The drop was sheer on the eastern side, inside the crescent, and the scree on the outside slope of the crescent was only good for chasing rainbow lizards.

Even though it was a beautiful route between Ithcommon and Gyllenhale, most faeries preferred to fly inside the cool canopy of trees below. And since the Masquerade was in two nights, the White Forest faeries were far too busy for scenery or rainbow lizards, and the ridge was deserted.

"I'm sure none of the Elders can empath our thoughts up here," Brigitta said, calmer now in the open air. She sat on the ledge and pulled the slice of honeyroll from her pack.

"Mind too suspicious," said Minq, pointing to his head with one lengthy ear and wiping off a place to sit with the other.

"Cautious," Brigitta clarified, and waved as Jarlath appeared over the southern curve of the ridge. "Like Jarlath."

She watched his sinewy body sail through the air as nimbly as any faerie who had grown up in the White Forest. Yes, he was healthier and happier inside the protected realm, but he carried within him a wariness she knew he could never shed. It was one of the reasons she trusted him.

"So," she teased as he landed next to them on the ridge, "excited about the Masquerade?"

"I've been planning my costume for moons," he said dryly.

They were agreed that most faerie festivals were frivolous. And at the last Twilight Festival, Roane and Thistle's over-enthusiasm during a hoop flute dance had embarrassed him, and he had lost them on purpose.

"The Festival of Moons is just like any other festival," explained Brigitta. "There's new music and dances and inventions."

"And food!" said Minq, fluttering up on his translucent wings. "Pie and berryroll and tingermint candy and lyllium suclaide."

"Stay focused," said Brigitta, and he fluttered back down.

"Food good," he mumbled, rubbing his belly with an ear.

"This festival, though, starts with the Masquerade," Brigitta continued. "Everyone dresses up in costumes, so it will be hard to tell who is who. If I can figure out how to temper my Water energy, maybe I can disguise myself as an Air Faerie and paint my wings as a Perimeter Guard."

"Is that even possible?" Jarlath asked.

"Well, it will take a lot of effort," she admitted, "but I've been doing it the other way around for moons, tempering my new Air so that only my Water energy is noticeable."

"Is that your only plan?" Jarlath scratched at his chin.

"It's my best plan," Brigitta said. "I'll start practicing right away."

"What about me?" asked Jarlath, kicking at a loose rock in the mountainside.

"You can pretty much be you," she laughed, "you're not the bad influence here."

"What do faeries dress up for anyway?" he asked as the rock broke free and they all watched it tumble down the side of the cliff.

"Why do they do anything? For the fun of it." Brigitta remembered some lesson she had learned in one of Auntie Ferna's Lore and Lineage classes. "A long time ago there was more emphasis on the symbolism of the Gray Months transitioning into the Grow Months. Everyone dressed in gray cloaks with colorful clothes underneath, and halfway through the Masquerade they would strip the cloaks away."

She pulled her knees up to her chin and stared out over the Earth Realm to the Center Realm, where she could just make out the sun glinting off the Hourglass. "But now it's just an excuse to make silly costumes and dance until the sun rises."

"What did you go as last year?" asked Jarlath softly, distracted by something on the horizon.

"Best costume!" Minq hooted. "She rockdragonfly."

"Can we get back to our plan?" Brigitta asked. "We've got less than two suns to figure this out. Jarlath?"

Beside her, Jarlath's breath was still and his eyes vacant. A moment later he shuddered and was fully awake again.

"What was that?" asked Brigitta. "What just happened?"

"Nothing, nothing." He rubbed at his eyes. "All those relays, flying back and forth to the Center Realm, you know." He waved her questions off and took a steadying breath. "Go on."

"Well . . ." She hesitated, now worried she was putting far too much pressure on her friend.

He raised his eyebrows playfully and she laughed.

"I can't go dressed as a Perimeter Guard," she continued, "that's not a costume, so I'll have to disguise myself as a Perimeter Guard *inside* of a costume."

"Disguise inside costume!" Minq said, impressed in spite of his misgivings. "Double disguise."

"Then it's just a matter of sneaking into the Hive," said Brigitta. "Well, that and keeping everyone distracted long enough to steal the scepter and make our escape without notice."

"Yeah," said Jarlath, "there's that."

"Okay, so I'm still working on the how," she said. "But I do know the when."

They stood up and walked south along the ridge, hatching the rest of the plan as they traversed the trail.

"At the end of the evening's events there's a processional," she explained. "It will be High Priest Fozk up front, then Elders, Apprentices, and Wisings. The scepter is kept with the Wisings until the processional, during which the newest Wising lights it and hands it up the processional."

Lost in the memory of her last Festival of the Moons,

Brigitta smiled. "Actually, it's quite pretty. The scepter grows in brightness as it goes up the line of faeries. It's like watching a star being born."

"So, you're saying," said Jarlath, looking a bit pale, "this scepter light trick is a big deal and the whole forest is going to fall into a panic when the scepter goes missing?"

"The Elders won't let that happen," Brigitta assured him. "They'll think of something. And if they don't, Minq can go into the Hive with some important question. When he finds them all upset, he can suggest they use Ondelle's hourglass necklace instead and tell everyone the change is a symbol of creating traditions for a new era or something. The point is, if we enter the tunnel just as the main entertainment begins, it gives us four or five moonbeats to trick the Wisings into giving us the scepter and get as far away as possible."

"Huh," said Jarlath, clearly impressed. "You've thought of everything."

"Not everything," she said. "I have no idea what happens after we leave the White Forest." She put a hand to her chest where the hourglass necklace used to lay. "Or how we'll protect ourselves."

"That's why you have me," said Jarlath, flexing his arms. "You're the brains; I'm the muscle."

Below them, a swell of blossom bells sounded from Gyllenhale, their echoes bubbling up to them on the breeze. They stood quietly listening to the soothing chimes surrounding them like a joyful spring. Brigitta closed her eyes and inhaled the sound, gathering strength from the momentary peace.

Since Brigitta had promised Thistle she'd lend a hand with her Masquerade costume, she bade good-bye to Jarlath and Minq and headed for Dmvyle. Thistle had given herself the task of helping out in the little nursery that had sprung up in the home of Dwinn and Cairys, parents of Duna, the little destinyless faerie Brigitta had first met in the Elder chamber before she and Ondelle traveled to Noe.

Duna was no longer the only destinyless child, however. A crystal-eyed Air Faerie boy named Tustin had been born in Thachreek, and the two mothers spent most of their spare time together. Cairys was a nervous little Fire Faerie. Her Earth Faerie spouse, Dwinn, worked in the marsh farms, which was how he had met Granae and Thistle. Tustin's mother, Brea, was a calming presence for Cairys, especially since she could now share her concerns for her child's future with someone who understood.

Thistle, who was technically "destinyless" herself, had taken to the children immediately. And when a pregnant Water Faerie woman from Easyl showed up to the cottage in tears, it was Thistle who had the idea to start a "Destiny Nursery" away from the rest of the faeries, so as not to upset the other parents and children. Thistle and Granae were positive that if they all observed carefully, they would find appropriate Life Tasks for Duna and Tustin. If they could do so in Mabbe's Hollows, Granae reasoned, they could certainly do so in the White Forest.

With time, thought Brigitta as she headed for the nursery, *there will be so many unmarked faeries flying around the forest that it won't matter anymore.* But if it made the families feel better, and gave Thistle something to do, Brigitta was all for it. And it was clear that Thistle loved the crystal-eyed babies without fear or prejudice.

As it turned out, Granae had done a fabulous job costuming her daughter as a baby rainbow lizard and herself as a matching mother rainbow lizard. She had even sewn little bubblebug costumes for Duna and Tustin. The cozy cottage was filled with laughter as Granae snipped at loose threads and adjusted Thistle's striped tail.

"You don't need my help," said Brigitta to Thistle. "Your costumes are better than most. Prize-worthy, even."

"You think?" asked Thistle, eyes sparkling above her pointy lizard lips. She picked up the destinyless Duna and zoomed her around the room, popping her lips like a bubblebug calling to its friends across the lake.

It broke Brigitta's heart to see her so happy. She reminded Brigitta of Himalette, who was already losing that innocence, and Brigitta couldn't help thinking that some day Thistle would lose hers, too.

"You are a masterful, magical Clothier, Granae," said Brigitta, truly impressed.

"No magic," Granae held up her hands, "just seasons and seasons of helping out in Mabbe's Hollows."

Unaware of the misty-eyed melancholy that flickered through Granae's eyes, Cairys and Brea laughed as Thistle swerved and bubbled her way about the cottage. When Granae pulled back from adjusting the hem of Tustin's costume, her hand went to her forehead, and she gazed into the air, stunned. A moment later, and Thistle fell into the same trance. If it weren't for Brigitta's quick reaction, Thistle would have dropped Duna on the floor.

A moonsbreath later, they both shook themselves awake again.

"Okay," said Brigitta, handing little Duna to Cairys. "One of you has to tell me what's going on. Jarlath did the exact same thing today."

"Did what exact same thing?" asked Thistle distractedly.

"That thing you just did, like you weren't there for a moment," explained Brigitta. "How often does that happen?"

"I—" said Granae, looking down at the scissors in her hands as if she didn't know how they had gotten there.

Brigitta removed the scissors from Granae's grip and set the faerie woman down on a stool, while Cairys, balancing Duna on her hip, produced a wet cloth from the kitchen and placed it on Granae's forehead. When Granae looked up, there was something dulled about her eyes, something missing.

"What just happened?" Granae asked, grabbing Brigitta's tunic. "What did you see?"

"I don't know, you just sort of went . . . blank," was the best she could describe it.

"Blank," Granae repeated, nodding. She nabbed Thistle and pulled her to her bosom, stroking her hair. They sat there rocking in silence, staring out at nothing.

"Why won't anyone tell me what's going on?" demanded Brigitta.

Duna burst into tears and Tustin followed suit. The two mothers carried their little bubblebugs into the next room, singing and cooing to quiet them down.

"It's the voices," said Granae in a hushed tone, hugging Thistle tighter as she trembled. "The ones Mabbe trained all of us to tune out."

"The echoes of the Ancients, you mean?" asked Brigitta. "They're speaking to you now?"

"No," said Granae, her face pale with worry. "They've stopped. I mean—I think—they're gone."

"I'm not being selfish," Brigitta told her reflection in her bedroom mirror. "It's for the good of the forest." She leaned in closer, challenging her reflection to disagree. "It's my destiny."

Her reflection imitated her motions, and then both of them sat still, waiting for the other to continue. She missed her Thought Mirror, the one item in her Apprentice chambers she wished she could have taken with her.

"I'm the same faerie who left for Noe with Ondelle," she said to the mirror. "I haven't changed, not really."

She squinted at her reflection and spoke back to herself as the mirror. "Haven't you? Through our actions aren't we defined?"

It was something Ondelle had once said to her. She reviewed her recent actions. The old Brigitta would never have stomped off in anger at Gola. The old Brigitta hadn't been as distrustful of others. The old Brigitta wasn't so full of secrets.

And now she was asking others to keep secrets for her. All because she didn't want anything to interfere with her plans to leave the forest. Although, it hadn't taken much to convince Thistle and Granae to keep silent about losing touch with the Ancient voices. At least for the time being. No one wanted to spoil the festival. Obviously, the Elders had to be told, and Granae agreed to call a meeting with them as soon as the festivities were over.

"After Jarlath and I are long gone," Brigitta said to her reflection.

Jarlath. She needed to see him as soon as possible to find out if he, too, had lost touch with the Ancient voices. Granae had said that hearing the voices was like living near a stream. The sound could be ignored, as it was constantly flowing in the background. Over time, she'd stopped noticing it . . . until it went silent.

Thistle hadn't been as sure. She could tell something was missing, but she had also been trained from a toddling to block it all out, whereas Granae had been Brigitta's age before Mabbe's ruling came down. Brigitta imagined for Thistle it was more like losing the whisper of a forgotten dream.

Roane never said much about what went on in his head. Brigitta had watched him intently during supper, and it could have been her imagination, or Himalette's ability to talk enough for four faeries, but Roane had seemed unusually quiet.

Regardless, it only served to make her departure more crucial. They could live without destiny marks from the Ancients, but the Noe Watchers were the only faeries who could perform dispersements when any faerie died.

She shuddered at the thought of no more disperse-ments, faerie spirits wandering their forest, unable to let go of their elemental energies for the next generation. No released energy, no new babies. Duna and her crystal-eyed companions would be the last of their kin unless Brigitta could fix things.

Was she mad for thinking that she was the one who was supposed to put everything right? Or that she even could? For taking it upon herself to steal the scepter and visit the dragon?

"You are not like Hrathgar," she whispered.

Her own image looked back at her suspiciously, and rightly so, as she had buried a secret so deep inside she could almost pretend that it wasn't there. She had an ulterior motive for not telling the Elders what had happened to Granae and Thistle. She didn't want Fozk to change his mind and rush off to find the Eternal Dragon. Not now.

She wanted to find the Dragon herself.

She knew for certain that Ondelle had released Water energy into her before she was born. Water energy Ondelle had gotten from that Ancient faerie. She was now convinced that Ondelle's own Fire and Air had been given to her in the same manner, forced upon her by High Priestess Freena. It was why Ondelle's own mother had denied their bond.

It was why Ondelle had detected Brigitta hiding in the passageway when she and Kyllia, Tilan, and Dinnae had spied on the Elders' spell rehearsals all those seasons ago. It was why Brigitta had felt such a connection to Ondelle, why Ondelle's Air energy felt so at home coursing through Brigitta, and why the High Priestess's memories settled inside of her like they belonged there.

And it was why Brigitta knew she had to get to the Eternal Dragon first, so it could take her to the bottom of the sea. She hadn't told anyone yet, not even Jarlath, that there was something else she had felt during Ondelle's memory.

"That faerie trapped inside the bubble?" she said, placing her hand to its reflection. "She has one element left, her Earth, and it belongs with me."

Chapter Five

Ondelle scanned the Center Realm arena, gripping her scepter so hard her knuckles had locked. If the White Forest faeries weren't so preoccupied with their festival preparations, they might have noticed the panic in her eyes. She looked to the ground beneath the platform. The open spell seed was still there. Of course it was still there.

It was exactly the kind of spell seed Hrathgar had used all those seasons ago when she had tried to steal the power of the Hourglass. And a moment earlier Ondelle had seen a resolved Vivilia carrying it toward the platform. As requested, Vivilia had left for Dead Mountain five suns earlier to check on the banished faerie, and now Ondelle cursed herself for her curiosity and concern for her old friend. Concern was only natural, of course, but one faerie's well-being could not eclipse the well-being of the entire White Forest.

Open on the ground in front of her, the spell seed had obviously been used somehow, but to what end she had no idea. Had Hrathgar put a spell on the Hourglass? On Ondelle and the Elders? On all the White Forest faeries?

"By the Dragon, Hrathgar," she hissed, "what have you done?"

She had to find Vivilia, but there was too much activity going on around her, too much energy to separate. She took equal breaths Air and Fire and laced them together into a seamless ring. She held the energy ring steady, readying it for quick action.

Ondelle loosened her anxious grip on the scepter, breathed from her belly, and scanned the arena once again. She felt a fluttering around the inner edge of the Fire Faerie grandstand like a drunken shadowfly. Vivilia! Without hesitation, Ondelle threw her looped energy, the ring expanding out to form a long, round tunnel. When it reached Vivilia, she ensnared her and felt for an opening through which to empath her thoughts.

What Ondelle felt was more than an opening; it was an empty vessel ready to receive. So, Hrathgar had used Vivilia as transportation to get the spell seed into the White Forest. Her old friend was clever, but Ondelle was quick-thinking. She could use Hrathgar's vessel, too.

She raised her hands and closed her eyes, whirling the lasso seductively around Vivilia's mind, preparing a thought-loop. Thought-loops were tricky and usually had to start with the subject's original thought. But, with Vivilia's empty mind, Hrathgar had almost made it too easy for Ondelle. She opened her eyes again and sent a thought forth. *I must find and protect Brigitta.*

In her enchanted state, the sprite repeated through the tunnel of energy, *I must find and protect Brigitta.*

I must take her this spell.

I must take her this spell.

There was no time to consult the Elders about the use of Blue Spell. The Dragon had given her all the permission she needed and the life-long task of protecting the energy's destiny. Ondelle's life was cut shorter with each use, but she couldn't think about that now.

By the power of the Eternal Dragon, Ondelle called as she lifted her scepter, gathered her forces, and shot a Blue Spell message across the arena straight into Vivilia's heart. A look of shock registered on the sprite's face, and then she disappeared in a quick poof of blue.

Lying in bed the next morning, Brigitta practiced forming Air and Water energy rings and stretching them out within her own mind, thought-looping a meditation of silvery scales skating to and fro. The image slid back and forth, circling her thoughts, as she contemplated the latest memory, which had come to her in the early morning hours as she tossed and turned, plagued by her secrets.

This proved the authenticity of the memories, she decided. No one had taught her to thought-loop. It wasn't something a Second Apprentice would ever learn on her own. Yet there she was with the knowledge of how to perform it, and here she was practicing it in her own mind. It didn't feel like she had just learned how to use it, either. She had *remembered* how to use it.

She shivered as she also recalled Ondelle's fear and panic on the day of Hrathgar's curse. She now understood how and why Ondelle had sent the Blue Spell protection through Vivilia, but she didn't understand why Ondelle had never told her about it. She hadn't found that memory.

"When the time is right," she said to her herself, the silver scales still sliding back and forth.

She dropped the thought-looped image and sighed. She couldn't stay in bed practicing spells all morning, so she got dressed and joined her family. Attempting to appear as awake and happy as possible, she spent the morning molding tingermint taffy with her Momma, polishing jars for her Poppa's new moonbeat moths, and feigning interest in Himalette's Masquerade costume: a pink, large-bottomed thunderbug she had designed to chime when she shook her behind. Himalette flew around the front yard, entertaining her family and neighbors with her tumbling, tinkling dance.

"You know, Himmy," Brigitta teased, "with a bottom that big, I would expect more of a big *BONG*."

Himalette smirked and shook her rear in her sister's direction, sending the Tiragarrow children into fits of laughter.

Brigitta looked to the sky. "Well, I should get moving if I'm going to meet up with Jarlath," she said to Pippet, who was handing out samples of taffy to neighbors with Roane quietly tagging along behind her.

"You're certain you feel up to it?" Pippet asked.

Neither of them had mentioned Brigitta's outburst from the other day, but there was a palpable tension now, a tension that saddened Brigitta because there was nothing to be done about it. She couldn't risk getting letting her guard down. What would her mother say if she found out the truth?

"Yes, I'm certain."

"You can always come find us if you need us," Mousha offered, nabbing his fourth taffy from Pippet's tray. "Orl Featherkind offered to watch my booth if necessary. I don't mind missing anything. Not for you."

"That's sweet, Poppa." She kissed his cheek. "I'll keep that in mind."

She gave Pippet a quick hug, grabbed her bulging pack, and was out of Tiragarrow before anyone could see the tears stinging her eyes. She wiped them away, trying not to think about how much her parents would worry after she went missing, and flew down along the southern tail of Spring River. The rushing of Precipice Falls comforted her and she paused for a moment to watch the waters churn before heading east toward Gola's to meet up with Jarlath and Minq.

As she skirted past Rioscrea, she made up her mind to confide in the old Drutan. To make things right with her and tell her everything. Ondelle had trusted her. Who knew what secrets they had shared? Brigitta grew determined to prove herself worthy of Gola's trust.

Beneath all of these thoughts festered a darker notion. There was a chance Brigitta might not return from her quest, and she did not want those angry words to be the last Gola ever heard from her. She did not want to be remembered as the second faerie to break her heart.

She reached the small clearing in front of Gola's tree, where Minq and Jarlath stood looking more than a little anxious.

"What's wrong?" she asked as she landed.

"We can't find Gola," said Jarlath. "And look."

He pointed to the cauldrons in front of Gola's tree-home, from which her chatterbuds usually greeted them with their tinny chorus. The four cauldrons were empty but for a few handfuls of soil.

"She's probably trading them at the market today," said Brigitta. "She's been talking about doing that for moons." She gazed wistfully at the abandoned cauldrons. Gola had been giving more and more of her possessions away. "I'll fly up and try to catch her on the path. You wait here in case we miss each other."

Before they could suggest otherwise, Brigitta was off, following the narrow trail from Gola's to Bobbercurxy. It was perfect, she thought. She could tell Gola everything on the stroll home. Even the part that she hadn't confessed to anyone else. Gola had already told her it wasn't her place to interfere with faerie destiny, only impart knowledge where, and when, she could.

But Gola was not at the marketplace, and her few friends, an old Fire Faerie Weaver named Krisanna and an Earth Faerie Potter called Valance, had not seen her in several suns. Brigitta streamed back to Gola's tree twice as fast.

"Where else could she be?" she asked Minq and Jarlath upon her return, now as concerned as they were.

Gola was not in the habit of wandering much past her gardens, other than to Bobbercurxy and, every once in a while, to the Center Realm. But someone always traveled along to assist her.

"We've been down to the river and out to the fire flower farm," said Jarlath.

"What about the market at Rivenbow?"

"Too far," said Minq. "Never go by self."

They all turned to consider Gola's tree-home. Under any other circumstances, none of them would have thought about entering it without her permission. Not even Minq. And although Gola had never left a note for them in the past, they decided to check inside to see if she had.

They were met with a dark, chilly room. Nothing had been brewed or baked in her kitchen that day. The bed was made and the whole space was unusually tidy. As Jarlath opened the curtains, the light caught some stones strung above the hearth.

"Are those her moonstones?" asked Jarlath.

"No, no, they can't be . . ." said Brigitta, moving closer. There were four of them, and they were shaped exactly like Gola's moonstones, strung along an identical thin black strap. But these stones had no starry shimmers and looked as if they were formed from dark clay rather than the night sky reflected in a pool of water. Brigitta touched one with a pinky finger and its absolute stillness sent a shiver through her heart. She braved a closer look and wrapped her hand around one. Nothing happened. No visions, no energy pulling her in.

"If they are her moonstones, one's missing," she murmured. "Look."

Minq and Jarlath moved to either side of her. With his ear, Minq lifted the strand of stones off the hearth and gazed at them, moisture dotting the edges of his eyes. Drawing in a shaky breath, he placed the strand around Brigitta's neck.

"What are you doing?" she said, fumbling for the stones. "Those are Gola's!"

"She left for you," he said.

"What do you mean *left* for me?" asked Brigitta.

"What are you telling us?" asked Jarlath, seizing Minq's arm.

"She old Drutan," he said, blinking his beady eyes at them. "She gone to root." He waved his ear toward the forest. "Out there."

"No, no . . . no . . ." The room started to spin and Brigitta grabbed onto a chair as Minq and Jarlath both reached out to steady her.

"I . . . I . . . She can't!" Brigitta burst into tears. "I haven't told her I'm sorry!"

Minq hugged her with both ears and Jarlath wrapped himself around his two friends, tears engulfing them all.

"She know," Minq said between sniffles, "she know."

👁👁

It was horribly wrong, Brigitta thought as she entered the Center Realm, that there could be such celebration with Gola taking root all alone out there in their forest. But there the White Forest faeries were, laughing and singing and dancing along, oblivious to the pain that made Brigitta's insides feel as though they were collapsing in on themselves.

As soon as they landed in the wide sandy path surrounding the grandstands, she, Minq, and Jarlath were drawn into the excited flow of faeries, like leaves into a river. The noise and motion and color were too much for her, and she began to panic, unable to breathe under her costume mask. Jarlath reached out and pulled her to his side, linking his arm through hers. Minq stepped to her other side, placing an ear against the small of her back to guide her along.

With all her heart, she wanted to postpone their journey to Forever Beach, but when would they get another chance to distract nearly every faerie in the forest? No, after the festival, the scepter would be under Fozk's nose again, and Granae would tell him about the Watchers losing touch with . . . the Watchers!

Brigitta spun around to look at Jarlath, his tree head bobbing along in the crowd. His eyes were sunken into the mask, so she couldn't see his expression, and she was too distraught to empath it.

Losing Gola that day made their choice of costumes

seem cruel. They were both dressed as trees. Brown fabric wrapped their bodies, leaves and branches criss-crossed their faces, and a nest sat on Brigitta's head. Underneath the Masquerade costume, she was disguised as a Perimeter Guard, the colors and markings on her wings carefully rendered in feather paints, which now appeared to her as too crude to fool anyone.

In her worry and grief over Gola's disappearance, she had forgotten to ask Jarlath about the Ancients. She hadn't even stopped to get a sense of any change in him. She had barely been able to get her costume on and get to the Center Realm. And now she was surrounded and being jostled by faeries pouring into the fairgrounds. The heat was nauseating, and her heart quickened. She had to pull herself together, or they wouldn't be able to get the scepter in time, and they'd never have another chance.

She stopped walking and Minq and Jarlath stopped along with her as faeries jostled them from all sides. Instinctively, Brigitta reached for her hourglass necklace, but instead found the lumps of lifeless moonstone hidden beneath her costume. Still, they were oddly comforting with their absolute absence of energy. Perhaps that was why Gola had left them for her. Maybe she had known all along that Brigitta was going to leave, had perhaps even chosen to root so she could give Brigitta the comfort of her silent stones. That would be just like something Gola would do, protecting Brigitta in her secret and humble way.

She rubbed at the stones through her costume. Gola was still with her. And like Ondelle, she would always be with her. She could find strength in that.

As her heart and breathing slowed, Brigitta became more conscious of her surroundings. Cooking contestants thrust culinary treats into the hands of every reveler, Traders called from tables lining the outer grandstands, and at the entrance to the arena, a hoopflute orchestra played as children held a leaf race overhead, the air from the instruments tossing the flutterscarves about.

"This way," she said to Jarlath and Minq, leading them around the Fire Faerie grandstand. She gazed over faerie heads as she navigated past hundreds of brightly colored tents and peeked into the arena at the costumed aerialists. Her eyes landed on the Hourglass of Protection. It was two-thirds empty. And no one seemed concerned.

They grabbed some taffy off of a passing tray and some tarts off another. Under cover of the chaos, Brigitta led Jarlath and Minq through the crowd, behind the Fire Faerie grandstand, and into the brush, hoping the tunnel entrance in the old tree stump hadn't been blocked off by the Elders.

Luckily, when they arrived, the only difference was that the stump was now covered in more vines.

She dumped an armful of goodies at Minq's feet. "Have at it."

For a moment, it seemed his unruly appetite had been curbed by his sadness, but a moonsbreath later he had downed two pipberry tarts.

Brigitta lit the lower quarter of a globelight and handed the light to Jarlath, who spread open the vines, squeezed through the crack in the stump, and disappeared into the tunnel. The leafy vines shook closed behind him.

She stepped up to the stump, and then turned back to Minq. "Be careful you don't pass out from over-digestion, Minq. Pace yourself."

He waved her off with his right ear while he wiped his hands and mouth with his left.

"And stay away from anything with lyllium in it," she warned, slipping into the trunk.

Hands tracing the dark walls, Brigitta made her way toward the glowing light ahead. When she reached Jarlath she pulled him around and studied his face.

"What?" he whispered.

"Your eyes look different," she said. "Are different."

He shrugged and looked away, up the tunnel. "We need to get going; we don't have a lot of time."

"I know about the Ancient voices, Jarlath," said Brigitta. "Granae told me." She placed a hand on his arm. "Is that what's been going on with you? Is that what you've been keeping from me?"

He whirled back around. "And you have no secrets from me?"

His accusation caught her off guard, and she fell back into the wall of the tunnel, creating a little avalanche of pebbles and dust. They both paused and listened until they were sure no one had heard.

"I'm sorry . . ." he continued and shook his head, "I'm just . . . these past few days . . ." He gestured helplessly.

"Are the voices gone completely?" she asked. "Have you really lost touch with them?"

He let out a sigh. "Maybe. I don't know. Does it matter right now?"

Brigitta thought about this. There would be no more dispersements for the dead if it were true, but what did that matter if they lost their forest entirely? There would also be no empathing him to get to the Ancients as she had done to change her physical form in Noe.

"I get it," he said when she didn't answer. "You only cared about me for my connection to them."

"Ha, ha." Brigitta swatted him.

They considered each other a moment longer. There was nothing to do but trust.

"Give me a chance to cloak my Water and focus my Air," she finally said. "And then . . ."

He nodded. "Yeah. And then."

Two Wisings, Lalam and Bastian, were sitting in the gathering room of the Elder Chamber in simple white tunics streamed with shimmering gold. Their hair flickered gold as well, like the morning light catching on Green Lake. They were passing the time making shadow figures on the wall as Brigitta and Jarlath observed them through the entryway from the crack in the stone wall on the other side of the hallway.

Lalam was about twice Brigitta's age and slender for an Earth Faerie, but solid. His wings were a barky brown, and his sun-warmed skin housed a subtle strength. Bastian had the lighter tones of an Air Faerie, slender teal wings, and eager yellow eyes.

Elder Mora and First Air Apprentice Na Tam were putting the final touches on the crystal box that held the scepter. They were not costumed at all yet. Na Tam wiped away some small speck of dirt on the surface of the box while Elder Mora added a touch of light to the air surrounding it. They stepped back to admire their work.

"I like it," Elder Mora said. "Subtle, yet . . . enchanting."

"Your first Masquerade as Air Elder." Na Tam nudged Elder Mora.

Mora emitted a very un-Elderlike giggle and nudged

Na Tam back. "And yours as First Apprentice."

Arm in arm, Mora and Na Tam left the chamber and Brigitta and Jarlath pulled away from the crack, slipping up against the wall. It was almost too easy, Brigitta thought. Bastian, the young Air Wising, had little mind training at all. And Earth Wising Lalam was a sweet and gentle man whom she judged open to suggestion. She just had to create the right thought-loop to keep their minds occupied. To make a thought-looping between two people without their consent, the thoughts would have to be verbalized, and the loop would have to make sense.

Because of what she now knew through Ondelle's memories, she was confident she could do it, but the whole idea made her uneasy. It will be a harmless trick, she told herself as they made their way downward, through the passageway, to an exit between two bookcases outside the Apprentice chambers. No one will get hurt.

They spiraled upward through the main passageway, and just before they rounded the curve that led to the Elder Chamber, Jarlath pulled back, but it was a moment too late. Perimeter Guard Master Reykia of Rivenbow flew toward them. Brigitta almost let her Water energy slip, but caught it back again carefully, like closing the gap between a pair of cupped hands.

"What are you doing here?" Reykia asked Jarlath. "And who are you?" she demanded of Brigitta.

"Ferris of Erriondower." Brigitta bowed slightly. She peeked through the costume leaves around her face, hoping her Watcher friend's name would bring her luck.

"The Elders approved her to join the guard," said Jarlath. "Dervia spell-cast the marking on her wings so she'd be recognized as one."

"Why wasn't I told?" barked Reykia. "We agreed on a system for guard selection."

"She was ready," he said, "and they figured you'd need the help tonight."

Conjuring Ondelle's benevolence, Brigitta emanated a hint of warm calming Air. Just a slight change in energy, not enough to cause suspicion.

Reykia composed herself and studied Brigitta. "Well, yes, I suppose I could use you on the periphery tonight."

"She's here to serve," encouraged Jarlath.

"Service is my highest endeavor," added Brigitta.

Jarlath coughed to cover a laugh.

"Fine," Reykia said, eyeing them one last time. "Follow me."

As she turned back around, Jarlath reached up with balled fists and struck her on the back of the head. She immediately crumpled to the ground.

Brigitta's surprised eyes shot to Jarlath's, and she clamped her own hand over her mouth to stifle a scream. This was not part of the plan.

"She'll be okay," he said. "I promise."

Slipping her hands away from her lips, Brigitta stood there in shock.

"I'm sorry," he said. "Old habits. I didn't know what else to do."

"Well, don't do it again," said Brigitta, bending down to make sure Reykia was all right. She was still breathing at least.

"It's a good trick, though," he said. "You should learn it."

She fired him an irritated look from beneath the bird's nest in her tree branches. "Let's just do this."

Jarlath nodded as she stood up, closed her eyes, and

took a deep breath. On the exhale, she let her Water energy go, swirling and mixing it evenly with the Air, creating the end of the loop, a ring that could be stretched out to form a tunnel. When the end of the loop felt sturdy enough, she opened her eyes.

"Just get the Wisings talking so I can set the loop."

They fluttered the rest of the way up the passage to the Elder Chamber. The two Wisings stood up to greet them as they entered the main room. Lalam's brow knit in confusion, but Bastian remained happily ready to assist.

"Perimeter Guard Ferris," Jarlath gestured vaguely at Brigitta, "and I have been sent to escort the scepter into the procession."

Wising Bastian smiled and turned to gather the box, but Lalam held him back with an arm. "I thought Reykia was to do it?"

"Reykia had to go out to the perimeter," said Jarlath. "I'm sure it's nothing to worry about, though." He turned to Bastian. "Which side of the box do you wish to stand on for the procession, left or right?"

Bastian turned to the older Wising and asked him, "Right or left?"

As soon as Bastian asked his question of Lalam, Brigitta's mind sprang into action. "Left or right?" she repeated to Bastian, tenderly looping the end of the energy ring around his mind. She stretched the ring into a tunnel and looped Lalam's thoughts, "Right or left?"

"Left or right?" repeated Bastian cheerfully.

Lalam hesitated, as if trying to remember what he was about to say. "Right or left?" he said, turning his eyes from Brigitta to the other Wising.

"Left or right?" asked Bastian.

They repeated the questions to each other, over and over, caught in the thought-loop. Jarlath crossed his arms and eyed Brigitta suspiciously.

"They'll be okay," she said. "*I promise.*"

"Seems a conk on the head is easier," Jarlath muttered.

"Any of the Elders can easily stop the loop if it doesn't wear off on its own," she said, stepping back to marvel at her handiwork.

They retrieved Reykia from the passageway and hid her behind a wooden chest. Brigitta removed the scepter from its crystal case, pulled the soft cord that held the fabric of her tree costume on, and wrapped the scepter up in the cloth. With the cord, she tied up the bundle and slung it across her back.

"We've got about three moonbeats before the Elders come looking for the scepter," she said, straightening the branches across her face.

There was a groan from behind the chest.

Jarlath pulled Brigitta by the arm. "We've got less time than that."

The two of them swooped down the passageway back toward the tunnel entrance. As they turned to duck between the bookshelves, someone emerged from within the tunnel and they all startled to a halt.

An amber-toned sprite hovered in front of them. It was Vivilia. She glanced back and forth at Brigitta and Jarlath as voices echoed behind her in the tunnel. She turned to call to the voices.

"Wait!" Brigitta whispered sharply, parting the leaves in front of her face.

Vivilia smiled, the corners of her eyes curving up like ribbons.

More voices called from the direction of the Elder Chamber. It sounded like Reykia was conscious and the thought-loop broken. Brigitta pleaded to the sprite with her eyes.

Vivilia nodded and pointed upward. The two faeries followed the path of her finger. At first, Brigitta didn't notice anything but rocky ceiling. Then, Vivilia took a deep breath and blew. As the little breeze hit the ceiling, a portion of the rock wavered. It was some kind of hidden space in the roof of the cave spellcast to appear solid. In a moonsbreath, Brigitta was up and through the hole with Jarlath right behind.

It was dark and tight, with just enough room to open her wings. Plenty of room for a sprite, she thought as she felt her way with her hands, not wanting to risk using the globelight. Muffled voices sounded from beneath them. Then, unmistakably, the high whine of Minq's voice. Brigitta cringed and hoped he could manage to keep their plan a secret. She didn't know if someone had found him dozing and he had squealed, if their plan was still in effect and he was playing his part, or if somehow the Elders had gotten wind of what she and Jarlath were up to.

The shape of the sprite tunnel was odd. First it shot straight up and then angled sharply. Several wingbeats later, it angled down again, as if they had flown up and over something. Maybe another tunnel or the entrance to the Hive. It curved once more and Brigitta was sure they were now flying parallel to the ground. She stopped and crouched on her knees, the tunnel too shallow to stand. She removed the tree branches and nest from her head and misted her mind out, working through the cracks and minuscule spaces within the rock, then the dirt, to the open air.

"We're about twelve hands deep," she said, relighting the globelight. The tunnel stretched out in both directions. Roots had been cut or tied back to keep them out of the way. "Have you felt any other passages breaking off?"

"No," said Jarlath, crouching next to her and removing his own headpiece. "It's more like a channel then a tunnel."

Brigitta tightened the straps of the bundle on her back, making sure the scepter was secure. "I guess we just follow it," she said.

"Do you trust her?" asked Jarlath.

"Ondelle did."

They continued along and in a few wingbeats the tunnel ended at a wall of stone. They pushed at it together, but it wouldn't budge. Confused, they looked back the other direction to see if they had missed something. Then Brigitta looked up and smirked. She blew at the ceiling and it wavered.

"This way," she said, flying up through the spellcast image. As soon as she did so, her globelight went out. She rubbed her hand over it and nothing happened.

They climbed and climbed until Brigitta was more than sure they were above ground level, yet they still climbed. She stopped for a moment and hovered in the air.

"We should have emerged already," she said.

"I was thinking the same thing," said Jarlath.

There was movement beneath them, and light. Brigitta sucked in her breath and shielded her eyes. A moment later, Vivilia scurried past, glowing like a torch.

"Follow me," she said in her small sprite voice.

It was a world within a world, nestled in the widest section of an enormous uul tree. All Brigitta could say while she gazed upon the sprite village was, "How is this possible? How can this be?"

Jarlath patted her shoulder. "Now you know how I felt when I landed in the White Forest."

There were fissures crafted into the trunk that let in natural light. The lines worked with the tree's natural shape, along and between its winding fibers. The light inside was a celestial blue, as if the night sky itself had found its way into the trunk. And what first appeared to be stars above were simply slowly dancing specks of brightness that floated overhead.

There were a few hundred sprites, male and female, who were hard to tell apart. They had reddish and yellowish tones to their skin, and eyes and hair of shifting colors, deep reds and earthy browns and mossy greens. Even Vivilia's hair had grown tawnier since entering the tree, and her eyes grew darker and darker with every moonsbreath.

The sprites didn't seem to have individual homes; they just sat about wherever it was convenient. Some worked crafts, some puzzled over solitary games, some played music or read or drew. It looked like a giant playspace, only there were no children. And Brigitta wondered, had she ever seen a sprite child?

There was a patience about them, as if they were all waiting for something. Nothing was particularly organized, but neither was it disorganized. Everything just was.

All of it was counter to the impish nature she had assumed of them. That most of the White Forest faeries assumed of them. It dawned on Brigitta that perhaps they didn't know anything about the sprites after all.

For instance, the sprites didn't even seem concerned that Brigitta and Jarlath were standing there gawping at them. As a matter of fact, other than several curious glances, they pretty much ignored the two intruders.

"Um," Brigitta turned to Vivilia, "they don't seem surprised about us being here."

"No," was all Vivilia said.

She led them to what Brigitta assumed was the main entrance, as it was the widest trunk hollow leading out of the village. Even at that, there wasn't room enough for Brigitta or Jarlath to open their wings, so they scrabbled and hauled themselves up through the thick branches that formed another kind of tunnel.

When they emerged from the uul tree, they followed Vivilia up and through the canopy to a small wooden bench secured to a branch by vines strung into the trees. As they sat, Brigitta got her bearings. It was dark to the north, but to the south she could make out the twinkling lights of the festival through the leaves and hear the faint cheers and laughter of celebrating faeries. Apparently, news of the stolen scepter hadn't reached them yet.

"Thank you," Brigitta said to Vivilia.

"I don't know why you did it," added Jarlath, "but, yeah, thanks."

The sprite touched the top of Brigitta's hand with her own and smiled. There was a devotion in that touch, a loyalty, something so sincere that Brigitta was nearly overcome. But before she could say anything further, Vivilia had slipped away from the bench.

"Three dusk owl hoots means all clear," she said and disappeared into the leaves.

They settled in to wait for the sprite's signal, anxiety brewing in Brigitta's stomach. She didn't want to think about what lay ahead. What she had gotten them *both* into. And now Vivilia was caught up in her schemes. Or had she been caught in them since the beginning? Brigitta's arms prickled in the cool air as unanswered questions filled her mind.

Something about Ondelle's memory of the day the stone curse hit the White Forest nagged at her. Ondelle had used Vivilia to transport her own spell, just like Hrathgar had, probably *because* Hrathgar had, to protect Brigitta. But if Ondelle had given the Water energy to a different faerie, then Ondelle would have protected *that* faerie and sent *her* into danger. Brigitta would have been turned to stone like all the rest.

The problem was, Brigitta didn't know whether she was the way she was because Ondelle had made her that way, or if Ondelle had entrusted her with the Water energy because she had *known* Brigitta was destined to have it. But how could she have known when Brigitta hadn't even been born yet? And if it wasn't her destiny, what did that say about her attraction to that faerie's Earth energy, waiting, at the bottom of the sea?

What was so special about her energy anyway?

Three dusk owl hoots sounded beneath them. Brigitta shook her head clear and pain shot through her temples. She grabbed the sides of her head, wondering if living with Ondelle's memories would ever cease to hurt so much.

"Are you all right?" asked Jarlath.

"Yeah, it's just . . ."

"It's just what?" Jarlath was still waiting for Brigitta to finish her thought when three additional hoots, slightly more adamant, sounded from below.

"We gotta go," she said and took to the air. She flew ahead of him, cutting the air efficiently, curving northeast out of the trees and heading toward the reed forest where no faeries would be this time of night, especially during the Masquerade. But just because the Masquerade had continued, it didn't mean no one was searching for them. And why shouldn't they be, after what Jarlath and Brigitta had just done?

"Jarlath," she finally spoke up as the tall reeds enveloped them in a grassy sound barrier. "Am I doing the right thing?"

He buzzed through the blades and disappeared, then poked his head back through them. "I don't know, but you're doing something."

"But am I being selfish?" She felt for the scepter on her back, a reminder of the reality of what she had done.

Jarlath fluttered toward her and looked her in the eyes. "You're being very brave, that's what."

"But there's more," she confessed. "You were right. I haven't told you everything about why I need to go—"

He put his hand up. "It doesn't matter. I trust your decision."

Something Ondelle once said sprang to her mind. *There are no right and wrong choices, only the choices themselves. We must make them and go on.*

She nodded and they continued, making a beeline through the reed forest. They skimmed quickly through the soft lowland brush that was the far eastern side of the Earth Realm and jetted toward the dense trees that acted as a buffer between their homeland and The Shift. A waning Great Moon sat low on the horizon, the smaller Lola Moon crescent chasing after her.

This far from the Center Realm, Brigitta and Jarlath

could no longer hear the festivities. It was quiet but for the low exhales of the Singing Caves. In the moonslight, their dark mouths spouted from rocky mounds, calling to each other with every breeze, like earthy ghosts. It was impossible not to stop and listen to them.

"It sounds like dream songs coming from the center of the world," said Jarlath.

Brigitta murmured assent before taking off again. Jarlath followed as she flitted back into the trees and kept a steady pace for several moonbeats. This was the third time she was leaving home. Only this time, she didn't know if she'd be welcomed back.

They made The Shift in good time and scouted the area for Perimeter Guards. There were none, and the Great Moon had disappeared, leaving the smaller crescent to light their way. They stepped into the rocky moat under the Lola Moon's eerie orange glow.

Jarlath shook his head as he looked back and forth across the expanse of earth. "We would never have gotten away with leaving our perimeter so unguarded in Noe."

"It's not their fault they've never known real danger," said Brigitta, feeling the need to defend her kin.

"Well, tonight," he said, "I'm grateful for their ignorance."

Brigitta stopped in front of the protective field and Jarlath nearly ran into her.

She turned around. "You're sure about this? You don't have to come, you know. You can say I spellcast you to do my bidding."

"No, I can't." He smiled, and for a moment, even without their starry-ness, his eyes reflected their signature mischievous spark. "That would mean admitting you could overpower me."

"Ha, ha."

Jarlath suddenly turned serious. "You do need to promise me one thing, though."

"What's that?"

"Whatever happens, you stick to your plan. If for some reason I can't go on, or . . . or . . . just promise you'll go on without me."

"Don't say that. We're in this together."

"This is bigger than me, Brigitta," insisted Jarlath. "Don't ever let me hold you back. Promise me, that's all. Please."

"All right," said Brigitta. "Fine."

Jarlath eyed her skeptically.

"I promise," she said, hand on her heart. "But it won't come to that. It won't."

He wrapped his left hand around her right and they turned toward the wavering field. Each took a deep breath, and they stepped through.

It only took a moment to cross the cool streams of the field. And then it was done. They were on the other side: slightly darker, definitely chillier, and spoiled by a foul odor that made Brigitta scowl.

"I forgot about the smell," she said, gazing the rest of the way across the dirt moat.

"Huh," said Jarlath. He turned back to look at the White Forest with its shimmering leaves punctuating the night. "That was undramatic."

Brigitta laughed and then realized they were still holding hands. She let go and busied herself by straightening her pack and the scepter strapped alongside it.

Jarlath placed both his hands against the field and pushed. He bounced and wobbled against it.

"It feels like pushing against a wall of water." He pulled his hands out and examined them. "But it's not wet."

"You can't get back inside without a White Forest Perimeter Guard. Not as long as the Hourglass spell holds, at least."

"Well," said Jarlath, puffing up his chest, "since you're the only White Forest faerie I know who can go in and fetch one, I'd better take good care of you."

"You'd better be nice to me, too," Brigitta pointed out. A movement in the distance, on the periphery of the White Forest, caught her eye. "We'd better get going."

They hastened into the Dark Forest and were quickly swallowed into its thickness. Brigitta halved her globelight and gave one side to Jarlath, which he tucked away in his pack. She lit hers and they were on their way. She preferred not to travel at night, but she didn't want to stop until they found a safe spot to sleep either. Something far enough from the White Forest so they couldn't be tracked down by the guards, if they dared to come after them. She wasn't sure that they would.

The plan was to journey north for a few moonbeats, then turn due west and simply keep flying until they met Forever Beach. According to the map she had retrieved from Gola's wall, it would be a long stretch of coast to search. But she would recognize the Dragon's beach from Ondelle's memory. She recalled the large plateau at the foot of the mountains and the distance from it to the V-shaped stones.

The trees opened up a bit, allowing them to fly for brief

moments of time, but they still kept close to one another, for the forest was writhing with movement and teeming with sound. Snorts, growls, and screeches followed them as they moved further and further away from The Shift.

A loud hum stopped them mid-wingstroke.

"Sliverleaves!" called Jarlath, dropping to the ground.

"I don't think so," said Brigitta doing the same. She shaded her globelight and squinted into the trees.

When the hum had ceased, she turned back to Jarlath. His body shook as he gripped an old frore dagger that she had never seen before. She held her globelight to his face and stared at him for a moment, his eyes harder and colder than they had been earlier that night, almost menacing.

Before she could ask him about the dagger, a swarm of hairy black beetles shot into her light, startling them both. Brigitta dropped her globelight half, and the beetles immediately descended in a thrumming mass, enveloping the light.

In the abrupt darkness, Jarlath retrieved his own globelight half and set it to a low, warm glow. "Shoo!" he called, kicking and stomping at the beetles.

His foot landed on one with a sickly crunch. All at once, the beetles stopped shaking and humming and looked up at him. Dozens of angry beetle heads cocked, waiting for him to make another move. Then they looked up at the other globelight half shining in his hand.

"Oh, no you don't." Brigitta snatched the globelight from Jarlath and snuffed it out. The world went black and there was a flurry of little wingbeats and prickly beetle legs on Brigitta's face and arms. She shrieked and brushed them away. A moonsbreath later and they were gone.

Both she and Jarlath stood breathing quietly for a few

moments, listening to the hum and scuttle as the beetle swarm moved on. When she was sure they were alone again, she relit Jarlath's globelight half and aimed it at the ground. Her half was gone.

"Bog buggers!" she swore. "Not one night in the forest and I've already lost half a globelight."

"We won't need it," Jarlath assured her. "After tonight, we'll travel by day."

All the menace she had detected in him had disappeared, and the glint in his eyes had returned. She had to be careful, she thought, the Dark Forest was full of tricks. She didn't doubt it could turn them against each other if they didn't watch out.

They stumbled on, and it wasn't long before they found a modest hollow in a tree. Brigitta managed a decent wall of dustmist, with a bit of firepepper for extra measure, to conceal the hole in the tree. They snuggled into their blankets, and before long Jarlath was fast asleep.

Of course, she thought, this was nothing to him. He'd slept in worse conditions. Much worse. This fact didn't comfort her, though, and all the tumbling thoughts and foggy memories and conflicting emotions, both hers and Ondelle's, nagged at her as she listened to the throaty sounds of the Dark Forest beasts.

Chapter Six

Ondelle stumbled into the cottage as Fernatta of Gyllenhale opened the door.

"Ondelle!" Fernatta cried, helping her old friend into her gathering room, which doubled as her classroom, and into her high-backed storytelling chair. "Sit here. I'll fetch you some tea."

When Fernatta returned with a mug, Ondelle was leaning back, eyes closed, looking less like a High Priestess and more like a frightened old woman.

"I cannot . . ." Ondelle began. She opened her black moon eyes, watery with pain. "I cannot hold this Water energy any longer, Ferna. It is taking my strength, and I am using up the Dragon's Gift in order to conceal it. It must be released."

Ferna placed the mug in Ondelle's hands and pulled up an old mushroom chair beside her. She dropped into it with a heavy sigh. "I know, I know . . . and I feel terrible for saying such a thing, but I wish I didn't."

Ondelle placed a hand on the sturdy Earth Faerie's shoulder. "I am so sorry to burden you with all of this. But I trust you more than any other faerie in the forest."

Fernatta placed her own hand over Ondelle's. "I left Elderhood all those seasons ago to avoid these sort of things. I *impart* knowledge through my Life Task. Keeping secrets is counter to my nature. It pains me to do so."

"Sometimes we must do the uncomfortable, and absorb the pain, to maintain peace and balance in the forest."

"Uncomfortable is one thing," Fernatta pointed out. "Hiding the truth is another. How do you think Hrathgar's village-nest would feel knowing we banished the innocent and good in her just because we didn't know how to deal with the bad?"

"And you would prefer they share your suffering?"

"I . . ." Fernatta started, then dropped her hands into her lap and shook her head.

"It was a long time ago, Ferna."

"I still live with our decision every day."

Ondelle, too, often thought of the good Hrathgar, alone with her dark self up on Dead Mountain. She wondered if the two Hrathgars were still alive at all. She thought of Hrathgar's family and friends and neighbors busy at the marketplace or preparing for the next festival, going about their daily lives. The only decisions they had to make were which color featherpaints to swap for their bundle of reeds or how much candleweb spinning to do in exchange for a basket of seasoned gundlebeans.

None of them had any idea how Ondelle had been tortured over the past several seasons with the task of marking, no, *condemning*, another faerie to her fate. She was about to create a lonely life for some young faerie. A life of making the same hard decisions Ondelle had made, of seeing the world without innocence.

"No one else knows of my energy's origin," explained Ondelle. "Who else can I turn to? I just need assistance in this endeavor, a confidant."

"Endeavor?" Fernatta said. "That makes it sound like nothing at all."

"If it helps any, I've decided to transfer only the Water," said Ondelle, staring out Fernatta's window into the trees. "I will not subject the child to unnecessary turmoil. She will have enough burden soon enough."

"But what of your instructions?"

"I will release the other elements when the time is right."

Fernatta stood up and paced the room. After a while, she paused. "I'm not sure how I feel about that," she finally said. "On the one hand, the child will live a more normal life, and you will live a longer one. But in the end, won't she require these gifts? I love you as a sister, Ondelle, but I cannot sacrifice my nephew's child's safety for you."

Ondelle stood and made her way to her friend. She took her hands in her own and gazed into her face, rounded over the years, but with the same kind eyes of her youth.

"I will keep watch over her," said Ondelle. "I will check in with her through our shared connection. I will protect her as I live, and when I no longer live, I will protect her even then."

"I have to ask," said Fernatta, "is this merely your personal fears speaking? We both know what would happen if you sacrificed one of your own elements, let alone both."

"Honestly," admitted Ondelle, "I am no longer sure." She smiled a sad, ironic smile. "But if you do not trust my instinct in this, tell me now, and I will bestow all three elements at once."

"And leave me to watch over and protect the child?" asked Fernatta. She let go of Ondelle's hands and moved to the window. Outside, the Gray Months' melancholy hues were surrendering to the Grow Months' brighter ones. "I don't think I could make such a decision."

Brigitta and Jarlath woke early and had a quiet breakfast of dried berries and honeyroll while still stuffed inside their tree. They didn't want to waste time cooking anything. Afterward, Brigitta gathered the firepepper and dustmist and she and Jarlath were on their way.

The forest was as she remembered: strange wet moss choked the trees, ivy thorns pointed out menacingly, and sour Dark Forest smells poisoned all spirit. But it was a little less frightening than the first time she had left her forest. Perhaps it was because she was prepared and had more tricks up her sleeve, perhaps it was because it was her own choice this time, or perhaps it was because she was with a dependable friend.

She would not drop her guard, however, she told herself as they flew, hiked, pushed, and climbed over the branches and brush all morning. She admired Jarlath's ability to focus. He did not fill the air with unnecessary chatter, or even speak when one of them helped the other through a narrow space or lifted brambles out of the way. They worked well together with Brigitta's sense of direction and Jarlath's vigilance.

His silent trust was a relief, as she was in no mood to discuss the guilt she felt around her secrets, the growing strength of Ondelle's memories, or her new knowledge of her Auntie's part in her destiny. Instead, she concentrated on moving forward, creating a rhythm and breathing to it. Determined not to stop until lunch. There was nothing she could do but continue with her plan.

Hypnotized by her own motion, she moved onward as if through a passageway that had been cut through the trees just for her. At first she thought it was merely directional instinct, but after a several moonbeats, she realized the forest was actually tunneling around them. Walls of thick trunks, branches, vines, and leaves had slowly formed on either side as they traveled. Even the ground was swimming with ivies. She hovered in the air, looking back at the way they came, and forward again at where they were headed.

"What's wrong?" asked Jarlath, doing the same. "Oh."

"I don't like this," said Brigitta. "I feel like we're being wrapped up in a—"

The word "cocoon" sat on her tongue like a spoiled gundlebean. Minq had assured her the carnivorous caterpillars kept to their nests in the northeastern side of the forest. But what if he were wrong, she wondered as she scanned the tunnel for sticky caterpillar threads. What if things had changed in the Dark Forest since he had left?

No silk strands stretched across the branches, which was a relief, but as Brigitta pulled back a giant leaf to reveal a tangle of impenetrable forest, a horrible knot formed in her stomach. There was no way out save forward . . . or backward. And if anything like a carnivorous caterpillar did come through the forested tunnel after them, they would be trapped.

"Jarlath," she whispered, "listen."

He wrinkled his face in concentration. "I don't hear anything."

"Exactly," she said, "nothing. Nothing at all."

She couldn't really see the forest closing in on them, but she sensed it. In tiny, incremental shudderings, it was squeezing them in.

"We should turn back," she said, gesturing behind them. Nothing but forest tunnel as far as the eye could see. "Let's find another way."

They fluttered back, retracing their wing-beats, traveling slightly faster. Again, Brigitta felt the forest squeeze.

"Calmly, breathe," she said. "Don't let it know you're afraid."

"Don't let what know I'm afraid?" asked Jarlath. "And who says I'm afraid?" He forced a laugh to demonstrate just how not afraid he was.

As they flew, it was impossible to deny that the twisted forest tunnel was growing narrower. Finally, Brigitta stopped again. "No, no, we're going the wrong way. We must have gotten turned around."

"This is the way we came," Jarlath insisted. "I swear it."

"I can't feel the direction any longer," said Brigitta, trying to keep the panic out of her voice. "Let's go up."

As they looked up, they instantly knew that was not an option. The top, sides, and floor of the forest were the same wall of impenetrable greens, reds, and browns, of prickles and burrs, of bark and branch. There was no sky, no ground, no sound.

Until.

From far down the tunnel of forest, the vines shook, the branches trembled, and the tunnel began closing in.

"Come on!" Brigitta screamed and grabbed Jarlath's hand. There was no room to fly, so she trudged through the forest's tentacles, pushing and grunting and thrusting her way forward, dragging Jarlath after her.

"It's swallowing us up!" she shrieked, pulling his hand, which suddenly felt much too rough and bony. She squeezed around only to face a solid wall of forest. She was holding on to the end of a tree branch.

"Jarlath!" she called as the forest closed in around her. "Jarlath!

She kicked and screamed, tore at the trees until her fingers were cut and bleeding. She did not dare sit down for fear the forest would close around her and she'd suffocate.

For the Great Moon, cried a voice inside her head, *use what you know!*

She didn't know if it was Ondelle's voice or her own or a combination of the two, but it stopped her struggling.

At least breathe, she thought, and then said it out loud. "Breathe."

In, out went Brigitta's breath. In, out sighed the forest. "Okay."

The air was dark and bitter and heavy. She did her best to concentrate, to balance all her energy by conjuring images of something powerful and steady. Silver scales came to mind, swimming back and forth, back and forth, in a warm current. She held the image until she was collected and focused enough and then sent out a tentative mind mist, seeping in through the slivers of space in the twisted mass of forest encasing her. Slowly, through the tiny spaces, her mind mist drifted, on and on, on and on.

There was no end.

Just as she was about to break the mind-mist connection, she sensed the trees loosening up, like untying a knot. She drew her mind mist back as the loosening approached. And then she could hear the unraveling, gaining momentum, twirling toward her.

A moonsbreath later, the forest opened up and she was looking through the barky, leafy tunnel into a flowered meadow. Before the rift could close again, she quickly stepped through. As she did, a vine snagged on the scepter secured to her back and yanked it from her shoulders. She spun around, reaching into the trees, but the scepter had vanished, and the forest threw up its massive wall once again.

"No!" she cried, pulling her hands away, but not before several thorns snagged her fingers and a branch sliced into her arm.

"No! No!" she shrieked at the wall and then collapsed to the ground in despair. How could she have let this happen?

She sat there for a moment feeling sorry for herself before turning to face the meadow. It was abnormally sunny, and she had to shield her eyes from the sudden brightness. She stood, squinting into the harsh light, as she gaped at her surroundings.

"Impossible."

She was standing in the lyllium field outside of Tiragarrow.

"Impossible," she repeated, whirling around and around.

It was exactly like the field outside of Tiragarrow. It even sounded like the lyllium field she used to lay in practically every day. It had the same buzzing, chirping noises, and the same dragonfly wing flutters. But there was no actual movement. Just the sound of movement. And this field was bordered by a most unwelcome forest. A thick and spiny thing.

"Jarlath?" she called as she stumbled through meadow. The shape of it was just as her lyllium field. The breadth and pattern of flowers the same. She stomped on the ground and reached down to touch it. It was dry and hard and rocky. It should not have bore any lylliums at all.

When she straightened back up, a winged figure was sitting in the middle of the field. It didn't seem to be moving, so she tentatively flitted toward it. It was definitely faerie-sized, but she couldn't tell the color of its wings. Or its hair. Or detect any of its other features. It was like she forgot what it looked like even though it was right in front of her. Even as she grew closer, she knew she could see it, but nothing specific about it registered in her mind.

When she was but moments away, she called out again, "Jarlath?"

The beast, definitely a faerie, stood and faced her.

Its features were her own.

Tall and lanky, with olive skin and auburn hair split into two haphazard hairtails on either side of its head, it wore a green tunic and carried a brown pack on its back.

Brigitta's hands flew to her face, and she landed roughly in the meadow, staring at the Brigitta before her. She wasn't sure if she should be afraid or not. She had spent so much time speaking to herself in her Thought Mirror, she was used to being scrutinized by her own image. Was this creature some kind of wild Thought Mirror?

"Are you me?" she asked.

"Jarlath?" the other Brigitta squawked and cocked her head.

"Uh, definitely not," said Brigitta, backing away.

"Jarlath?" it squawked again, then awkwardly chomped its lips as if it were using a mouth it wasn't used to owning. It hopped up and down a few times, trying out its legs as well. It wiggled its fingers and cried out in glee.

Assuming it wasn't going to attack her, Brigitta put her hands on her hips. "Who are you? What happened to Jarlath?"

Her strange twin cocked its head in the other direction until it was parallel with the earth. It blinked at Brigitta with its eyes one above the other.

"Yeah," said Brigitta, backing away. "I can see you're not going to be any help."

The beast straightened its head, blinked a few more times, but remained where it was. Frustrated, Brigitta screwed up her face and stuck out her tongue at it. The beast stuck out its own tongue, long and purple, like a worm.

"Ewwwww." Brigitta shrank away.

It hopped up and down more adamantly, squawking like a fat bird calling to its mate. Brigitta glanced around the field to see who or what it was calling to. When she turned back around, the odd beast was directly in front of her, staring. She leapt back, still unsure whether the thing was dangerous or simply annoying.

As slowly and calmly as possible, Brigitta stretched out a tentacle of Water energy to see if she could empath its thoughts. Its mental walls were strangely solid for something that appeared to be a complete idiot. Then, its body parts began to flicker; one moment its arm was an arm, and the next moment she could see the forest behind it.

"What are you?" Brigitta demanded.

"Are you," it repeated, this time sounding a bit more like a faerie girl and not as much a clueless bird. Its face moved through a series of other faces: her Momma, Ondelle, Auntie Ferna, Fozk—as if trying them all on for size. Then it went back to her own face and squawked happily, flapping its arms.

Was it stealing images from her mind? She backed through the field. Even if it wasn't dangerous, it was a horrible thing, and it wasn't getting her get any closer to figuring out where she was, what had happened to Jarlath, or how to get the scepter back.

"Well, nice to have met you," said Brigitta finally, eyeing her strange doppelganger. "I hereby dub this Oddtwin Meadow. And if you aren't going to help me, Oddtwin, I'll just be on my way."

She moved closer to the edge of the meadow, and the Brigitta beast moved with her, keeping perfect pace.

"You're worse than my little sister," Brigitta joked nervously. For a moonsbreath, the oddtwin's face was that of Himalette's. Then it was back to her own.

"Stop that," Brigitta insisted as she scurried away.

"Stop that," the oddtwin repeated, following her.

Brigitta stopped, and the beast stopped. Then, it began to convulse. For a moment, it shook so hard it was completely blurred, and Brigitta couldn't tell one body part from the other. When it stopped shaking, it had four arms and four legs. It scrunched up its face, grunted, and a loud popping sound filled the air as a second beast burst from the first.

Two hopping, squawking Brigittas now stood in front of her.

"That can't be good," she said.

The two beasts hopped toward her and cocked their heads. Their movements reminded her of Roucho, her Poppa's featherless delivery bird, and suddenly a shower of broodnuts fell from the sky.

"Ow," said Brigitta as one cracked on her head.

"Ow," said the oddtwins.

Brigitta reached down and picked up one of the nuts. It certainly looked just like a broodnut. She cracked it open and a black beetle flew out, like the ones that had stolen her globelight. It dove at her face, and she frantically waved it away.

The other two Brigittas began to convulse.

"Nice oddtwins," she said, slowly moving away from them. "Good oddtwins."

She was now backed up against the forest wall. As she felt her way along the branches and trunks and ivies and leaves for an entrance of any kind, the beasts started to shake so violently it seemed the earth would open up beneath them. And again when they stopped there were twice as many arms and legs than there should have been.

"That's enough, really," said Brigitta. "I get it, you like to imitate things."

Again there were popping sounds and a moment later, two more Brigittas flew out. This time, they landed on all fours and hissed up at her.

"Bog buggers," Brigitta swore as she moved faster along the forest wall, pushing and shoving to no avail. She turned and flew, searching and searching for some way inside.

Pop! Pop! Pop! Pop! She glanced back in time to see eight Brigittas trailing her, some flying, some crawling, some hopping.

Her heart pounded as she picked up speed. Pop! Pop! Pop! Pop!

There was no way back into the forest. The only way to escape was up. She hovered in the air as dozens of oddtwins scurried toward her.

Pop! Pop! Pop! Pop!

Risking the winds, she fluttered higher and was immediately catapulted back into the wall of trees, grazing her cheek with a sharp branch. Warm blood trickled down her face as she untangled herself.

Pop! Pop! Pop! Pop!

There were now over a hundred beasts after her, but a moonsbreath away.

"Stop!" she called and threw her hands in the air. To her surprise, the creatures stopped mid-flight, mid-hop, mid-slither.

As they all stared at her, little gashes grew across their right cheeks, and blood began to drip from them. Only the blood was black instead of red. Brigitta wiped the blood from her own cheek and examined her hand. Red.

If this meadow somehow manifested things from her own life, maybe she could manifest something on purpose. Something useful. Something to help her escape.

But the meadow kept getting things wrong, so it had to be something simple. Something nonliving . . .

She glanced up. She needed something to help her navigate the winds.

When she looked back down, all the oddtwin eyes were still on her, studying her. She took a deep breath, filling herself all the way to her belly. With every bit of concentration she had, she released her breath and visualized a *wind-winder*. She felt the soft white cords of it, woven from sun-bleached reeds from the marsh farm. Another breath and she visualized each perfectly spellcast square of it. One more and she encased this vision in a cocoon of air, protecting it. She felt its lightness, its balance, and opened her eyes.

Every oddtwin cocked its head at her.

And then.

All at once, they started to convulse.

"Oh, hagworms," she swore. "Bog bugging hagworms."

These things were going to double and double until

she suffocated underneath them. She turned and flitted along the trees. There had to be a way out. There had to be a vulnerable patch of forest somewhere. And then she saw it, up ahead, hanging from a branch: a wind-winder.

She squealed, flew as fast as she could, and snatched up the net, kissing it with a grateful smack, just as the field exploded in multiplying oddtwins. She flew straight into the center of the meadow, with oddtwins close behind. As she flew she loosened and expanded one of the wind-winder's squares and tucked herself inside, buffeting on the wind. The net wobbled while she spread it out in a globe shape. She'd never actually used one before, only watched as the Perimeter Guards practiced.

Hands slightly apart, palms facing each other, she quickly brewed up a patch of balanced air. It was like blowing glass, only without the glass, just the shape of the air. The first one slipped through her fingers, and she gathered it back up. Once it was steady, she slipped it into one of the net holes.

Below her, the lyllium field was completely covered with oddtwins, crawling and slithering around each other like a nest of bugs. A few dozen flew in circles about their heads and cawed up at her as she formed two more patches of air. But she was still flying too low to go over the forest, so she beat her wings, grunting her way higher against the heavy dark forest air.

She filled two more net holes, but still couldn't get control of the wind-winder and was hurtled toward the trees by a sudden gust. Thrusting both hands up, she created two air pockets, one in each hand, and lay them in place just before she collided with the thorny branches. The wind-winder kicked in and the gust was absorbed into the net.

She filled the remaining net holes and fluttered away from the trees. Below her, oddtwins tried to give chase, but the winds were too strong. She wobbled around until she got her balance. It was tricky, and physically exhausting, to fly, concentrate, and keep each net hole filled with conjured air. But still, she managed to get herself higher than the trees and make her way over the forest, hoping she could find Jarlath within the thickness of it.

Encased in her wind-winder, she fluttered along the border of the field, seeing nothing but twisted trees, trees, and more trees. She widened her route and went around again, and again, refilling each net hole as her air pockets dissolved. But she couldn't maintain this forever, she was already more than tired, and there was no place to land. Either she would have to risk crash landing in an impenetrable forest, or go back to the lyllium field and face the horde of bizarre Brigittas.

Three air pockets collapsed at once, sending the wind-winder eastward. Brigitta molded the air between her hands once more as she drifted further away from the meadow. She backstroked her wings, trying to gain purchase, until movement caught her eye. She shifted direction and fluttered toward the motion.

Sitting among the trees was what appeared to be a massive nest. Beasts scuttled along its sides like giant hairy ants, carrying various items in their pincher mouths: branches, fruit, and other bugs. In the middle of the nest stood Jarlath. And in his hands was the scepter.

He didn't see Brigitta above him at first. Balancing in the mess, he carefully poked the scepter into the nest as he eyed the buggy beasts scurrying about their tasks.

"Jarlath!" Brigitta called from above. "Oh, thank the Dragon!"

Jarlath looked up eagerly, but the rest of him stayed completely still. "Don't thank it yet," he said carefully. "And watch out. You do not want to get stung by one of those guys."

As if to demonstrate, a furry little black beast climbed up the inside of the nest on eight spindly legs. When it reached the top, one of the enormous ant-like creatures slashed at it with its rear end, barely breaking ranks, and the little beast tumbled back down into the nest, landed against some debris, and did not get back up.

"I'll lower myself slowly and you get into the net. Just pull evenly on two connecting sides of a square."

"Gotcha," said Jarlath, keeping watch on the beasts circling the nest. His expression grew puzzled. "Where did you get that thing?"

Brigitta maneuvered herself directly over Jarlath and, with careful wing flutters, descended straight down. "Long story," she said.

As Jarlath reached for the net, he pulled too harshly and disturbed two air pockets. The wind-winder tumbled away, and Jarlath held on as they slid toward the side of the nest. Above them, the beasts stopped their scuttling and peered over the edge, antennae circling in the air.

"Get in!" Brigitta screamed, and Jarlath opened the square enough to crawl inside. They tried to coordinate their flying, but it was too cramped for both of them to fully open their wings.

The beasts began scurrying down the sides of the nest.

"Grab my waist from behind," instructed Brigitta, "and beat your wings in exactly the same rhythm as mine."

Jarlath did so and Brigitta swung them up, patching the air pockets in the net as they climbed, higher and higher, out of the reach of the bugs.

"Now you can thank the Dragon," called Jarlath, his heart pounding behind her.

"Not until we find somewhere to land," she said. "You scout, I need to concentrate on keeping this thing in the air."

They drifted northwestward. It was easier to fly with both their weight and wings working together, but still exhausting for Brigitta's mind. She needed to rest soon or they would certainly crash.

Four air pockets dissolved at once.

"Jarlath!" Brigitta called as they slipped in the air.

"We have to go north," he said.

"North?"

"Toward the mountains," he affirmed. "It's the quickest way out of the forest."

She conjured more air pockets to replace the ruined ones, but they were weaker. "We'll have to fly lower," she said, "or the wind will destroy all my work."

They descended and headed north, Brigitta's strength dwindling until she could no longer conjure any new air pockets. The remaining ones in the net holes would have to hold until they could land.

"Up ahead!" called Jarlath. "I see a plateau!"

Brigitta squinted into the horizon and indeed there was a plateau, which would make for an easy landing, if they could reach it before the wind-winder collapsed.

"Hold on," she said, more to herself than Jarlath.

From behind her, she felt Jarlath shake his body as if to restart it for the final stretch. He tightened his grip on her waist and beat his wings with hers. Together they flew, as steadily as they could, toward the plateau. But, one by one, the air pockets gave way, and the wind-winder grew more and more unstable. They tossed and twisted toward the cliff, the last few air pockets dissolved, and they spun backward into the side of the plateau.

They hit hard, Jarlath taking the brunt of it. He let go of Brigitta's waist and they both grabbed for something, anything, on the steep plateau to steady themselves. Jarlath found a handhold and reached for Brigitta. Together they stretched one of the wind-winder squares open and helped each other out. As they shook themselves free, the contraption flew from their hands like a frightened bird.

Brigitta looked up to the top of the plateau. "It's not so far!" she shouted above the wind. "We can do it!"

Jarlath nodded, his face scratched and smudged with dirt. Then he grinned. "Yeah, we've been in worse situations!"

It was true, and suddenly, they burst into laughter. The kind that was part relief and part disbelief. They caught their breaths and examined the dark forest spread beneath them. The hissing, writhing, reeking dark forest was not so menacing from above.

"You first!" Jarlath gestured upward.

They half-scrabbled, half-flew, fighting the wind up the side of the plateau, and pulled themselves over the top, falling to the ground between two tall stones. They lay face-down in the dry scrub, breeze chilling their skin, arms and legs and minds numb.

Brigitta turned her head so that she and Jarlath were facing each other, a few pokey reeds tickling her neck. "Wanna camp here for the night?"

"I thought you'd never ask."

With great effort, they hauled themselves up and were

met by hundreds of standing stones, like giant haphazard teeth bursting from the earth. After rewrapping and attaching the scepter to Brigitta's back, they walked carefully among and around the stones, a few dozen hands tall, half as wide, but not very thick. Brigitta grabbed the edge of one of them and tried to shake the thing. It didn't budge.

"What do you suppose these are?" asked Jarlath, circling another.

"I don't know," said Brigitta, brushing at the stone's sandy roughness with her palm. "But they'll protect us from the wind."

"Do you think this is natural or faerie-crafted?"

"I'm not sure," said Brigitta. "They do feel sacred, but kind of . . . dead?" She walked all the way around one, contemplating its uses.

Jarlath pushed at another one with both hands, then leaned into it with his shoulder. "They seem sturdy enough."

Brigitta walked around the object again, fingers lingering on the stone. "There's an echo of faerie energy here. Like a place that has been swept, but some dust lingers."

She rounded the corner, faced him again, and grinned. "As long as those oddtwins can't reach us up here."

"What are oddtwins?" asked Jarlath.

"Well, that's what I call them."

They fluttered and roamed through the numerous standing stones while Brigitta related her story of the lyllium field and the strange mimicking beasts that multiplied like firesparks. As they moved further into the seemingly endless stretch of stones, everything else disappeared from view, and their voices dulled as if entering a cave.

When she finished the part about visualizing the wind-winder into being, she asked, "So, how did you end up in that awful nest?"

"When we were separated by the forest," began Jarlath, "it basically swallowed me up and spat me back out in there." He held up his arms and examined the tree-branch and thorn scratches, now sealed with dry blood. "I was terrified; I thought I had landed in some giant bird's nest." He shivered. "Thank Faweh it was only deadly poisondarters."

"Yeah," laughed Brigitta, "thank Faweh."

"Still," Jarlath continued, "I couldn't fly out! I kept getting blown toward the sides of the nest."

"What about the scepter?" asked Brigitta. She stepped around a standing stone and froze.

"Oh, I found it lying next to me. I was trying to dig my way—" Jarlath ran into Brigitta. He peered around her.

They had come to the end of the plateau.

Below them, a raggedy carpet of forest transitioned into a long stretch of flat, golden land. Above the stretch of gold, a vast and endless world of shifting blackness that met the sinister clouds and sky in a distance so far away it seemed impossible.

Brigitta's hands went instinctively to her chest for her hourglass and instead found Gola's lifeless moonstones. Tears sprung to her eyes as she clasped them to her heart, holding Gola close.

"The Sea of Tzajeek," she said.

Chapter Seven

"Whatever you are planning, I won't let you do it," said Elder Ondelle, sitting down on Second Apprentice Hrathgar's bed.

"Hmmm," said Hrathgar, dropping into a chair in front of her Thought Mirror, "I don't recall you ever having stopped me from doing anything before."

"I will go to the Elders," said Ondelle.

"Really? Run to the other Elders for help?" Hrathgar laughed and turned to the mirror, studying the contours of her face. "And I always thought you were the strong one."

"Asking for assistance is not a weakness."

"Maybe not," said Hrathgar, "but being disloyal to your friends is."

"You were the one who left us, Gar," Ondelle pointed out. "For a long time. And yes, if it comes to the good of one friend and the good of the whole forest," Ondelle caught Hrathgar's eyes in the mirror, "then my duty lies with the forest."

The eyes reflected in the Thought Mirror glanced toward Ondelle, startling her. Something flickered behind those eyes, something frightened. Something trapped inside that couldn't escape.

Hrathgar quickly turned away from her mirror to face Elder Ondelle. Her eyes now mimicked the cruelty in her smile.

Ondelle stood. "What have you done with her!" she demanded.

"Whatever do you mean?" asked Hrathgar.

"You are not Hrathgar!"

Hrathgar waved Ondelle off. "Don't be silly, of course I am. I've changed, is all. I know things. I've been places no White Forest faerie has ever been before."

As Hrathgar spoke, she rubbed at something underneath her tunic. She slid it out and dangled it on its strap in front of her own face, admiring it. "I have more knowledge, more power. I will not be an Apprentice for long."

Ondelle gazed at the stone, drawn into it. Before she could stop herself, she reached over and touched it. Images swarmed her mind: *her hands on a young blue Water Faerie's face, a woman with skin like a tree, a circular vibrating ring, thought-looping across the arena to a sprite* . . . and in a moonsbreath the images scattered.

"Anything interesting?" Hrathgar smirked as she tucked the stone back into her tunic. She leaned closer to the shaking Ondelle. "Perhaps you saw your own woeful end?"

"No . . . no . . ." stammered Ondelle, backing toward the door. "I saw yours."

It was Hrathgar's turn to be shocked. She caught herself and began to laugh.

"A girl," said Ondelle, more to herself than to Hrathgar. "I sent a young girl . . ."

She fumbled for the door. As she yanked it open, Hrathgar called after her. "I look forward to meeting her some day!"

Ondelle slammed the door and leaned against it, Hrathgar's laughter vibrating through it from behind her. The air felt thin; she couldn't breathe. Her hands flew to her throat. She looked up and around frantically, trying to find someone who wasn't there. Gasping.

Brigitta snapped awake. Jarlath was leaning over her, snarling, hands around her throat. A moonsbreath later, he pulled his hands away, and stared at her, dazed.

She sat up, choking fresh air into her lungs. "Jarlath! What in Faweh?!"

"Are you all right?" he asked, blinking in confusion. "You cried out in your sleep."

"You were trying to strangle me!" she accused, rubbing at her sore neck.

"What?" He shook his head vehemently. "Why would I do that? You were having a nightmare or something. You cried out. I just joggled your shoulders to wake you up."

Brigitta leaned back on her elbows and stared at him. He looked back at her, eyes only full of concern. Had she been having a bad dream? Why would he have been choking her? It didn't make any sense.

But it wasn't a dream.

She sat up again and hugged her knees to her chest. "I was having one of Ondelle's memories."

"In your sleep?"

"Yes, you know that happens."

Jarlath twisted around and sat cross-legged in front of her, pondering this. "Then how do you know they're not dreams?"

"I just do," she said defensively.

He nodded agreement, but there was hesitation in his motion.

"Well, it *was* a little different this time," she admitted. "Ondelle and Hrathgar had a fight and Ondelle started choking. Then, it was like she was looking for someone. And I had the strangest feeling it was me."

"You see?" he said, visibly relieved. "A bad dream." He lay back down with his arms under his head. "Maybe all your own memories and emotions are getting mixed up with them?"

Brigitta only shook her head. It was not a dream. She could tell the difference. She knew that memory was of the night Hrathgar tried to steal the power of the Hourglass. Ondelle had warned the other Elders. Hrathgar was overtaken by her evil side, then was split in two, and her two selves were banished to Dead Mountain.

Was Ondelle trying to warn Brigitta, too?

"My neck," she said, rotating it around. "It hurts."

"You probably strained it getting up to the plateau," Jarlath said, "or using that wind-winder."

"I guess," she said. She didn't want to talk about it any more. Something wasn't right.

"I'll take watch now," she told him. "Your turn to get some rest."

The sky was already lightening by the time Jarlath's breath turned to the deep and rhythmic cadence of sleep. Brigitta ventured closer to the edge of the plateau, leaning up against one of the stony pillars and gazing across the black sea as it licked the sand. A faint rushing sound glided through the air and she grew excited by the prospect of touching that water.

She flew back to where her traveling companion slept curled beneath a petrified pillar, and her heart trembled as she watched him sleep. If anything were wrong with him

. . . if he wasn't the real Jarlath . . .

Had he been replaced by some oddtwin? No, she thought, those things couldn't string two words together on their own, let alone have a conversation. But she could still feel his hands around her neck and see the maniacal look in his eyes. And she couldn't shake the image of Hrathgar, terrified, in the Thought Mirror.

What was it if it wasn't something that happened back in that bug nest? How long had he been acting strange? Did it have something to do with losing touch with the Ancients, or, and she shuddered to even think of this, had he been duping her the whole time, working for Croilus and spying on the White Forest? Her gut told her, no, it couldn't be. It was something else.

And she didn't feel safe any more.

There was a little *blurping* sensation inside her mind, as if a bubble had popped in her head. She kneeled down and put her hands on the ground to steady herself.

Hello, a soft voice intruded. A voice she didn't recognize, but which sounded as if shaped from her own thoughts.

"Hello?" she called out loud.

Hello, the voice inside her head said again, accompanied by movement behind one of the stones at the edge of the plateau.

Brigitta picked herself back up and crept around the stones to find a beast huddled against one of them. Its skin was so light it glowed, and so thin she could see veins and organs within and a dark shape reverberating in its chest. Its eyes were bulgy black, like large wet pebbles, and its nose resembled a snake's, just two small pits in the center of its face. There were two slits in each side of its head instead of ears, and the skin over its lips was swollen and bluish, though its mouth was shaped much like her own. For clothing it wore only short trousers made of rough green plants.

It shivered as it held up its hands, palms forward, five webbed fingers on each.

I being Narru, it said without moving its mouth. *You hearing me?*

She nodded as the beast tottered forward into the gathering light, and she decided it was a male beast. He steadied himself against the closest standing stone.

"What do you want?" asked Brigitta.

Want? he asked, pulling his hand away and sifting through the grains of sand that had come loose in it. When he looked back to her face, he blinked a few times, lids closing sideways across his eyes, like curtains. He seemed quite young. She had no idea how young, he just had a childlike energy about him, curious and frightened.

"Where are you from?" she asked, more gently this time.

He smiled. *Pariglenn, Flota of the Saari. Having you knowing of this place and Saari?*

She couldn't have heard that right. "Pariglenn?" she asked. But as soon as the word left her lips, she recognized some of the Saarin's features from the mural at Croilus when they had found the Purview. The mural of the World Sages. This boy was from one of the ancient civilizations.

"But that's across . . ." She gestured out to the sea. "How in the Dragon's name did you get here?"

He gestured wide with his arms. *Going through a great—*

His face registered shock and pain and he fell forward to the ground. Behind him stood Jarlath with the scepter.

"Jarlath!" Brigitta cried, rushing to him and grabbing the scepter from his hands.

He grinned at her. "I knew that thing would come in handy!"

"What have you done!" She kneeled down to Narru and felt his head. There was a nasty bump on the base of his skull.

"What do you mean?" said Jarlath. "I was keeping this thing from attacking you."

"He wasn't attacking me," she said. "We were having a conversation."

"I hate to break it to you," said Jarlath, "but you were talking to yourself. You were not having a conversation."

"He was talking to me in my mind," she explained.

"Would you listen to yourself?" he cried.

"I know what I heard."

"And you can trust anything you hear in the Dark Forest?"

"This is different," she insisted. "Don't you remember his kind from the mural at Croilus?"

Jarlath's hands went to his head and he groaned. "For Faweh's sake, Brigitta, what is wrong with you?"

"What's wrong with you?" she retorted. She bent over to look into Narru's unblinking eyes. They had a thick film over them that she hadn't noticed before.

"He was putting some kind of spell on you," continued Jarlath in a gentler tone.

With her pinky finger, Brigitta gently touched the Saarin boy's cheek. It, too, had a thick, transparent layer over the skin.

Jarlath pulled her back. "You'd better not get too close."

"Stop it, Jarlath, he's not going to hurt me."

"You're right, he's not." Jarlath pushed Brigitta aside and, using his hands and feet, rolled the strange beast toward the edge of the plateau.

"What are you doing?" Brigitta fluttered over to Jarlath and yanked on his arm. Without the protection of the stones, the wind whipped at her wings as she struggled to pull him back.

"What does it look like I'm doing?" said Jarlath with a shove. "Getting rid of the ugly thing."

"You can't do that!" she cried. "He hasn't done anything wrong!"

She pulled harder on Jarlath's arm until he turned and snarled at her. "Do you want my help getting to your Dragon or not?"

She let go of his arm and stepped back. "Jarlath, please!" she begged him.

"You are so naïve. No wonder your forest is in danger." He turned back to the mysterious boy from Pariglenn and gave one final shove with his hands.

The Saarin fell over the side and Brigitta dove after him, getting under his body and catching him. He was heavier than he looked, dense with muscles, and she plummeted several wing-lengths until she could catch her balance. She fluttered frantically in the gusts of wind as she climbed back up. Jarlath simply stood on the edge of the cliff, arms crossed, scowling at her.

With a heave, she pushed the boy back up over the top of the plateau, his limbs flopping like dead fish. As his body fell over, something on his right hand caught her eye.

"Let's see if you can do that again," said Jarlath, sticking his foot on Narru's stomach.

"Wait! Look!" Brigitta held up the Saarin's hand. On his two middle fingers were matching rings, identical to the ones the Nhords had used to get through their Purview to find Brigitta in the Valley of Noe.

"Oh." Jarlath's expression softened, and then his shoulders slumped as, all at once, the anger drained from his body. He looked down at his feet as if the anger were puddled there.

"I'm sorry." He looked back up, dark hair whipping across his face. His deep blue eyes had regained their usual warmth. "I guess . . . I'm a little rash sometimes. I was just trying to protect you."

The Saarin moaned and shifted himself into a sitting position. His curtain eyelids opened as his hand went to the back of his neck. Thick lips pouted beneath his confused expression. *Much unfriendly.*

Brigitta helped the boy up and led him back to the protection of the stones. Jarlath followed in silence.

"Narru, this is Jarlath," she said, holding her hands out between them. "He can't hear you in his mind, so he thought you were going to hurt me."

The Saarin stared intently at Jarlath with his moist eyes. Jarlath shifted uncomfortably. *You being right. He having no hearing.*

"Well," said Brigitta as Jarlath and the Saarin regarded each other. "Maybe we should have some breakfast?"

Narru slipped behind one of the giant sand teeth and pulled forth a knapsack. It was brimming with dried fruits and salted tubers the likes of which Brigitta had never seen, even in the lushest White Forest farms. They were bright and fragrant, incongruous with the hazy morning above and threatening forest below.

At first, Jarlath wouldn't eat any of the Saarin's food. But, not wanting to appear rude or distrustful, Brigitta took one bite of everything Narru offered, and several bites of something he called lingomana, which had a crisp, tangy outer peel and a sweet pulpy inside. Her delighted sighs finally convinced Jarlath to taste it.

My sharing, your sharing? asked the Saarin in Brigitta's mind.

"Oh," she said, laughing, "you want to try something of mine?"

The Saarin nodded happily and Brigitta dug out some honeyroll for him. He crumbled it up in his fingers, enjoying its texture before filling his mouth with it. If he could have gone cross-eyed, Brigitta was sure he would have from sheer pleasure.

"This is all very nice," grumbled Jarlath. "But don't we have an important mission?"

He was right, of course. It had just been nice for Brigitta to forget herself for a while in Narru's cheerful energy. "Narru," she started, placing a hand on his, "we need to know where you got those rings."

"Puh," he said out loud and nodded. He popped his lips a few more times and felt them with his fingers.

My Foundings, he said, *having ring guarding.* Brigitta repeated what he said to Jarlath.

"Foundings?" he asked.

You not having? the Saarin said. *The ones of your keeping. Protecting and feeding, knowledge giving.*

"You mean parents?" asked Brigitta. "Our parents raise us, take care of us."

Sure, yes, making like that. Gatamuel and Sarilla. He having ring gifting and he giving mate Sarilla ring gifting. Now I having ring gifting. One for me, one for my mate giving.

"I see," said Brigitta, not bothering to translate for Jarlath, who was losing his patience beside her. "But do you know where the rings come from originally?"

Saari tellings of ring giftings from faeries.

"Yes!" Brigitta cried, wanting to hug the young Saarin.

"What?" demanded Jarlath. "What did he say?"

"Just a moment," Brigitta told Jarlath. "Narru, did a little fuzzy light come to you and did you go through a Purview to get here? A large round metal structure?"

The Saarin grinned wide with his bubbly lips. *Five sun risings past, floating light coming and playing with my thinking. Light helping me searching for Blood Seed. Making of Pariglenn. Heart of land.*

Little floating light coming to right Saarin. Narru patted his chest proudly. *No Saarin land walking like me. I practicing in light and dark, land walking.*

In the growing daylight, Brigitta translated as the Saarin explained that Flota of the Saari was his home, a series of floating and ever-changing islands off the eastern coast of Pariglenn. Ever since the Great World Cry had overrun Pariglenn with the element of Earth, the Saari spent the majority of their time in the ocean, as the land on Pariglenn was so fertile that everything grew faster than the residents could cope with. All of the beasts on Pariglenn itself either flew or dug and were constantly on the move.

Staying on land, being still, and you being buried, said Narru.

The small moving islands prevented the vegetation from growing too quickly, but also kept the communal Saari vigilant, as they were always adjusting to the rearrangement of their neighbors. The motion of the waves and tides were incorporated into all aspects of their lives. They were so accustomed to the movement of the water, however, that they were susceptible to "land sickness."

Not I, Narru said, eyes shining with pride, *I practicing land walking in secret. I going ashore and climbing trees.* He held up a webbed foot and extended some claws from each toe, grinning. *Much sharp from tree-climbing.*

Since the first time he had heard the tales from his *ersafounding,* his grandmother, Brigitta deduced, the young Saarin had been obsessed with finding the ancient Blood Seed, the "heart of land" as he called it, from which all roots on the continent supposedly began. The myth was that whoever found the origin of the roots would have the power to transport himself across Faweh. He felt a calling to find this Blood Seed, and his preoccupation with it made the other Saarin "concerning" for him.

"I know the feeling," muttered Brigitta.

Little floating guiding me to Blood Seed. Making purpose. Much meaning to me. So much, looking for origin even in dreamings.

It took Narru three suns to reach the center of Pariglenn, only stopping for brief naps in the trees, fearful he would be suffocated by the overgrowth if he slept too long. When he reached the center of the continent he found what looked like a red barren hill, but on closer inspection, discovered it was a mound of thin roots, so tightly interwoven he could climb them. And when he did, he was met by a round, silver structure engulfed in the roots. The whisper light slipped through it, and it began to hum and twist, loosening itself. The roots dropped away to reveal silver carvings shifting around the ring. He followed the whisper light through and landed on the plateau.

When he finished his story, he smiled. *Little floating making mind knowings.* He pointed to Brigitta. *I knowing being with you.*

Excited by the similarities, Brigitta related her experiences with the Purview in Noe and the Nhords, who came from the northern continent of Araglenn.

"Jarlath, Narru!" she exclaimed. "There must be a Purview on each continent. That's how everyone else came to visit the faeries in Noe. I bet there's two more to be opened, one on Carraiglenn and one on Storlglenn!"

"So what if they're all opened?" asked Jarlath, crossing his arms in front of him. "How does that help us right now?"

"I don't know," she admitted, "but I know someone who will." She turned to her new friend. "Narru, how would you like to come with us to find the Eternal Dragon?"

As Brigitta and Jarlath packed up their belongings, the Saarin chipped away at the top of the plateau, and then buried the cores, seeds, and stems of his food.

"I don't think anything will grow up here," Brigitta told him.

Not doing for growing, he answered, *doing for feeding. Land hungry.*

"Oh, well," she shrugged, "I guess if that keeps it from eating us . . ."

"Hey," asked Jarlath from around one of the stones, "have you seen my knife?"

"Where did you leave it?" asked Brigitta, wrapping up the scepter once again and strapping it to her back.

Jarlath got down on his hands and knees and wiped at the ground. "I didn't leave it anywhere; it was around my leg!"

"Maybe it fell off somewhere?" she asked.

"You've been with me all morning, you know I haven't been anywhere." He stood back up and paced around the standing stones until he came back and faced the Saarin. "You!" he accused. "Open up your bag!"

"Jarlath!" Brigitta scolded him.

Narru gazed up from where he squatted on the ground, and Jarlath kicked a fruit core out of his hands, sending it flying off the cliff.

"Open your bag!"

Narru gestured at his bag and Jarlath ripped through it, pulling out a water canteen, more fruits, berries, nuts, and tubers. No knife. Jarlath stood there and scowled, breathing heavy through his teeth, nostrils flaring, as if he were about to charge.

"Jarlath," said Brigitta with all the calm she could muster, "maybe you should sit down for a while?"

Without warning, he lunged at her. But before he could reach her, he froze, his eyelids fluttered, and he fell to the ground.

The Saarin's bulgy eyes bulged even more. *You powerful telling at doing*, he said in awe.

"That wasn't me," she said, rushing to Jarlath's side. She felt his face and neck; he was alive and breathing. "I have no idea what just happened. But it's not the first time he's acted so strange. I'm really worried. Something's been wrong with him for a while."

I sensing your mistrusting. The Saarin lifted a flap on his leafy pants and revealed the frore dagger embedded flat against his skin, as if in clay. He peeled the knife off, leaving a dagger-shaped impression on his thigh, which he rubbed to reform the skin.

Maybe you should keeping. He handed the knife to Brigitta.

Against her better judgment, and everything she had promised herself she wouldn't do, Brigitta settled her breathing and sent a mind mist out to empath Jarlath's thoughts. What she felt was a dark barrier, and something confused and frantic behind it. Like the real Jarlath was trapped beyond her reach.

Then, she sensed that he sensed her, on the other side of the barrier. Just like when Ondelle had sensed Hrathgar's good inside the mirrored eyes of Hrathgar Evil. Brigitta sent tendrils of mind mist to search for a way inside, but there was no way to get through.

When she pulled away she realized the morning had passed and they were still on the plateau. She had no idea what to do. Some spell had been cast on Jarlath and she didn't even know when it had happened, how it had happened, or who had cast it. She had to get him back home to the Elders as soon as possible. One of them might know what to do.

But as she gazed out to the sea, so close now, the thought of turning back dissolved into grief. "Oh, Jarlath," she murmured at the expanse of water.

Before they had crossed The Shift, he had made her promise that she would go on no matter what. "You knew something was wrong, didn't you? You made me promise because you knew." She almost laughed, thinking about how furious he would be if she ignored her promise. She sniffed before she even realized tears were falling down her cheeks.

When she turned back around, Narru was wiping Jarlath's face of dust so tenderly it gave her a kind of hope.

There was something comforting about the Saarin, like there had been something comforting about Abdira and Uwain. Like they were all connected. Like they were meant to find each other.

"Narru," she said, "I don't think he's coming out of this spell. Not without help from someone who knows more magic than I do."

Finding this helping now?

"I'm going to leave him here," she said, attempting to sound braver than she felt, "and come back for him later."

I helping, said the Saarin. *Leaving of foods and water in case waking.*

"Good idea." Brigitta looked around and picked up a chalky black rock. "I'll leave a message, too."

They moved Jarlath behind one of the thicker standing stones to protect him from the wind and bundled him in a blanket. Brigitta set up a dustmist camouflage for good measure and on the stone in front of him scratched with a rock:

WAIT HERE

KEEPING MY PROMISE

BACK SOON

"I'm sure he'll be fine," she said, choking back further tears. She leaned down and kissed the top of his head. "Come on, Narru, before I change my mind."

The young Saarin was right about his adaptation to land.

A tremendous climber, he was limber and lithe, using the extended claws on his fingers and toes to dig into the rock face. Still, it was terribly windy and slow going. Brigitta flew next to him in case he should lose his footing, which he did several times, but the mind-connection between them made her anticipate each fall, and she caught him after he had barely left the rock. By the time they hit the forest floor beneath the plateau, it was well into the afternoon.

Odd, said the Saarin, once they had rested for a bit. *Land being so still and quiet.*

"Quiet?" asked Brigitta, shivering as she listened to the thrum and hum of the dark forest beasts and bugs. "Hardly. Listen to all those things."

Not beasts, land itself. Not earth growing like Pariglenn. He put his hand to the ground, like feeling for a heartbeat, and smiled.

"Maybe some day I'll take a trip to Pariglenn, and you can show me where you live."

Yes! The Saarin stood back up. *Shall we seeing Dragon now?*

Narru sprung along on the backs of his feet, almost like a frog, as Brigitta hiked and trudged and flew through the thick forest. Traveling with Narru reminded her of her journey to Dead Mountain with Himalette. Curious and excited, Narru didn't seem to realize how dangerous the forest could be.

"Narru," asked Brigitta, "do you have giant caterpillars on Pariglenn? Or giant frogs? Or giant beasts of any kind?"

Saari giants of Pariglenn, he answered. *Many giant beasts swimming in far out deep water. Only small beasts living on earth land. Much too quick earth land. All beasts swallowing up unless moving.*

"Swallowed up?" said Brigitta, and the Saarin nodded. "Perhaps I wouldn't like it then."

The woods were dense, the thorns sharp, sticky webs and spittle caught on their hands and faces and Brigitta's hair, but they still managed a steady pace. They grew quiet, saving their energy for moving through the forest, until the trees began to thin and a new sound, a muffled and gusty roar, filled the air.

"Shhh, what's that?" asked Brigitta. She hovered in the air and listened to the rhythmic rumbling beyond the trees.

Narru leaped up and down with his hands in the air. "Puh!" He popped his thick lips together. "Puh! Puh!" He pointed ahead of them excitedly.

The waving, his words reverberated in Brigitta's mind, *sea calling.*

Narru raced ahead of her, through the last of the trees, and she pushed herself to keep up with him. The roaring grew louder, the air colder, and the forest broke away.

They were met with a stretch of blustering sands that extended north and south into the distance until devoured by rocky mountains that shot into the sky, impaling the large grumbling clouds overhead.

Not being in sea since five sun risings! said Narru, and he leapt through the spinning sand dervishes, scattering pebbles and shells with his long feet.

"Narru, no!" Brigitta fluttered after him, squinting as the sands pelted her face. "Wait!"

Ignoring her calls, Narru splashed into the dark waters and disappeared.

"Narru!" she called again as she reached the water's edge. "Narru!" she cried desperately.

She landed in the wet sand, away from the wind-blown grains. The sea that she had thought was completely black was nothing of the sort. It was dark blue, darker than Jarlath's eyes, with grayish foam that rode the crests of the waves and sinister shadowy plants that stole what little light filtered down from the skies. She could see nothing past them, had no idea what might lie underneath.

"Bog buggers." Brigitta paced back and forth, dodging the water as it lapped the shore. She leaned down and stuck her hand in a small wave as it approached and the icy coldness of it shocked her.

If Narru hadn't been drowned by the sea's weeds, he had certainly frozen to death. Or been eaten by something. Whatever lived in the sea.

Her mission suddenly returned to mind. The Eternal Dragon!

She ripped the scepter from her back, conjuring Ondelle's memory. She had to summon the cliffs. Flitting back over the whirling sands, she buzzed up the beach where she thought the rocks should be. Sure enough, there they were, just like they had been in Ondelle's memory.

She felt vindicated and relieved. The Elders were wrong. It was not simply a matter of exhaustion and grief. She would summon the cliffs and the Dragon, and the Dragon would save Narru and Jarlath and the White Forest!

Her heart pounded as she approached the V-shaped stones. Like she remembered, they were about three hands high and flat on the top, like long narrow platforms.

She unwrapped the scepter and lifted it over her head, bringing it down hard into the sand, which accepted it easily. And then the sand took hold, like a baby's mouth around its thumb. She let go, and the scepter stood there on its own between the rocks.

She fluttered back toward the beach and waited for the rumbling to begin.

A little sand storm licked at her wings.

The waves crashed and rolled onto the shore.

The stones were still.

"Come on!" yelled Brigitta. "I did what I was supposed to do!"

Nothing. The stones remained exactly as they were, and a moment later, the scepter spat itself out into the sand.

Perhaps she hadn't shoved it into the sand hard enough. She flew back up to the rocks, picked up the scepter, and thrust it back in.

The rocks were still. A moment later, and the sand spat the scepter out once again.

Brigitta! came Narru's voice in her mind.

She whipped around to face the water just as the little Saarin leapt from the sea and bounded up the beach toward her, panic on his face. *Coming, coming up to beach!*

"Narru!" Brigitta cried. "Thank the Moons, I thought you were gone."

When he reached her, he grabbed her arms with his slick wet hands, claws extended, snagging her skin. *Coming up to beach! Many not-beings!*

"Ow!" she cried, and as she pulled away from him she saw something emerging from the water.

She and Narru leapt over the two platform rocks and squished themselves as flat as possible. Brigitta eased up to the space between them and peered through. More than one something was emerging from the sea. A whole flock of colorless winged somethings advanced together, as if to a piece of music only they could hear. Dozens and dozens and dozens of them appeared, lining up in formation along the shore. Amassing like shadowflies on a honeyed branch.

Faeries, Brigitta realized. Faeries larger than Brigitta had ever seen. Lifeless, yet somehow moving. Enchanted dead. As they emerged, each found a position on the shore and stopped, face forward, expressionless and waiting.

It took almost a moonbeat for all of them to gather on the shore, and once they had, they shuffled to part in the middle. A shimmering bubble rose from the sea and floated up the beach, landing between the parted faeries.

The bubble popped.

Brigitta's world wobbled around her, and she had to sink her hands into the sand to steady herself. For standing on the beach, in one of his ridiculous purple robes, was Croilus of Noe.

Chapter Eight

The Dragon sped past Ondelle in a silver streak, and the water around her cleared. In front of her was another bubble, just like her own, and a young faerie was trapped inside. She had dual elements, Water and Earth, and looked eerily familiar, but larger than any young White Forest faerie would be. Her eyes were closed, and her face relaxed, as if enjoying a gentle dream. Most definitely alive, she breathed long, slow breaths, but beyond that, Ondelle had no idea what state she was in or how long she had been that way.

The Eternal Dragon sped by again, this time clearing the waters farther behind the encapsulated faerie. Beyond her stood row upon row of colorless faeries without bubbles. Ghostly things, although not translucent; solid and organic, like living statues.

The Dragon circled around the rows of faeries and headed back toward Ondelle. She caught Its eyes and was instantly lost in their abyss. For a moonsbreath, it felt as if her mind were about to leave her body. It was so frightening, yet so exhilarating, that when the Dragon turned away, disconnecting her from Its powerful gaze, she slumped to the ground.

When she arose, there was a new orb upon her scepter. Still in a daze, it took a moment before she realized what the Dragon had done. The orb was beautiful, sparkling like a newborn star. It was her destiny; it was her charge.

"Welcome," spoke the faerie in the bubble.

Transfixed by the Dragon's Gift, Ondelle had not noticed the faerie awaken. With her eyes open, she no longer appeared so young. Deep and bright crystal blue, they held both innocence and wisdom. Joy and pain.

"I am Ondelle of the White Forest." Ondelle bowed, not sure what was custom when an elemental faerie met an Ancient for the first time.

"I am Narine of Noe," the Ancient said. "Please, stand for your knowing."

The High Priestess straightened up, ready to receive, her scepter grasped with both hands. Narine fluttered toward her until their two bubbles touched. She spread her hands forward and the bubbles mingled, then merged. A warm vent of air wafted into Ondelle's watery cocoon and Narine took hold of the orb.

A sudden burst of energies and images flooded Ondelle's being until Narine placed a hand on her arm, and they subsided into a gentler flow. Still, they were such disconnected thoughts and feelings and memories and dreams that she could not make any sense of them.

"Do not try to sort them as they come, nor force a meaning," said Narine. "It takes its own time for a body to figure out how to live with its knowing."

Ondelle nodded as Narine pulled her hands away. Her skin grew cold without the Ancient faerie's touch. Narine then pressed her hands upon her own chest and belly. They settled and her body quivered a bit. Her hands appeared to sink into herself, reaching inside to extract a nebulous entity.

She slowly moved the entity through her bubble, and it pulsed in the air like a heartbeat. She held it up to Ondelle; it was her Water energy.

Ondelle gasped. She had no idea elements could be extracted from living faeries, only ascended during dispersements. Did this mean Narine was no longer alive? And how could she be anyway, it now dawned on Ondelle, after one thousand season cycles?

Narine released the element to Ondelle, who took it in her own hands. She couldn't exactly touch it; she more held the air around it as it swirled and beat in front of her.

"This you are to give when the time is right," said Narine. "As my energies were given to you before you were born, so you will pass your three on to a new faerie for the future of Faweh. Above all, these energies must be protected. They are the last of their kind."

While the Water energy seeped into Ondelle's being through the palms of her hands, Narine pulled her bubble away and they became two again. The Ancient faerie girl drifted back to her original spot on the ocean floor, and then took root, with the haunting formation of Ancient faeries behind her.

"But," Ondelle called to Narine as the energy dissipated into her being, "how am I to give it and to whom?"

"You will know when the time is right," said Narine. Now bonded solely with her Earth energy, she appeared smaller and more fragile and somehow, farther away. "And when the time is right, you will know."

Brigitta opened her eyes, shook her head, and shivered in

the cold dark air. She lifted her face, neck throbbing, and a layer of sand stuck to it. Wiping it with her hand, she tried to recall where she was and the last thing that had happened before—

"Narine!" She bolted upright and spied over the rocks in front of her to the beach beyond.

Then she remembered the last thing she had witnessed before being assailed by Ondelle's memory: Croilus and a force of entranced Ancients. But why would the Ancients obey him? What had he done to them and how had he done it?

She recalled the bubble Croilus had been encased in, just like the one in Ondelle's memory. Did that mean Croilus had been visited by the Dragon? Had Croilus called up the rocks on the beach?

She looked down to the space between the rocks, hoping it could tell her something. But the hole she had made earlier that day was already refilled with sand.

Croilus left Noe with Mabbe's scepter; it had allowed him to travel through the Purview. Perhaps Croilus had known exactly what he was doing and where he was going. Perhaps his plan had always been to get Mabbe's scepter renewed by the Eternal Dragon.

Did that mean Croilus now had the power of Blue Spell?

Had the Eternal Dragon made a mistake?

Brigitta?

"Narru!" She twisted around and saw the Saarin scrambling down from a tree in the forest.

Thinking you disappearing like Jarlath, he said, shaking with relief. *Thinking I being alone.*

A wave of pity washed over her. The poor stranger

had discovered much about the outside world in a short amount of time. What she had discovered a few season cycles ago: the world was not a safe place.

She was very glad to see him, but troubled by the memories now crowding her head. She didn't even know where to start.

"Narru," she said urgently. "What happened? Tell me everything."

Man faerie flying with not-living faeries. He pointed toward the mountains. *All going away.*

"How long ago?"

Long as your sleeping.

"The man faerie in the purple robe," she tried again as gently as possible, "did he have a scepter with him?" She held up her own. "Like this one?"

Oh, yes, having like that. He nodded.

Something else occurred to her. "All those faeries were colorless, right? Like spirits?"

Narru nodded. *Not-living.*

"There wasn't a young girl faerie with bright blue eyes and silvery hair and green wings?"

No faerie as her I seeing.

Brigitta leapt up and grabbed her scepter. "We have to find her." She turned to the Saarin, who blinked his sideways eyelids at her. "You have to find her."

Without a bubble encasing from the Eternal Dragon, it would be impossible for Brigitta to find Narine in the bone-chilling water. It would be too dark and murky to see, even with a globelight, let alone breathe. Narru, on the other hand, was built to swim in the ocean.

She described what she could from Ondelle's memory of her visit with Narine and asked Narru if he thought he could communicate with her.

Yes, this I believing. He nodded emphatically. *And when you speaking in mind body with me, we speaking to Narine.*

"Wait, you mean I can empath your mind and speak with her through you?" she asked.

Yes, you speaking with Jarlath in earth body. Speaking with Saarin in mind body.

"Narru, I can't understand half of what you say, but I think you're making complete sense."

The day had grown dim and windy. They trudged back down to the shore, holding their arms across their faces to protect against the pelting sands. A gust came off the water, yanking at Brigitta's wings, so she turned and walked backward, throwing them wide so that they wrapped around her, keeping the sands away. As she pushed her way to the shore, she studied the mountains to the north and the long plateau where Jarlath was hidden.

"Narru," she said, "Croilus went that way?"

Yes.

A heavy pang of guilt shot through her heart. "Hold on, Jarlath," she said.

She hoped for his sake they could find Narine. Imagine, she thought, Narine herself! Friend to Gola, daughter of the High Sage. Certainly she would know how to help them.

As the sand storms dissipated, and the beach transitioned into lapping waves, Brigitta turned back around and sat upon a small log, calling for Narru to stop. She removed the remaining globelight half from her pack, lighting it up to demonstrate, then breaking it into smaller slices and handing one to him.

He shook his head, amused. *Saarin own light making.*

"If you say so," she said. He waited as she stuck the slivers of light into the sand, little crescent moons glowing up at them. Then she closed her eyes and misted her mind out, tentatively reaching for his, as unfamiliar and awkward as a first kiss.

When she reached his mind, she allowed a few drops of Water energy to trickle into the space behind his eyes, and they settled there, almost as if sitting down in a chair that had been pulled out just for her.

This is how you all communicate, she said as it dawned on her. *By visiting each other's minds.* It made good sense for creatures whose homes were always shifting on the sea.

She sensed his mind assent without any words. It was obvious Narru was adept in this giving and receiving of "mind body" talking. It must be instinctual to the Saari. Effortless, like breathing.

Amazing, she said, her own thoughts reverberating in his mind.

Opening your eyes, he said.

She did, and she could somehow see him and the ocean beyond at the same time she could see her own self through his eyes. He viewed the world in what she could only describe as a tender light. His eyes took in far more detail and depth and color than a faerie's eyes did.

All right, she thought inside his mind, *I'm ready.*

Through the Saarin's eyes she dove into the water. It was murky, but he was built to move and live in it. His body emitted a glow that extended evenly through the gloom. She felt no shock of coldness, no fear of drowning, no sting when the salty wetness hit.

He was skilled at holding her mind with his, even more so than Ondelle had ever been. It felt like he was holding the "hand" of her mind, keeping her there. He propelled himself forward with powerful webbed feet, breathing through the slits in the side of his head. Traversing the sands, back and forth, they dropped farther and farther away from the beach. He swam one direction, then the other, methodically searching until finally he paused and shook his head.

No breath holding, he thought to Brigitta, *dizzy making.*

Brigitta almost laughed. She hadn't realized she'd been holding her breath. She exhaled and counted off in rhythm, like a lullaby, and the Saarin swam to it, comforted by her sing-song voice. Below them, shelled beasts scuttled across the sea floor, and in front of them, strands of mottled greenery stretched up, reaching for light, as tiny critters hid within.

He turned left and swam for a stretch, and then right. A large shape appeared, glinting in the dark water. As he swam toward it, Narine's figure came into view, encased in exactly the same manner as Brigitta had seen in Ondelle's memory.

Narru swam to within arm's length of Narine's sweet face. Even though her eyes were closed and her body still, Brigitta could tell Narine lived. Somehow, she had been protected all these season cycles, frozen in time, never aging like Mabbe had.

Hello? Narru called tentatively and poked at the bubble. *Are you awaking?*

The faerie inside shuddered, took a deep breath, and blinked open her eyes. Brigitta was shocked to see that they were now crystal white. Her shocked expression was mirrored on Narine's face, whose mouth dropped open when she found Narru in front of her. She placed her hand against her encasing.

"You're not—" She stumbled for the words. "Are you from . . . from . . . Pariglenn?"

Yes, Brigitta's mind reverberated his answer. *Narru from Flota of Saari. And being with me faerie Brigitta from the Forest of White.*

Speaking in Narru's mind body, Brigitta added. *I'm on the beach.*

Narine's eyes couldn't get any wider. "You'll have to pardon me, I have no concept of time any longer." She broke into a wide grin. "Nevertheless, how joyous this occasion!"

She moved forward and threw her arms toward Narru's head. Her bubble expanded to include him, and Brigitta could feel the comfort of its warmth.

Narine's grin quickly faded. "Where are the rest?"

What do you mean? said Brigitta.

"I sense only my Air and Water."

That's me, said Brigitta. *Ondelle gifted me with your Water before I was born, then later, she gave me her Air.*

"What of her Fire?" asked Narine, now looking more than concerned. "And what of the Earth I gave to Croilus to take back to the White Forest? Where are those?"

Brigitta's heart dropped to her stomach.

Croilus isn't from the White Forest, she said. She could feel herself tensing up in Narru's mind body, and him struggling to keep her there.

"But I thought with the Saarin here . . ." Narine struggled to locate the question. "So, you have not come to disperse us? Faweh is not balanced?"

What? Of course not, said Brigitta, *that's why we've come to you.*

It was several moonsbreaths before Narine spoke. And even then, she took Brigitta by surprise by easing herself down on the ocean floor with an, "Oh."

What do you mean, Oh? Panic rose in Brigitta's chest.

Slowing breathing, Narru thought to her. *Calming thoughts.*

She tried to calm herself, but she could not believe this was Narine, the Ancient faerie from Noe. And now that she was just sitting there on the ocean floor, stripped of all her elements, she didn't seem any wiser than Brigitta herself. Even after all this time, Brigitta thought dejectedly, she was still just a girl.

You're supposed to be the one with all the answers, Brigitta accused.

"He had the Dragon's Gift in his scepter . . ." Narine stared off into the darkness of ocean. "He said he would take my Earth energy to the White Forest."

To steal your other energies! Brigitta exclaimed, her mind dizzy, her connection to the Saarin slipping away. She refocused herself on Narine. *He had no destiny markings, no element of his own!*

"That had been foreseen for the White Forest faeries. I assumed he had come just in time." She looked back up at Narru. "Who is this Croilus faerie?"

He's from Noe, said Brigitta. *He's a descendant of Mabbe. He tried to overthrow her.*

"What?" Narine sat up.

That's whose scepter he had, continued Brigitta. *That's how he tricked you.*

"That's not possible!" Narine stood, eyes wild. "Mabbe would have to be—"

One thousand season cycles old, confirmed Brigitta. *I met her myself. She was but skin held in place by magic. She's gone now, swallowed up by the River that Runs Backwards.*

"Oh, Great Moon." Narine trembled as she placed her hands on Narru's shoulders and looked into his eyes, searching for her faerie kin sitting alone on the beach. "I have given myself away: my elements, my knowings. But this was orchestrated a long time ago, you understand, by consensus of the Ancients. And now . . ." She closed her eyes and emitted a pained laugh. "This is how I'll spend the rest of Faweh's seasons. That was the risk we took all those moons ago."

Not understanding, Narru spoke up. *What this meaning?*

Narine opened her eyes and let go of his shoulders. "The Dragon gave Croilus his gift, and I've bestowed mine. That's the end of it. The knowings are spent, the elements released." Narine's encasing slipped from around Narru and the cocoon of warmth vanished with it.

No! said Brigitta sternly, startling both Narine and the Saarin. *I have not lost Ondelle and my friends and my family for Croilus to win. For the White Forest to be destroyed. I will get your Earth, and I will take back the Dragon's Gift.*

"But how?" asked Narine.

I don't know, but I will do it or die trying. What choice do I have?

I doing with Brigitta, the Saarin said, placing his palm against his chest.

Narine took a deep breath and nodded. "I have nothing left to gift you," she finally said. "I have no energy left for transference and no recollection of the knowings. As the last of them was given, so they were forgotten. I may appear solid, but truly I am an echo of myself."

What do you mean? asked Brigitta.

"I mean," said Narine, "my own destiny has been served. I can tell you pieces from my life, but forgetting is all I have left to do. I'm sure what happened to Mabbe was horrifying . . . Ancients weren't meant to live this long. It was a great sacrifice to cast the spell that kept me here."

She shook her head sadly. "I was hoping to be released to the ethers rather than sit on the bottom of the sea in perpetual ignorance."

Recalling some bit of her past, she abruptly pivoted to search the waters around her. "And soon the Dragon will claim what's left of my memories." She returned her attention to Narru and attempted a smile, but Brigitta could see she was truly frightened. "My gift back to It."

Then tell me what you do know, said Brigitta, *and I will do all I can to make things right.*

"I can tell you that all my energies will be attracted to each other," she began, "especially now that they are all released. You will sense the others as you approach, as they will sense you. They were meant to find each other again.

"I wish I could tell you what was in the knowing I gave to Croilus." She searched the waters again. "It will settle itself in him in a matter of moons, depending upon how much his body fights it. There are ways of provoking him so that the knowledge never completely settles. I do know the last of the Blue Spell will be useless to him unless it does."

Then we will have to make sure it never does.

A vast shadowy movement shifted behind her in the distance. Narine's body jerked, and for a moment her expression was blank. She shook herself back to attention. "Never does what?"

Faerie girl mind-body slipping, informed Narru.

Brigitta focused all her energy on staying connected with Narine. *How do I provoke someone to keep him from a knowing?*

"Give him something to be unsettled about. A potent dilemma."

What about all the Ancients? Where have they gone?

"The Ancients . . ." said Narine, turning all the way around in a circle, noticing their absence for the first time. "Oh."

Man faerie leaving with non-living faeries, said Narru, gesturing toward the shore. *Going to mountains.*

They were somehow under his control, added Brigitta.

Narine opened her mouth to speak, but the dark movement returned, zigzagging in their direction. Her eyes glazed over. "I—I don't know."

Can we stop Croilus from controlling the Ancients? asked Brigitta.

"If they are connected, and he is killed," Narine said slowly, sifting through her broken memories, "they will be destroyed along with him."

As if being doused by cold water, Narine grew suddenly lucid. "Destroyed, Brigitta, not dispersed. The fifth element lost forever."

Then what do we do?

"You could still balance Faweh—" she started.

The dark shape grew closer, and her voice drifted away again.

" . . . even if it is too late for us . . ."

The shape swam into view: a silver- and green-scaled mountain of a beast.

". . . maybe that would be enough to appease the Dragon . . ."

Brigitta? called Narru nervously, backing away from Narine.

How do we balance Faweh? Brigitta asked, urging him to stay.

"How?"

The beast tunneled into a mass of sea weeds, Its tail flicking through the water behind it.

Narine's eyes glazed over for a second time. "Birds," she said in a faraway voice. "I remember great white birds."

Not remembering long, said Narru as they watched the Ancient girl struggling to piece a memory together. *No sense making.*

"No," Narine said, voice fading, "the birds are important."

A sudden shift in the water thrust the Saarin backward, and he grabbed hold of two long rubbery plants to keep from floating away.

"You should go," Narine murmured and closed her eyes.

Narru clawed at the sandy floor with his feet, pushing away from Narine.

Calmly, so I can stay with you, said Brigitta. *It's all right, Narru.*

All right being for you, he thought, *sitting on beach.*

She concentrated on staying with the Saarin, comforting his mind. The shape wound its way around within the sea weeds, and Narru twisted in the water, trying to keep an eye on it. She could feel his heart pounding, his panicked breath, and then, their connection ceased.

Alone on the beach in the dark and cold, Brigitta stood up from the log, jolted into her surroundings. On the shore, Narru rushed from the water and scurried on all fours, backward, like an upside-down spider. As she hurried to assist him, a monstrous head burst up from the sea on a neck of bright silvery-green scales. Long and slender, the neck stretched up and up, towering over them.

Brigitta grabbed Narru by the shoulders and they

stumbled back as the beast's eyes opened, pulling them into Its limitlessness. Frozen in place on the beach, Brigitta and Narru held onto each other, thoughts scattered and useless.

The Eternal Dragon gave a great snort, and then opened Its mouth and inhaled.

Every last bit of warmth, every last bit of color, every last bit of light trembled and loosened and crackled until it all broke away and was inhaled through that awesome mouth. For a moonsbreath, Brigitta could see and feel nothing, as if floating in a void. And then, it all snapped back into place and the Dragon was gone but for a large round ripple on the surface of the water.

Brigitta and Narru sat clutching each other in the wet sand, speechless.

Dragon giving warning? the Saarin finally spoke, voice trembling.

"I don't know what that was," said Brigitta, unable to let go of Narru, "except another sign that we are on our own."

After they picked themselves up and dusted off the combination of sand and mud, they made their way wordlessly back up the beach toward the forest. Brigitta had no idea which was less dangerous at night, forest or beach, but she did not want the color sucked from her world again, let alone all her memories. She was done with Forever Beach.

They moved along the edge of the forest until they came across a portion of wood that had been wrenched away. A stray piece of purple fabric waved from a broken branch, and Brigitta plucked it off.

"Croilus . . ." she whispered, holding Narru back as she scanned the trees. "I don't feel anything. Narine said I would." She pulled at Narru. "Come on, there's nothing for us here."

As they traveled toward the plateau, she hoped upon hope that Jarlath was all right. She thought about the Ancient voices, the ones Mabbe had forbade the Noe faeries listen to. Croilus had listened to them and they had driven him mad and then brought him here. The Ancients had wanted all of Narine's elements to be united in one faerie with the last of the Dragon's Gift, so they could finally be dispersed when Faweh was balanced.

She doubted Croilus had such unselfish plans.

A wet blast of sand from the beach startled Brigitta from her thoughts. The plateau loomed in front of her. Night had cloaked them in with no stars to lead the way. It was either fortunate or unfortunate that the Saarin's skin glowed.

"Is there any way to turn yourself down a little?" asked Brigitta, looking up to the top of the plateau, which seemed higher and farther away than it had earlier that day.

Narru examined his hands and feet and smiled. *I being good lighting.*

"Yeah, but right now you need to be good hiding." She removed an extra tunic from her pack. "Put this on, and use the hood."

With her tunic on, he looked like an old faerie woman. Splashes of brightness shone from his fingers and toes as he grappled with the rocks. He and Brigitta used all their strength to fight the current of air as they ascended. She sent the Saarin scrambling ahead in case he lost his footing. But he didn't fall this time, and she silently thanked the Great Moon, as she doubted she had the energy to catch him.

A few moonbeats later, and they pulled themselves over the edge of the plateau, scurrying behind one of the great standing stones to get out of the wind.

"Do you remember where we left Jarlath?" Brigitta whispered, unsure of why she felt the need to do so.

Leaving him here, Narru said, pointing to the stone next to them.

"Here, but—" Brigitta twisted around. Sure enough, her scrawled message was still on the stone and scattered footprints marked the ground.

And then she felt it, a pulling, a longing. A part of her wandering lost.

Brigitta. Narru yanked on her tunic sleeve.

A few wingbeats away, Jarlath stood leaning against the side of one of the great rocks. He appeared winded, confused, but otherwise unharmed.

"Jarlath!" Brigitta called and fluttered toward him.

He stared, almost past her, as she approached. And just before she reached him, several other figures appeared around him, large and ghostly.

The enchanted Ancients.

They took up the space on either side of him as Brigitta dropped to the ground, and when she wheeled around, more landed behind her, closing her and Narru up in the circle.

"How lovely to see you again, Brigitta of the White Forest." Croilus stepped out from behind them and flashed his sickly smile. "I believe you have something for me?"

As the Ancients herded Brigitta and Narru together, moving as one entity, she scanned their faces. They looked bewildered, as if not understanding why their bodies were doing what they were doing.

"Narine's energy!" cried Brigitta. "It belongs with me." She held up her hands as they closed in. "Ancients, can't you feel it? I am your kin!"

"They can't feel anything any longer!" Croilus's self-congratulatory laughter filled the air. "Not if I don't let them."

The old Noe faeries stopped moving and stared not at, but through Brigitta and Narru, who pressed his trembling body against her, fingers clawing her shoulder. A few of the Ancients parted and Croilus was there, angular face flushed with victory, scepter in hand.

"They are my servants," he said smugly. He tapped the closest one, a stout male with a beard that tapered to a point just below his chin. "Bags of skin held up by my goodwill."

Brigitta forced herself to look at the Ancient. Everything about him was colorless, probably lost to the Dragon Itself over time. His wings were longer than Brigitta was tall, but empty of life, and there was no hint of crystal or sparkle in his eyes. Croilus was right; there was no Ethereal energy among them. No energy of any kind . . . except . . .

She snapped her attention back to Croilus. Yes, Narine's stolen Earth energy flickered beyond her reach. Unsettled, the energy flustered inside him. Beads of sweat formed on his forehead even though it was chilly on the plateau. She met his eyes. A fleeting frantic look came over him until he blinked it away and scowled.

He's frightened, Brigitta thought to Narru.

Emboldened, she straightened up, remembering Narine's advice. "They won't harm me," Brigitta said to Croilus, "and you cannot control them."

As she said this, she felt him falter, and a tension released from the throng of Ancients. They were like puppets, but Croilus didn't own them as well as he wanted her to believe. The knowing had not settled in him.

She leered at the old Watcher, mustering all the conviction she could. "They will turn on you when they realize the evil in your heart."

He panicked and swung around maniacally, and the Ancients tumbled away. "Get her energy!" he cried. They stood there, looking at him almost curiously. He spun around, focused himself on Jarlath, and repeated his command. "Bring it to me!"

Jarlath broke away and streamed toward Brigitta with a battle cry, slamming into her and knocking her backwards. She stumbled to the edge of the plateau, and as she regained her balance, Jarlath leaped through the air and landed on top of her, pinning her to the ground. She struggled to loosen her wings from beneath her.

"Jarlath!" she cried, pushing at his chest. "It's me, Brigitta!"

A moonsbreath later, Narru rushed at Jarlath, but he deflected the Saarin with a well-placed kick, and Narru tumbled back into one of the standing stones. Jarlath lifted a rock from the ground and brought it up over his head as Croilus shrieked with glee.

Brigitta softened her voice and attempted a futile mind mist. "I know you are in there, Jarlath. And I know you'd never hurt me."

She stared into the frightening dark-blueness of Jarlath's

eyes as he held the rock above his head, arms quivering with indecision.

"Jarlath," she whispered, "please, no."

With an anguished cry, he brought the stone down on the thin upper bone of Brigitta's left wing, and she both felt and heard it crack. She screamed in pain, writhing underneath him. He lifted the stone again, this time aiming for her skull, his face contorted, eyes wild.

A gust of wind streamed up from behind him, the stone flew out of his hands and sailed over the edge of the plateau. He twisted away and Brigitta shoved him off of her, the top of her left wing hanging useless.

She tried to stand, but was too dizzy with pain. It pounded around her injury like a separate heartbeat. Another gust swept Jarlath off his feet, and he struggled in the current of air to regain his stability. In a frenzied struggle with an invisible foe, Jarlath managed to swing himself out of the wind, and he collapsed to the ground huffing and puffing for breath.

Brigitta followed the wind as it retreated to its source. Hovering next to a crumbling stone was High Priest Fozk of Fhorsa. He turned his attention to Croilus and the Ancients as she fought to stay conscious. Two ropes of air twisted out of Fozk's hands like snakes and wrapped themselves around Croilus's body.

Don't kill him! thought Brigitta frantically as the world faded away. *You'll kill the Ancients!*

Chapter Nine

Ondelle brushed her long black hair in her mirror. Her Thought Mirror. She held her image's gaze and numbed her mind, muddying her thoughts so she wouldn't have to listen to them.

Her image stopped brushing and dropped her hand into her lap. "Really, Ondelle?" she said from the mirror. "You think you can hide your own thoughts from yourself?"

Ondelle set her brush on the table below the mirror and folded her hands. "Sometimes it is best to be without thought."

"You were destined as a sacrifice," her image blurted.

"We are all destined to sacrifice ourselves in one way or another," she responded.

"She won't be strong enough with just the one element," Ondelle's image accused, then leaned toward her. "You are disobeying the Ancients and the Dragon Itself!"

Ondelle stood up and slammed her hand down on the table. "She's a child! And I was charged to protect her! What would you have me do, leave her all alone with enough power to destroy herself?"

"You managed as a deodyte."

"She will have an acceptance I never had. She will gain the trust of her forest."

"You cannot control her destiny, Ondelle," the image

said quietly, playing with the brush in her lap.

They sat there in the silence of that truth.

The image spoke again. "Just be certain your motives are not self-serving."

Ondelle sat back down at her mirror. "I will protect her as necessary and bestow the gifts when it is time." She grabbed the edges of the mirror and spoke into her own black moon eyes. "But I will not allow her to be feared and abandoned by her own kin."

Brigitta! a voice called inside her head, and then her body was hefted up, weight tugging on either side of her.

"Brigitta!" a familiar voice cried close to her ears.

Minq!

Startled awake, Brigitta struggled to stand, turning to hug her friend.

"Oh, Minq, I'm so glad to see you!" she cried, grabbing his face and kissing him on the nose.

"No time!" He pulled at her.

It took a moment for her to get her bearings as Minq tugged at her from one side and Narru from the other.

In front of them, Fozk stood with his noose of air extended and loosened. It surrounded Croilus as he swirled his scepter wildly to keep it at bay. The airy ring twisted in on itself, knotting up and bursting apart. The Ancients whirled around, tumbling through the gusts of air that ricocheted off the standing stones. One shot of air struck Fozk, forcing him to the ground.

As Croilus and the Ancients retreated through the stones, the air continued to swirl about them, like water through channels in a river. Fozk's hair and tunic flapped wildly in the windstorm as he rose, lifted up his arms, and gathered the Air energy, shaping it into one large mass.

But something had tampered with it, expanding its force, and there was too much energy for Fozk to contain. The wind grew wilder, the stone in front of Brigitta cracked, and pieces of it pelted her body and face and injured wing.

"I can't hold it for long," cried Fozk, opening his arms to encompass more.

She looked to where Jarlath had been blown away from her. He sat on his knees, hugging himself and shaking in the windstorm. Brigitta held out her hand. "Jarlath, come with us."

He scowled at her, stood up on wobbly legs, and followed Croilus and the Ancients through the stones.

"No!" she cried and stumbled after him.

Another stone cracked and a large chunk of it slammed into the ground. She leapt to avoid it and a surge of pain ran from her broken wing to the center of her back.

Narru pulled her by the arm. *Too dangerous. Death making.*

"Jarlath!" Brigitta screamed, yanking herself away from Narru despite the pain.

"We must leave at once!" shouted Fozk. "We are no match for the stones!"

She turned to Fozk, wild-haired and wild-eyed, and felt the icy dagger of destiny. This moment, she had been here before.

When she had touched Gola's moonstone before leaving for Noe, Brigitta had been assaulted by visions. Crossroads, Gola had called them, marking decisions she would have to make. One of them presented itself now. But Brigitta had only seen the crossroad, not the decision itself, and she had no idea what to do.

"Brigitta!" Minq pleaded with her. He held onto the edge of a cracking stone with his hands and both ears.

When she looked back, Jarlath had disappeared. The world crumbled around her. Tears streaming down her face, she let Narru guide her to Fozk and Minq. With a snapping of his wrists, the High Priest released the Air energy he had managed to harness and formed a buffer of wind leading down the side of the plateau. Fragments of stone pelted them as they descended over the edge, Fozk carrying Brigitta in his arms, and Minq and Narru eyeing each other as they clambered down side-by-side.

Hunched over a log, Brigitta cried into her arms as Fozk set her wing, and Minq and Narru warmed dinner on the fire. They had made camp in a small clearing the High Priest had declared "safe enough" after he wove some dustmist and firepepper through the air.

No anger pricked at Brigitta that Minq had told the Elders where she had gone. She was too crushed about Jarlath. He would never have left her like that; she didn't care what she had promised.

"It was wrong to leave," she said through her tears.

"Puh," sounded the Saarin with a pop of his lips. *We Saari saying thing never wrong being, just other being.*

Brigitta lifted her head. "That's easy for you to say."

He stared at her, flames mirrored in his moist eyes. *I having no way home*, he pointed out. *Being that wrong?*

"I don't know." She crumpled back down again. "Maybe. How do you know *you* were the one supposed to follow the whisper light into the Purview?"

I being here, he said, *that how I knowing.*

Fozk paused in his task. "Are you going to share Narru's thoughts?"

"He doesn't hold my sense of despair," she said.

Fozk nodded and lifted his hands to create little airy cushions around the branch he had used to set her wing. He was gifted with the element of Air, yet she had never sought him out as a mentor, thinking he was somewhat fragile. Under his healing touch, however, she now realized his energy was simply lightly balanced, nimble, utilizing a quiet core strength. She considered what she knew of him: a gifted mind mister, more focused than the average Air Faerie, and a master of empathing.

Which meant, since he wasn't following her conversation with Narru, that the High Priest hadn't snuck into Narru's mind, nor hers for that matter. She twisted around, even though it pained her to do so, and looked into his sky-bright eyes, barely bluer than the pale skin and white hair around them.

"Thank you."

"You won't be able to fly for some time," he said, finishing the cushion and testing its strength. He moved to the fire to warm his hands. "When we get back, Adaire will tend to you. She is a more talented healer than I."

"I'm not going home," said Brigitta. "Not while Jarlath is still out there."

"You'd risk both your lives with only half your strength," said Fozk.

She was about to argue when Minq cut in, "You in no shape." He shook his head, ears flopping over his shoulders.

She knew they were right, deep down she knew, but she had to do something. She couldn't just leave Jarlath with Croilus. Back at the plateau, she had let him go because she had no choice. How could that have been a choice? Her wing was broken; she couldn't fly after them in the windstorm with the stones crashing all around. No, that wasn't the crossroads she had visualized through Gola's moonstone. The choice was much deeper, much more sinister than that. It wasn't just about Jarlath.

"High Priest Fozk," she said, closing her eyes and swallowing at the lump in her throat, "I have to tell you something. I have to tell you several somethings. And you have to believe them all."

Fozk pulled out a blanket and handed it to Brigitta, then spread one on the ground for himself. "I'm listening," he said, and gestured for Minq and Narru to dish out the meal, a broodnut mash mixed with some of the Saarin's tropical salts and dried seaweeds.

"I'm not crazy," Brigitta started, taking the proffered bowl from Minq's ear.

"I don't recall ever saying that you were," replied Fozk.

Brigitta didn't know where to start. If Fozk had gone to the Eternal Dragon like he should have after Ondelle died, none of this would have happened. Croilus wouldn't have a charged scepter or Narine's Earth energy. But no one, not even her, had known what Croilus was up to, so she couldn't exactly blame the High Priest for that.

"Croilus has the last of the Dragon's Gift in his scepter," she said. "He can call forth Blue Spell if his knowing takes hold. If his body can figure out how to live with it."

Fozk's expression remained still as Minq and Narru gathered closer.

"Go on," said Fozk.

"The High Sage's daughter, Narine, held back her elements when the rest of the Ancients transferred them to the White Forest faeries after the Great World Cry. When Faweh was ready to be rebalanced, her elements were to be united again in one faerie who would use the last of Dragon's Gift to lead the Ancients back to Noe to be properly dispersed. But Croilus isn't interested in dispersing Ancients with Blue Spell. He wants to control them for some horrible purpose."

She recalled the rhyme in the first Chronicler's book. A White Forest faerie would *travel back to times of old to make the balance right again.*

Something nagged at her. Something was missing. She couldn't figure out how everything was connected so the balance would return. The whisper light led them to Noe before the last of the Dragon's Gift was given. So that meant they had to balance Faweh *before* dispersing the Ancients. But maybe Ondelle had messed everything up by not gifting her Narine's Air and Fire energy when she was supposed to. And where was Narine's Fire energy now?

Both Brigitta's head and wing ached, and her mouth was dry. As if reading this thought, Fozk opened his pack and pulled out a canteen. Brigitta took several gulps of pipberry-sweetened water before continuing.

"I don't know what's going to happen now," she said as her tears came again. "I don't know what Croilus will do with the last of the Blue Spell. Or how he'll use the Ancients."

She rifled through her belongings and found the useless scepter. She unraveled it from its bindings and stared into the crystal on the end. "How can Faweh ever be balanced now? Without uniting the elements, without Blue Spell . . ."

She handed the staff over to Fozk. As he reached for it, something glinted inside of his tunic: his hourglass necklace.

". . . your necklace," she murmured.

He reached for it, as instinctively as she used to. The motion triggered a memory. One of her own memories this time.

"Ondelle's spell." She sat up straighter and pointed to his chest. "In the necklace! There's still some Blue Spell left!"

Over the next moonbeat, Brigitta related the story of how Ondelle had placed the whisper light into her hourglass for safekeeping and sealed it there with Blue Spell magic that would return Brigitta to the White Forest if Ondelle died in Noe.

The dark forest noises faded into the background, and time stood still as Fozk listened intently to Brigitta's tale. Minq and Narru huddled together by the fire, wide-eyed and silent.

"But Ondelle didn't die in Noe," Brigitta concluded. "That return spell she cast was never used. So, it's still in there, right?"

Fozk took the hourglass out from beneath his tunic, held it between his palms, and closed his eyes. The rest of them waited while the muffled rustles and howls outside their circle of protection returned to Brigitta's awareness once again.

She considered the dustmist and firepepper that temporarily kept the beasts at bay. It suddenly felt like weak defense. The wisest and most powerful White Forest faeries might survive in the Dark Forest, but what about everyone else? What about Himalette and her Momma and Poppa? What about little destinyless Duna and Tustin? Who among them could manage carnivorous caterpillars or devious oddtwins?

Fozk opened his eyes and studied the hourglass. He looked up and nodded. "It's quite shielded, but, yes, I believe it's still there."

"Do you think there's enough to renew the Hourglass?" Brigitta asked hopefully.

"I'm not sure," answered Fozk. "I don't know of an occasion in which Blue Spell was conjured for one spell and then redirected for use with another."

"But we can try, right?"

"With your help," he said. "The spell was intended for you, so only you can release it."

What being Hourglass? asked Narru.

She turned to the Saarin. "The Hourglass of Protection. It was a gift from the Ancients. It keeps our forest safe, but must be renewed each season cycle using Blue Spell."

If you renewing Hourglass, this lasting only one season cycle?

"Yes, it would be temporary, but it could afford us some time."

"If it works," added Fozk. He reached over and patted Minq on the shoulder, whose expression had grown grim.

No way making protection lasting longer? asked the Saarin.

"No," said Brigitta. "It only lasts one season cycle. We can't extend the protection any longer without more Blue Spell."

"Actually," said Fozk, "we can."

Brigitta perked up so quickly she startled Minq. She winced as she shifted her wing. "What do you mean?"

"There's a spell included in the original White Forest Chronicles by Chevalde of Noe to indefinitely extend the protection if necessary."

"How come we've never used that spell before?" asked Brigitta, incredulous.

"Because it completely shuts the White Forest off from the outside world," Fozk said. "Forever."

Even though Fozk had done a credible job of easing her pain, Brigitta's mind still kept her awake. She regretted declining the ceunias leaf Fozk had offered as she tossed and turned beneath her blanket, contemplating the choice that had to be made: risk the lives of every White Forest faerie, including her family, or shut Jarlath out of the White Forest forever.

And what about her friends in Noe? If their connection to the Ancients had been severed, they would be unable to disperse Nightwalkers or use the Purview. What if they, too, were somehow under Croilus's command? She shuddered at the thought.

Another thought struck her. She had no power in the White Forest. She wasn't even an Apprentice any longer. The Elders would decide what to do no matter what she had to say about it. Of course, she could refuse to release the Blue Spell to them, but what kind of selfish faerie would that make her?

Ondelle had protected Brigitta in her way, so that

she would not become an outcast among her family and friends, but Brigitta had managed to make everyone distrust and resent her all on her own. Perhaps that was part of her destiny as well.

She sighed heavily, exhausted by her own mind.

"You awake." Minq's small, high voice reached out.

"Yeah."

She sat up on her elbows and searched for her friend in the darkness. He was lying near the edge of the clearing by her feet. His ears stretched up and batted at some branches above his head where the dustmist wall had thinned.

"I sorry, Briggy," he said. "No go as planned."

"Does anything ever?"

"You happy we come for you?" he asked.

She dropped her elbows and sank into her blanket. The word "happy" couldn't find any purchase in her thoughts.

Minq lay his ears back down. "Fozk already know, back at Hive. Minq no betray you."

This information did not surprise her, but she wondered at it nonetheless. If Fozk had known she was going to steal the scepter, why in Faweh hadn't he stopped her from doing it? She curled her blanket tighter around herself, as if that would protect her from all that lay ahead.

"I still yours?" Mink asked, voice cracking.

"Of course, Mink," she answered. "And I still yours."

She took another deep breath, filling her belly fuller and fuller with it until she was certain there was no space left in her entire being. And then, she called forth her Water energy, which filled the minute spaces, the cracks and crannies, until she was so full she was numb.

Chapter Ten

It was all Ondelle could do to keep her hands from shaking as she took the jar from Perimeter Guard Gaowen of Thachreek and held it up to her face. A little fuzzy yellow light pattered against the glass as if attempting to communicate.

"Thank you, Trease, Gaowen," she said. "Please wait here for further instructions."

Trease looked relieved to be rid of the tiny light, but Gaowen's eager face leaned closer, begging for more information.

Ondelle simply smiled at them both. "I will return soon."

After she left the gathering room, her knees went weak, and she stumbled down the corridor to her personal chambers. She closed her door, pressed herself up against it, and opened the lid of the jar. The little light blinked up at her. Carefully, she moved farther into the room and set the jar on her dresser, then sat down on her bed, hands in lap. Waiting, heart pounding.

It had been many season cycles since she had received a new piece of her knowing, a morsel that had been tucked away until triggered by the whisper light. Until the moment the two guards brought the light to her, she had been certain that all of Narine's knowing had been evoked.

How had such a thing hidden itself so deep inside of her that she could not detect it?

As the light floated out of the jar and toward her face, a familiar energy filled the room.

Hello again, something chimed, not in her ear, but directly into her head. A tinkly, musical sound.

"Hello," Ondelle breathed.

The light dove and bumped up against her chin, her neck, and down her arm. Ondelle turned her right hand over so that the light rested in her palm. It gave off a blast of energy and she gasped.

Suddenly, she knew: she must travel to Noe and find the Purview.

And all of her, including the part that Brigitta housed, had to come with her. Narine's energies jostled for attention inside of her. They knew they were not long for this body, that she had been preparing to let them go. But first, she had to convince everyone in the White Forest that Brigitta was meant to be a trusted leader. That it was her destiny to be so.

The journey back to the White Forest was slow and steady, with Minq and Fozk taking turns assisting Brigitta, who could still not fly with her injured wing. The Saarin, rejuvenated from his reconnection with the ocean, easily kept up with them, though he grew more and more anxious the farther inland they traveled.

At one point they encountered a deep swamp with boggy waters that burned everyone's skin, and they had to trek around it. They wove their way, choking on its vile air, scorching their lungs as if inhaling firepepper.

They camped in a deserted cave the second night, throats too parched to speak, only to wake to the tiny tracks of beasts that had infiltrated the dustmist barrier. Later, they discovered the little beasts had made nests in their clothes and hair and the inside of Minq's ears. They were all covered in little red bites by late morning.

The following afternoon, they reentered the White Forest. They had barely stepped across The Shift when Roucho, Mousha's featherless delivery bird, descended and dropped a broodnut at their feet. Carved into the soft shell was a message. COME QUICK, JARLATH! ROANE IS NOT WELL.

The entire party hurried to Tiragarrow, Brigitta ignoring the pain and speeding herself along with wing thrusts despite Fozk's warning that she might cause permanent damage. She was frantic, because in all that had happened, she had completely forgotten about Roane. She had left his older brother, his only living relative, in the Dark Forest with Croilus. If she could not get Jarlath back safe and sound, she would never forgive herself.

It seemed as if everyone in the entire village-nest was nervously milling about outside her parents' cottage. As the High Priest approached, the Tiragarrow faeries parted, murmuring and pointing to the strange beast that had returned with them. Minq put an ear across Narru's shoulder protectively as they made their way through the crowd.

Brigitta burst into her parents' cottage, followed by Fozk and Minq, while the Saarin dallied at the door, overwhelmed by the sudden swarm of strangers.

"Where is he?" Brigitta cried into the empty gathering room. "Where's Roane?"

"Briggy!" Himalette streaked out of her bedroom and straight into Brigitta's stomach, sending her backwards into Fozk.

The shock to her injured wing forced tears to her eyes, and she tried to pull her frightened sister away, but Himalette held tight to Brigitta's waist, burying her face in her tunic.

"I was making his lunch," cried Himalette. "Momma and Poppa were with the Elders . . . his eyes, they went dark and he . . . he just stopped."

"Stopped what, dear?" asked Fozk, placing a hand on Himalette's head. She gave a heavy, sobby sigh and relaxed. She pulled her face away from Brigitta's chest, now moistened with tears. "Just . . . stopped."

"What do you mean?" gasped Brigitta. "He's dead?"

"No, not dead. Just not moving." She sniffed and shook her head. "Nobody knows what to do."

"It's not just Roane," a voice called from Brigitta's bedroom.

A moment later Elder Adaire stepped into the gathering room, her tunic sleeves rolled up and her face lined with worry. "It's Thistle and Granae, too. A few suns ago, they all simply . . ." She gestured helplessly and stepped aside so Brigitta and Fozk could take a look at Roane, lying on top of the covers of Brigitta's bed, breathing, eyes open, but seeing nothing.

"Fozk," said Brigitta, grabbing hold of his arm. "It's like what happened to Jarlath. Croilus has done something to the Ancients." She gazed upon Roane's innocent face. "And they're all Watchers, half-bloodline descendents of the Ancients."

He nodded solemnly.

"Do you think they will turn violent, like Jarlath?" she whispered.

"I wish I knew," he said, and then he patted her arm. "Perhaps at this distance, or from within the White Forest, Croilus cannot have the same effect."

"In Noe, the others . . ." Her voice trailed off. If Devin and Zhay and Ferris were in the same condition, they would be unprotected. She hoped Fozk was right about the distance preventing Croilus from having any power over them. And she hoped that the Nhords were with them, too. Abdira and Uwain wouldn't let anything happen to her friends.

"Brigitta!" cried her Momma and Poppa as they raced through the house to their daughter.

She pulled herself away from her thoughts as they approached, and it was as if she were watching two strangers. Her journey to the Eternal Dragon and back, and Ondelle's memories of them as young parents, had colored her feelings toward them. They looked so fragile and naïve to her now.

Her expression must have worried them, for they both slowed down and then stopped shy of any embrace.

"Fozk?" asked Pippet, grasping Mousha's hand without taking her eyes off her daughter. "Is she all right?"

"Her wing is badly injured," Fozk replied, "and the boy Jarlath was unable to return with us."

They carefully folded Brigitta into their arms, stroking her hair and rubbing her back. No, she thought, she was not *all right*. She didn't know what she was, but she felt strange, as if being pulled elsewhere. And even though her heart ached for the two faeries holding her, a part of her wanted to be pulled away.

Brigitta sat quietly in the meeting with the Elders and High Priest Fozk, watching the proceedings, detached, just a cloud observing the forest. Perhaps it was a way of protecting herself from having to make too many difficult decisions. Maybe choices were less like crossroads and more like logs in a river clogging its course. If one could just make a choice, the other logs would unjam, and the way would be clear.

She recalled how the knowing triggered by the whisper light had made everything clear for Ondelle. Brigitta wished for that kind of clarity for herself, for it to appear like magic, telling her exactly what to do.

She pulled her attention back to the room. The Elders and High Priest were discussing Chevalde of Noe's Impenetrable Spell, to be performed during twin full moons, which would lock the forest in its protective shell forever.

Or until Faweh was balanced once again.

"Yes, we'd be safe inside," said Fozk, "but without the ability to disperse the spirits of the dead, we would only be extending our inevitable extinction."

It was true. Without the elements ascending and transforming, no new elemental faeries would be born. And since the Watchers, the only ones who could perform dispersements, were all debilitated, and possibly dangerous, in a hundred season cycles or so, all that would be left of Faweh's faeries would be their feral kin of Noe. Frightened shadows of what was once a grand civilization.

Would future visitors from afar stumble across the White Forest, a strange protected area haunted by undispersed spirits of the dead? Would these travelers study the spirits behind the field like thunderbugs under glass?

"I don't think the question is whether we perform the magic or not," said Hammus. "I think the question is when we do it."

"I say the next full moons," said Adaire with authority. "Who knows what this Croilus faerie will be capable of once his knowing settles."

"It is not *his* knowing," Dervia pointed out.

"It doesn't matter whose it was," countered Hammus. "We cannot have his Blue Spell magic wreaking havoc on our forest nor our families terrorized by spellbound Ancients."

"I agree," said Adaire. "Let us be safe."

"But think about what we're saying," said Dervia. "You're dooming our younger generation."

"They're doomed regardless!" shouted Hammus. He lowered his head in apology and took a breath before continuing. "I'm sorry … this is hard on us all."

Mora, the newest Elder, placed a hand over his, and they resumed their discussion in a more subdued tone.

A strange pulse of air filled the space, pressing in on Brigitta from every part of the room all at once, though the Elders didn't seem to feel it at all. They began to fade from Brigitta's sight, and she shook her head. They came into focus once again, but quickly disappeared, and then she was looking across a great expanse of rolling hills leading to a breathtaking high narrow mountain that twisted into the clouds.

A throng of Ancients flew silently toward it like ghosts, and she gazed upon them with a mixture of anxiety and elation. As they passed in front of her, Jarlath floated by, caught in their tide. The harsh sunlight formed a strange halo in the distance, and it appeared as it they were all floating toward a ring of fire.

"Brigitta?"

Her attention was jogged back into the Elder chambers, all faces turned toward her, curious and concerned.

"Are you all right?" asked Mora.

"I know where Croilus is heading," said Brigitta as it dawned on her. She could still taste the air, as if she had actually been standing there across from the great mountain. "I could see it!"

"Perhaps you are too exhausted for this right now." Dervia turned to the others. "We need to contemplate this further. It is not a decision we can—"

"No," said Brigitta, startling them all.

Everything had suddenly clicked into place. Seeing Jarlath and the Ancients in that fiery ring had reminded her of when they used the energy of dispersing nightwalkers in Noe to get through the Purview. All the pieces of Narine in those whisper lights had the same message for Ondelle and the Nhords and the Saarin: open the Purview.

"You must do it on the next full moons," she said.

Her certainty and depth of command caught them off guard.

"You have something to share with us, Brigitta?" asked Fozk.

"Yes." She stood up, smiling for the first time in moons. "Yes!"

The logjam had been removed, and the course was as clear as a Green Season sky. "You will close off the White Forest," she told them, "and when you do, I will be on the other side."

There were five Purviews, Brigitta reasoned, one on each continent. Three had already been opened: the one in Noe, the one Abdira and Uwain came through on Araglenn, and the one Narru had used on Pariglenn. There were two left and no guarantee, after almost one thousand season cycles, that anyone would be around to open them on Storlglenn and Carraiglenn. No guarantee there were ears to listen and eyes to see the whisper lights when they came. And no guarantee any ears or eyes belonged to beasts as loyal as the Nhords or as curious as the odd young Saarin.

"I'm the only one who can do it," she said. "I can find Jarlath *and* the whisper lights using Narine's energy."

The Elders looked unconvinced, though the expression on Fozk's face was harder to read.

"Narine couldn't remember what she had given away," she said to him. "She hid knowings inside the whisper lights. If we open all of the Purviews, we can unite Faweh."

"Brigitta," said Dervia, "there is no proof that this is the case."

"*Travel back to times of old to make the balance right again,*" she said to Dervia. "We *all* have to travel back, someone from each civilization. And they each get there through a Purview."

The room grew silent but for Fozk's deep inhale. "Go on."

"I can help open the last two Purviews, balance Faweh, and break the Impenetrable Spell." As Brigitta spoke, she grew more confident and more excited. "I just need to find Croilus and get the scepter and Narine's Earth energy back before the knowing settles and he figures out how to use the last of the Blue Spell."

Before they could argue, she described what she had seen while connected to Narine's energy, the expanse of land and the great peak, and they referred to the map of Foraglenn left to them by the Ancients.

"Sage Peak," said Hammus, and the rest murmured.

"That would make sense," added High Priest Fozk.

"Why?" Brigitta peered down at the map. "What's so special about Sage Peak?"

"It's a sacred place," said Mora.

"A powerful place," said Dervia. "A place where the Ancient Sages used to connect to Faweh's energy. A place of clarity."

"It is written," added Adaire, "that its energy is so pure that every thought is magic."

"I wonder what he's up to?" asked Hammus.

"Nothing good, that's for sure," said Brigitta. "But if he's looking to connect to that pure energy, I'm sure he'll be disappointed."

"Why is that?" asked Dervia.

"Because nothing in Faweh is as it was before the Great World Cry," said Brigitta. "Didn't Dead Mountain used to be some kind of Sage retreat and Noe Valley a place of peace?"

"Let's hope he does more harm to himself than others, then," said Hammus.

Now that Brigitta had a way to find Jarlath and clarity in balancing Faweh, a plan quickly hatched from within her, as if channeling it from Ondelle herself.

"Narru, Minq, and I can go to Sage Peak for Jarlath and Narine's Earth energy and the stolen scepter. Then we'll travel to Storlglenn, find the whisper light, open the Purview, and figure out a way to travel to Carraiglenn through it. There, we'll locate the final whisper light, open the final Purview, and use it to return to Noe where we can call the Ancients so they can be dispersed!

"We'll have the scepter and the rings to get through the Purviews," Brigitta went on, practically giddy. "The Nhord rings and the Saarin's rings. We can do this!"

"But how will you rescue Jarlath?" asked Hammus. "Even without being under Croilus's spell, he may still be in a stupor like the other Watchers."

"Ondelle gave her Air energy to me," Brigitta explained. "If I can get to Narine's Earth energy before it settles in Croilus, I'm sure there's a way to give it to Jarlath. Then he'll be an Earth Faerie with an energy of his own. He won't need a connection to Ancient energy anymore!"

Hammus and Adaire shook their heads while the others contemplated this possibility.

"Crossing the water to Storlglenn, or any other continent for that matter, has never been attempted by any White Forest faerie," Mora pointed out.

"Neither had traveling to Noe," said Fozk, "before Ondelle and Brigitta left."

"Besides," said Brigitta, "I'll have Narru. He lives in the sea. He knows water like we know how to breathe."

"IF you can transfer Narine's Earth energy, IF you can steal the scepter back from Croilus, IF you can cross an ocean, IF you can find the whisper lights, IF you can open the Purviews . . ." Dervia threw up her arms. "Brigitta, that's a tremendous amount of *ifs*!"

"IF I don't succeed," Brigitta said, matching Dervia's intensity, "you will be no worse off in the White Forest."

"But you would be trapped out there forever," said Adaire, and Mora murmured agreement.

"We can't let you go," said Hammus.

"It is not your decision," said Fozk, surprising them all.

He addressed the Elders, but kept his gaze on Brigitta. "We should assume our headstrong Brigitta would leave regardless of whether she had our permission or not," he continued, something between sorrow and pride radiating from his bright eyes. "I'm sure you'll agree it is far better she go well-prepared and with our support."

Later that afternoon, while Fozk gathered ingredients the Elders believed she would need for her journey, Brigitta sat watching him inspect the plants in the Hive garden, an ample patch of fertile land behind the entrance mound.

The day was painfully beautiful, striking clear blue sky, faerie children playing in the festival grounds, the smells of lyllium and dragon flower and tingermint weaving up from the garden. On such a day, it would be easy for one to forget about everything outside the forest, like dismissing a dream. But not for Brigitta while Jarlath was still out there.

She thought of the journey back home and the time she'd lost, and hoped her new lessons with Fozk would help make up for it all.

"High Priest Fozk," she asked, "how do you keep yourself, well, all to yourself?"

"Do you mean am I not tempted to listen in on others' thoughts?"

"I would be."

"No, you would not," he said, bending to feel a starkiss

blossom before pulling the plant out of the ground with a graceful twist of his wrist. "You cannot master empathing otherwise. The ability to know must be balanced with the need to know."

Brigitta contemplated this as he gathered more plants. If he didn't read minds, he certainly had remarkable intuition. Maybe it was because he didn't attempt to invade others' thoughts that their emotions simply presented themselves to him. She wondered about her own selfishness and if she would only master her talents when she started thinking beyond her own desires.

The High Priest dusted off his hands on his tunic, leaving smudges of dirt. She decided that she liked how he worked with his hands, that he enjoyed being intimate with the earth. No small task seemed beneath him.

"Funny how knowledge appears to us sometimes, though," he said, dropping a few new seeds in to take the plant's place and patting the dirt back down around it. "For instance, did you know that the last conversation left in someone's Thought Mirror can be retrieved before the new owner uses it?"

He looked up from his task, eyes smiling. "If the previous owner sets the intention for it to be heard, that is. It's not that hard to do."

They looked at each other with new understanding, and Brigitta wondered at the breadth of Ondelle's cleverness. She had left him something in her mirror. Knowledge about who Brigitta was, perhaps. About her destiny.

"This was much harder to learn," he said, gesturing to the garden. "Elder Dervia has the natural gift." He placed everything in a basket and turned toward the Hive.

"I have no patience with plants or animals," Brigitta

said, hanging back, stalling for time, desperately wanting to know what message Ondelle had left for him. "Or faeries, really."

He chuckled, each sound a clear percussive beat. There was so much more to High Priest Fozk than she had ever given thought. And so much knowledge each High Priest or Priestess kept to themselves until the time was right.

Before entering the Hive, the High Priest pulled some ceunias root out of his basket and tossed it to Brigitta. "Give this to your mother in a tea before you give her the news."

When he had vanished into the Hive, Brigitta went to pick up Minq and Narru, waiting for her in the festival grounds with a group of children. She watched Minq from the shadow of the tree for a while before approaching. The faerie children loved him, loved wrapping themselves up in his ears, loved snuggling into his belly. It dawned on her that she had no idea how old Minq was, or how long he would live. She wasn't even sure he knew the answers to these things.

With him was Narru, who blushed shyly as the faerie children led him in a dance across the festival grounds. He had been accepted immediately among the young ones, even if the older faeries looked at him with suspicion. It was difficult not to trust him, though, with his large sideways blinking eyes and innocent smile.

Brigitta had brought seven beings home to the White Forest, and strange as it may seem, she felt closer to all of them than any White Forest faerie. Even her Momma and Poppa. No one cared for them as much as she did, and

since she had brought them there, she felt that they were
her responsibility. Losing Jarlath, she had failed them all.

After Adaire's skilled healing Brigitta had been
instructed to keep off her tender wing for as long as
possible, so Fozk had called on two Perimeter Guards'
assistance to see to Brigitta's transportation. As they
arrived, bronze brothers with magnificent purple wings,
she slid aside the fabric of the carry-cart to make room for
Narru. The large guards took flight, with Minq struggling
to keep up from behind.

This being nice forest home, said Narru, who had been
extremely quiet since entering the White Forest. *Not being
like ocean, though.* He put a hand to his forehead. *Stillness
making land sickness.*

"We'll get you back to the ocean," she said, taking his
other hand. It felt slick and cool against her own skin,
with fingernails like tiny black pebbles. "I promise."

When they arrived in Tiragarrow, Pippet set up an
enormous feast for Brigitta and her friends. Himalette was
there, and Mousha, too, strangely not in his lab puzzling
over smoking beakers. No one spoke of Roane or Thistle
or Granae, all taken to the Hive for "safekeeping." Pippet
laughed overtly at every little thing, not wanting to darken
the mood.

After supper, Himalette was dismissed to visit a friend,
and then Brigitta did as Fozk had said and made a tea
from the ceunias root for her mother and father, using
the excuse that it was a gift from the Elders, which they
of course could not turn down. But the calming effects of
the tea did not do much to dampen Pippet's howls when
Brigitta told her of her plan to leave the forest. Mousha
sank into his chair, deflated.

"No!" cried Pippet. "No, no! I will not have you leave us again!"

"Mother," Brigitta said, gathering her strength, "I'm going. I must."

"Then I'll come, too!" she cried. "You can't go alone!" Mousha held Pippet back and hugged her tight.

"You know you can't, Momma," said Brigitta, choking back her own tears. "You have to stay here for Poppa and Himmy."

"Why you, Brigitta?" begged Pippet. "Why you?"

"Because I'm the only one who can," she said. "My destiny was determined the moment Ondelle made it so."

Mousha nodded, lips pulled so tight they trembled, as he rocked Pippet in his arms.

"We've been poring over seasons of texts," said Adaire the following afternoon in the library with Fozk, Adaire, Dervia, and Mora.

Brigitta tried her best to concentrate. Her mother's pain deeply disturbed her, she couldn't stop thinking about the Watchers in Noe, and Gola, the one she always turned to for advice, had completely disappeared. The purple-winged Perimeter Guard brothers had checked for her, but Gola's home was empty, and no one had seen her in many moons. If she hadn't completely rooted by now, she would be by the time Brigitta, Minq, and Narru returned.

If they returned.

She held one of the moonstones between her fingers, wondering about the missing stone. If Gola had taken it with her, was there a way for her to find it with these ones? Could they call to each other like Narine's energies or like Ondelle did with the hourglass necklace? But the moonstones did not hum full of potential energy. They were cool on her skin and empty.

"Brigitta, are you listening?" asked Adaire.

"Yes." Brigitta refocused her gaze. "Go on."

"We believe you are the only one who can unlock the Blue Spell from the hourglass," Dervia said. "We also believe we have a way to get the Earth energy into Jarlath."

"Transformation," said Adaire. "You will transform Croilus's and Jarlath's energies."

"No small feat, we realize," added Dervia. "But we believe it is possible thanks to Ondelle."

"Transformation," Brigitta murmured, mulling over the idea like sucking on a piece of hard candy. She shook her head. "Without the help of the Ancients, I am not particularly adept at transformation in the best of circumstances."

"Then you will learn," Fozk said. "And perhaps Ondelle's memories will serve to speed the process. We have little time before the full moons."

As they excused themselves to attend to their duties, Brigitta realized that was the first time any of them had acknowledged that Ondelle's memories were real.

Her lessons began immediately after their meeting, and when Brigitta entered Adaire's practice chamber, two clay pots sat on the table, one red and one gold. Adaire explained that the more hollow or porous something was, the easier to work transference on it. She focused her energy and in a few moonsbreaths, proceeded to turn the red pot gold and the gold pot red.

"That's not exactly what you'll be doing to them, but it

matters not. It starts with one empty space in mind. If you can master filling one empty space, you can master filling all empty spaces."

"Elder Adaire, I mean no disrespect," said Brigitta, "but I don't think Croilus and Jarlath will be sitting around like clay pots for me."

"What if you approached them while they were asleep?" a voice emerged from the wall. It was Lalam; he had been standing there so quietly she hadn't even noticed him. A talent of the Wisings was knowing how to blend into a room until their services were necessary.

He pulled into the light. Kind hazel eyes shone down at her. There was no hostility there, surprising considering how Brigitta had last left him in the thought-loop.

"Wising Lalam," said Adaire, not even fazed that he had been listening in.

Brigitta wondered for a moment how many times a Wising may have been in a room without her realizing it. That was a trick she definitely wanted to learn. She thought of anxious little Glennis of Easyl, Himmy's friend who had Wising Destiny Marks. She could not imagine poor Glennis trying to be that still.

"You have a talent for transformation," Adaire continued. "Perhaps you can train with Brigitta each morning before she leaves?"

"Perhaps I could train with Brigitta each morning after she leaves as well."

"That is not possible," said Adaire. "You know very well you would be unable to return to the White Forest if you left."

"Until Faweh is rebalanced, you mean."

It wasn't quite a challenge, but Brigitta noted a slight

twinkle in Lalam's eyes, and she could tell Adaire did not want to admit she doubted Brigitta's success.

"Are you suggesting, then, that you accompany her?" asked Adaire.

"With your permission, of course."

Adaire sucked in a breath. No Wising had ever requested to leave the services of an Elder before. Not to Brigitta's knowledge, at least. Adaire's face turned a deeper shade of red before she blew her breath back out into the room.

"Speak with Fozk," was all she said.

Things were definitely other than normal in the White Forest. To Brigitta's surprise, Fozk approved of Lalam leaving the forest. The Wising sat quietly next to Narru and Minq, while the Elders and Fozk discussed this strategy.

"He has knowledge of Earth energy," Fozk pointed out to the Elders, "and is young and strong." He turned to Brigitta. "Do you have everything you need for all of you to make it through the Purviews?"

"Just," Brigitta replied. "We have four rings and the scepter. But if we can't get the scepter away from Croilus . . ."

"Then I guess we'd better get that scepter back," said Lalam.

"Then it is settled," said Fozk with finality, sending everyone away to prepare.

In the time she had left, Brigitta exercised her injured wing and completed what lessons she could with the Elders: weather manipulation and poison reduction from Dervia, healing and transformation from Adaire, smelting and quickening from Hammus, mind misting and empathing from Mora.

Narru himself got lessons in vocalization from Song Master Helvine so he could speak some of his thoughts, and Minq had some informal flying lessons from the purple-winged Perimeter Guard brothers.

The afternoon before they were set to leave, Brigitta and Minq, with the help of Glennis of Easyl, searched from Bobbercurxy to No Moon's Canyon for Gola the Drutan. They had no luck, as there were simply too many trees. To Brigitta's disappointment, the moonstones didn't lead her anywhere; they only kept her cool when she pressed them to her skin.

When it was apparent they were going to have to leave the forest without saying good-bye to their beloved Drutan, Brigitta and Minq sat on the edge of No Moon's Canyon and cried as Glennis expressed her sympathies to them.

"Glennis," Brigitta said when she finally ran out of tears, "promise me you'll come looking some times. Promise me if you find her you'll tell her I'm sorry . . . and . . . and . . . that I love her."

"If I find her," said Glennis carefully, placing a hand on Brigitta's shoulder, "I promise I will tell her."

Chapter Eleven

Ondelle wove her hands through the air in her practiced manner. She had performed the High Priestess's task of resetting the Hourglass of Protection dozens of times, and there was no reason for this time to be any different, but still, the spell must be cast precisely. She glanced at the Elders: Fozk, Hammus, Adaire, and Jorris each held their own miniature hourglasses. Each holding the space for the Dragon's Gift to do its work.

She closed her eyes in concentration. A moment later, something deep within her chest moved, like a sleeping animal stirring. Then the energy was pulled, nearly yanked forward. A small gasp escaped her lips as the energy was pulled toward the entryway and across the passage, into a fissure in the wall.

She felt it there, the connection, behind the wall. She opened her eyes.

Brigitta.

And something else. A call to action. Something part of her had been anticipating since she had entered Pippet's womb and transferred Narine's Water energy.

"Ondelle, are you well?" asked Elder Dervia.

"I just need some air," she said.

Fozk stepped up and held out his hands.

"No," laughed Ondelle, "the outside kind. You may all rest for a while. You've done well."

She made her way outside, heart pounding, and scanned the forest and festival grounds. The arena was bustling, the faeries happy, celebratory. She closed her eyes and reached out with Narine's energy. She did not like to spy on Brigitta this way, but this was bigger than either of them. This was their dual destiny unfolding. And for as long as she had been anticipating this moment, she felt completely unprepared. How could it be time? Brigitta was still a child.

She concentrated her energy in that spot deep within her chest. But instead of reaching outward, like one would do while mind-misting, she folded the energy inward, to the infinite side of herself. A moment later, and she was flying into the lyllium fields. Her heart broke as she, now seeing as Brigitta, flew low over the lylliums and touched the petals. An innocent gesture. The last she may ever perform.

Everything was about to change.

In the full two moons' light, Brigitta and her family, Lalam and his, Minq, Perimeter Guards Reykia and Gaowen, Fozk, the Elders, and the Apprentices and Wisings, including Glennis, who would be moving into the Hive soon, stood before The Shift. Entering the Dark Forest at night was definitely not Brigitta's first choice, but the Impenetrable Spell had to be performed with the full moons' energy.

Brigitta hugged her parents fiercely, but as briefly as possible. They wore brave faces for Himalette's sake, but Brigitta could feel their sorrow to her core.

"I'll be back, Momma," Brigitta said with determination before turning to her father. "You know I will."

"And a grand celebration we will have," said her Poppa in a voice choked with heartache. He kissed the top of her head.

Himalette hugged her next and handed her a small package. "Open that when you miss me," she said glumly, wiping her sleeve across her sniffling nose.

"Guess it will never get opened, then," joked Brigitta.

Himalette tried to laugh, but the sound got stuck in her throat.

"Come here, you big lola," Brigitta said, hugging her sister and kissing her cheek.

Auntie Ferna finally approached, but instead of hugging her, she kneeled down and looked intently into Brigitta's eyes, studying what she found. Then, she leaned in close and whispered into her ear, "Remember, Ondelle is within you. Always."

Then, Brigitta pulled away and nodded to the Elders, who nodded in return. They, too, had their brave faces on.

It was the first time Brigitta had ever left the forest with complete Elder consent, and she was leaving more prepared than ever before, with treated blankets and reinforced tunics, dried foods, dense breads, herbs, dustmist, firepepper, two globlights, four canteens, a smelting stone, healing kit, a real wind-winder, and Jarlath's frore dagger—distributed among the travelers' packs. In addition, Lalam carried a personal spell pouch around his waist.

Narru blinked his sideways eyes and wiggled his lips, testing them. "Good-bye," he said, then smiled shyly and waved.

Mousha held onto Pippet and Himalette tightly, as Brigitta and her traveling party stepped through the invisible barrier in the center of The Shift. Fozk took one end of the hourglass, and she took the other, holding it perfectly centered in the protective field.

"If this doesn't work . . ." A joke halted on her tongue as Fozk's icy blue eyes bore down on her.

"May the wisdom of all faeries be with you."

She nodded and they both closed their eyes. Brigitta misted her mind through her own body, down her arm. She misted out from her fingertips, lightly holding the hourglass, and into the hourglass itself, sifting through the sands toward the center where the protective field began.

Just as they had practiced, she met Fozk's mind mist right in the middle of the hourglass. They coiled their mists together, mingling their Air energies, and she used her Water to slowly fill in the empty space. They didn't rush; they let the energies blend naturally until there was no distinction between them.

Now, Fozk's voice reverberated in her mind.

Together they coaxed the Blue Spell forward. Brigitta thought the magic would resist, as if being woken from a long sleep. Instead, it burst forth so forcefully she was nearly knocked off her feet.

Then, the four Elders were with them, calling forth the Impenetrable Spell. Calling and calling until it emerged, an unshakable force.

"No!" she heard her mother wail, and she let go of the hourglass and opened her eyes.

The Impenetrable Spell quickly spread like gathering thunderclouds over the forest, thickening into a solid shell. And just before the shield sealed itself for good, something burst through it and collapsed to the ground with a sharp cry.

Lalam and Brigitta rushed over to see what it was. A young faerie with deep yellow wings was lying in the dirt moat. She stood up and smiled a dizzy smile.

"Glennis!" Brigitta hollered, "get back across or you'll be stuck out here!"

They both looked to the newly encased White Forest. By the expressions on all the faces on the other side, Brigitta could tell that it was already too late.

She turned angrily back to Glennis. "What were you thinking! You knew that would happen!"

"You wouldn't have let me come if I'd asked," Glennis said, brushing herself off.

"Of course not!" said Brigitta. "You have no business being out here!"

"I've just as much business as you," said Glennis.

"You'll get yourself killed."

"That's my risk to take."

Brigitta balled her fists. "We don't have enough rings!"

"Rings?" asked Glennis as Minq and Narru joined them. "What rings?"

"Looks like our party has grown by one Wising," said Lalam, straightening Glennis's pack.

Muffled voices came from the other side of the protective shell. Brigitta held her hand up to it. It was still transparent, but now solid. Smooth and neutral, like a jar. On the other side, her tear-faced mother pressed her own hand against it as Himalette clung to her waist, and Auntie Ferna put her arms around Mousha.

The Elders and Fozk appeared to be in a heated discussion about Glennis, as their glances suggested, but there was nothing they could do. The White Forest was impenetrable, and if Brigitta and her companions ever wanted to get back in, they had to face the gargantuan task before them.

"What's done is done," Lalam said, turning to Brigitta. "We'll figure something out along the way."

Brigitta nodded, removed her pack, and yanked out the healing kit. She grabbed a mossleaf patch and slapped it over Glennis's mouth, whose eyes bugged out in surprise.

"You will be quiet, do as you're told, and keep up with the rest of us," said Brigitta.

Glennis nodded and straightened up.

"Don't think I won't leave you behind if I have to."

Minq threw Brigitta a questioning glance as she hefted her pack, but she was not going to be soft on Glennis, no matter what any of the others thought. The Dark Forest was a dangerous place, and Glennis had just complicated everything. Compromised it, even.

She set her face as stone cold as she could. She had to be decisive. She had to make choices and move forward. And she had to tear herself away or she would never be able to leave. With one last glance at her loved ones, she took off toward the Dark Forest. "Come on, then."

She fluttered over the expanse of shifting dirt toward the trees. Minq and Narru bounded after her on their agile legs, with Glennis and Lalam taking up the rear. They slipped into the Dark Forest, cutting off their view of their home and kin.

"You have to feel the spaces first in order to move what's not there into them," said Lalam, face half lit from the globelight tucked into the tree branches. "Like that children's game, Ten-Go-Ten. You know the one."

Sleepy-eyed, the remains of their dinner before them, Glennis, Minq, and Narru watched from a log, as Brigitta and Lalam practiced in the scant area secured with a firepepper and dustmist wall.

Brigitta hadn't played Ten-Go-Ten in season cycles, but she knew what he was talking about. The game was played with two-toned stones on a grid, ten squares up and ten squares across. The object was to have all your stones on the board with the same color showing, and all touching in some way: diagonally, up, down, or across. Once you placed a stone, you could flip it over in any direction into an empty space, or jump over another player, flipping their stone instead.

Lalam drew a Ten-Go-Ten board in the dirt. "Everything has space that can be filled. I see objects in transformation as rearranging material into those spaces."

"But I still don't understand how you get them to move in the first place, once you've found the empty spaces?" she asked. "Adaire said she sifts them."

"Everyone finds his or her own way," he said, placing six different colored pebbles into the playing grid and staring down into them. As they all observed, one of the pebbles slowly turned from black to green. "I use rooting. I surround matter with roots and everything outside the roots is usable space."

Brigitta hadn't spent enough time in Earth energy lessons to study rooting, an advanced technique in which one's thoughts stretched out into limitless roots, almost like spider webs, allowing the faerie to detect an object's shape with the mind.

Brigitta sat down on her blanket, exhausted. "I don't have time to master rooting."

Lalam shrugged. "It starts with one root."

"You've been hanging around Elders too long."

Dinner complete, Glennis stuck the mossleaf patch back over her mouth and began to clean up. As Glennis focused on her task, with not a hint of complaint, a brief stab of guilt pierced Brigitta's heart. Perhaps she'd been too rough on Glennis. After all, it was her destiny to serve.

"To serve the destiny that awaits," Brigitta murmured, suddenly missing the hulking Nhord couple she had befriended in Noe. She hoped they were looking over the Watchers. She hoped they were all safe.

She looked around at her odd assortment of companions as they got ready for bed: a young faerie barely older than Himalette, a long-eared hairless beast with removable wings, a land-locked sea creature child, and an Earth faerie man she had tricked into allowing her to steal the White Forest scepter. A faerie she now knew to be reasonably skilled at rooting and transformation.

"Lalam," she said, "about the night of the Masquerade . . ."

"The thought-loop?" He smirked at her while he unraveled his blanket.

"Yeah." She crossed her arms and eyed him suspiciously.

"It was impressive," he said, slipping into his bedroll. He pulled the blanket around himself snugly and closed his eyes. "I would have looped me first instead of the novice Wising. That way, you could have taken me by surprise."

It took no time at all for Lalam to fall to sleep. In the meantime, Brigitta tossed around trying to find the best position for her newly healed wing, wondering why he had allowed her to thought-loop him in the first place. What had he witnessed, over the seasons, from his silent, concealed spaces in the Hive?

The young Saarin was falling behind. Lalam and Brigitta stopped to inspect him, and his skin was peeling, displaying more of his blue web-like veins underneath.

Land sick, he murmured in Brigitta's mind.

Around them the forest was dense and prickly, no water in sight. She examined the clouds through the tree branches and briefly empathed them, but they were forming in quick whispering curls, not dense wet masses. They spun in the air, teasing her with their lack of rain-ness.

"We need you, Narru," said Brigitta. "We can't cross the ocean without you, so hold on."

Holding.

Minq wrapped an ear around his shoulders to steady him as they plodded after Brigitta, Lalam, and Glennis.

"We have to find him some water," Brigitta whispered to Lalam.

A moonbeat later and Narru collapsed. Brigitta and Lalam carried him over to a blackened stump. Brigitta sat down, holding Narru's head in her lap.

"Take this." She placed a canteen to his lips and managed to get a few capfuls into his mouth. While she helped him drink, she became aware of a distant rushing sound beneath the thrum of the forest.

"The River That Runs Backwards," she said, head perking up.

They carried him through the trees, pushing branches and webs out of his way, until they were close enough to gather the water drops misting in the air. They gave him more to drink and wet him down, but even as the water absorbed into his skin, he remained weak and nauseous. "I don't understand what's happening," said Brigitta to Lalam and Glennis. "It's plenty wet here, but he's not getting any better."

"I don't think it's just the wetness, Brigitta," said Lalam, mixing a stomach-easing concoction. He broke open a leafy pouch and poured the sandy mix into his potion bowl. "From what you have told us of it, the ocean sounds like a very different world. His kind are not meant to stay on land for extended periods of time. This may be killing him."

"What are you saying?" Brigitta let Narru's head rest back in her lap, and she placed her hand over his burning forehead. "I must choose between saving Jarlath or saving Narru? I don't know how much time I have for either!"

"No, not choose," said Minq, twisting around a tree whose wetness he had been wiping off with his ears. He pulled his sopping ears to Brigitta and squeezed more water into her hands. "I take Narru ocean, you save Jarlath, meet for crossing."

"You mean we separate?" asked Brigitta, splashing the water over Narru's face.

"Only slow you down anyway," said Minq, wiggling his small wings. "This way we all have chance."

"I don't know, Minq," she said. "Just the two of you?" The last thing Brigitta wanted was to be separated from one more friend. It would ruin her if anything happened to either of them.

"I know Dark Forest," he said. "I know forest like inside of ear. And Saarin know ocean like skin on stomach."

"He makes good sense," said Lalam. "And I doubt Narru could scale Sage Peak."

"I . . . I . . ." Brigitta shook her head. She turned to Glennis. "What do you think?"

Glennis startled from where she sat, mossleaf patch still smeared over her mouth. She pulled it away slowly and grimaced as it pulled at her skin. She thought for a moment. "I agree with Lalam and Minq."

Brigitta let this information sink in. *Decisive*, she thought. *That's how to lead.* She looked at all their faces and then down at the dehydrated Saarin.

"All right." She turned to Minq and Lalam. "But where will we meet up again? We still have to decide the best place to cross."

She pulled a blanket over Narru as Lalam took out their map.

Brigitta had been using Ondelle's principle of approaching the unknown *one step at a time* to avoid getting overwhelmed. But there was no denying that sooner or later they were going to have to cross the ocean. The task seemed too distant, and unreal, seeing as finding Croilus and stealing the scepter and Earth energy was problematic enough. She knew nothing about Sage Peak's magic. Who were the last Ancients to meditate in its caverns, and what did they leave behind that Croilus could use against them?

Lalam, Minq, and Glennis grew quiet as they studied the map of Foraglenn, Glennis tapping a stick against a stone around the fire pit. Brigitta stared at the stick as it rapped out its rhythm. She followed it up Glennis's arm to the bright tunic she wore. She had seen it somewhere before.

"Glennis," Brigitta asked, "when did you get that tunic?"

Glennis looked down. "Oh, this? Just yesterday morning, as a matter of fact. Do you like it? It's for my Wising ceremony. Well, it *was* for my Wising ceremony. Look," Glennis pulled out a small durma, a ceremonial drum, "they gave me this, too. I mean, I know it won't really come in handy or anything, I just wanted something to remind me of home . . ."

Glennis's rambling faded into the background as Brigitta tried to access some memory of—*Glennis leaning over the side of a boat with yellow sails* . . . She instinctively reached for the hourglass around her neck, but instead, found Gola's moonstones.

That was it. The moonstone visions.

"We were on a boat," said Brigitta. "You and I were crossing the ocean on a boat."

"We were?" Glennis asked, putting her durma away. "When?"

"Lalam, where would we have gotten a boat on Foraglenn? We were in a boat, I swear it!" Brigitta was almost frantic, mind grasping at the image. She was speaking of it as if it had already happened, and that's what it felt like. A vague memory, difficult to hold on to, like smoke.

"All right, you were on a boat," he said. "But I have no idea where you would have found one large enough to cross an ocean."

Brigitta wracked her brain to no avail. She could not conjure more than the fleeting image of Glennis on board some unfamiliar vessel.

"Why don't we lay out our journey and go from there?" suggested Lalam.

They went back to studying the map. "Sage Peak first . . ." Brigitta murmured. "Then Storlglenn is this way, east . . . but our eastern coast looks too rugged. Perhaps there is easier access here, from Icecap Forest."

Narru squirmed in Brigitta's lap and moaned.

"Shhhh," she said. "You need rest."

"Mnuuuuh," he muttered, and then crawled into Brigitta's mind. *Icecap Forest,* he said. *Lodge of Eastern Months.*

"Lodge of Eastern Months." Brigitta looked up at her companions. "What's that?"

"No idea," said Lalam as Minq and Glennis shook their heads.

Stop on Trading Route, said the Saarin, *before Great World Cry.*

"Trading route? Is there a boat there?"

"Uhnnnngggg," nodded Narru. *Boats being in all sea lodges. All lands trading.*

"Narru," Brigitta said, "why didn't you tell us this before?"

Never saying boat needing before.

Brigitta, Lalam, Glennis, and Minq all studied the little patch labeled Icecap Forest on the map.

"Then that's where we'll meet," Brigitta said, decisively. "Four by land, two by sea."

Lalam, Glennis, and Narru had been warned numerous times from both Brigitta and Minq about the River That Runs Backwards. About its dizzying madness, about its powerful pull, about not getting too close. Seeing it for themselves was another matter, and even Glennis was speechless.

They held onto each other as they made their way, traversing its banks, looking for the best spot over which to fly.

When they arrived at a section that provided a high protection of cliff, Brigitta set up the wind-winder with Lalam's assistance so that it created a shell around Narru's body, leaving a cushion of air in every direction. He wouldn't be flying anywhere himself; the point was to hold him up and make him light so Minq could guide him along. They had no idea how long their spell would last. Brigitta hoped it was strong enough to get him all the way to the eastern shore of Foraglenn, but that was unlikely.

They huddled around him, each taking hold of the wind-winder, and flew as high as Minq was able with his weaker wings, before setting off over the river. The sound grew intense as they crossed overhead, no one speaking, no one daring to look down. It pulled at them, sending each one off in frightening gusts, but they held on.

When they dropped down on the other side, Brigitta hugged both Minq and Narru, using every bit of willpower to hold back her tears. "We'll see you in the Icecap Forest at the Lodge of Eastern Months."

She kissed Minq on top of his head between the ears. "Boat or no boat," she added.

"No worry," he said. "Take good care of Narru. Like brother."

"Wait a good five or six suns," she said, "and if we don't show, find some way to get him home."

"You show," he said.

A moonsbreath later and the two odd beasts were off, Minq pulling Narru by the hand, and Narru bobbing along in the wind-winder. Not long after, Brigitta, Lalam, and Glennis headed out in the direction of Sage Peak.

Brigitta silently flew up front, picking her way through the forest and keeping an eye on the leaves and branches to make sure they weren't tunneling around them like they had done to her and Jarlath. Glennis chatted away, asking Lalam all sorts of questions about the differences between Earth and Water magic and the pros and cons of being a Wising. Maybe she'd learn more out here from Lalam than from the Elders in the White Forest.

"Do you always like being a Wising?" Glennis asked.

"I am suited to it," he responded.

"What was the hardest thing to learn?"

"Patience."

Brigitta laughed. It would probably be the hardest thing for Glennis to learn as well. She broke through the next twist of trees and stopped. The other two halted behind her.

In front of them was the most enormous flower Brigitta had ever seen. Only, it didn't seem to be attached to any plant. It was just sitting in the middle of a clearing on the forest floor. It was inviting, large enough for all three of them to lie down and take a nap. Hundreds of orange stamens extended from the center, and layers and layers of bright yellow petals, like giant tongues, beckoned to be slid down.

"That looks like fun!" said Glennis. "I know we're in a

hurry, but can we try it just once?"

In some part of her mind, Brigitta knew they shouldn't, but that thought was quickly buried under another thought that didn't see why not. What was one more moonbeat, after all? They could always cut their lunch short. Or have it now. Only she wasn't sure if it was lunchtime. She wasn't even sure how long she'd been standing there staring at the strange flower. Or if she was hungry.

"Lalam." She spun around to ask if he knew how long it had been since breakfast, but he was no longer behind her. Instead, he sat on the ground stroking the anther of a stamen that had extended itself from the flower's center. As it nuzzled against his hand, its pollen rubbed off, sending orange dust everywhere.

"It's very soft," he said, brushing it up and down, a trail of orange dust settling on his tunic and in his hair. "And look." He pulled down another tendril next to him. Suckered onto the end of it was a blue-feathered bird about the size of Brigitta's head with long, stiff yellow legs.

"Huh," was all she could think to say. "Why would a bird stick itself to a flower?"

"I don't know," said Lalam, now stroking the bird, "but it looks peaceful, doesn't it?"

She had to admit that it did look peaceful with its eyes staring open blankly. Nothing on its mind. "It's very good at being still, don't you think?"

Before he could answer, the plant moved its tentacle-like stamen and snatched the bird away. It disappeared somewhere beneath the flower.

They both laughed.

"I think we scared it away," said Lalam, going back to petting the anther.

"Silly bird," said Brigitta. She scratched her head. There was something she was supposed to be doing, but she couldn't remember what. Maybe she had already done it.

She looked up at Glennis, now scaling the giant flower to get to the highest petal.

"Oh, yes!" exclaimed Brigitta, the rest of the world dropping away. "We were going to slide down the petals!"

Chapter Twelve

Ondelle staggered through the sand and collapsed halfway up the beach. The forest beyond was so dark she couldn't distinguish the individual trees. She didn't like that absence of light, did not want to enter the forest, but she knew she had to get off the beach. A fierce sandstorm was brewing, and she could sense something monstrous emerging from the depths of the sea.

Breathless, she struggled to get up. What was wrong with her? She had a scepter fully renewed with the great Dragon's Gift! She lived with more than half of Narine's elemental energy inside of her. She had her knowing.

Narine's knowing.

A sharp pain stabbed Ondelle in the temples and she cried out. The knowing couldn't settle; she had to rid herself of any resistance. But first, she had to move away from the shore.

She managed to push herself up on her hands and knees, and she crawled over the beach, the wind whipping up and pelting her face with sand. She closed her eyes and kept crawling until her hands felt earth and leaves. She pulled herself to the closest tree and hauled herself up off the ground, wondering if she'd be able to fly.

The Standing Stones. That was the safest place for her. How did she know about them? As soon as she questioned her intuition another stab of pain shot through her head. Ah, that was it. Trust the knowing. It would not settle otherwise.

To the Stones then. Without further hesitation, she took to the air, flying north along the edge of the forest. Concentrating on each wingbeat helped ease the pain in her skull as she climbed her way to the plateau and the protection of the Stones. She now knew them to be the remains of a gathering place, and she couldn't help smiling at Narine's memory of the serene lookout over Forever Beach, young Faeries and Saarin and Chakau'un lazing in the shade of the Standing Stones as their parents meditated together.

The wind picked up, knocking the memory away, and her headache returned. It drove into her temples and she fell against one of the stones, collapsing to the ground.

"Let go," she said to herself, trembling. "Trust."

To fight the cold, she wove a pocket of air around herself and breathed the warmth of her Fire energy into it. Even this simple spell brought pain to her head, and she leaned back into the stone. If this was what it would feel like each time one of Narine's memories came to her through the knowing, she dreaded her journey back to the White Forest. If she could but calm her mind enough. She took a deep breath and allowed any resistance to ride out on her exhale.

The pain of the knowing engulfed her. This time, it wasn't in her head. It was someplace so deep inside of her that her entire being was swallowed in grief. This knowing, a laceration on her spirit she would never be able to heal.

"No," she said. "Oh, Great Moon, no."

Her trust had bought her the truth. She picked up her

scepter, staring into the crystal with new awareness, trying to see that truth inside.

She now knew the truth of Blue Spell as this: that every time a White Forest faerie used its magic, she was transforming an Ancient's energy. The fifth element, Ether, had been bound to the Ancients, as the other four elements had been bound to the White Forest faeries by the Ancients to protect them against a world gone mad. The Eternal Dragon had fed on balanced elements, and with the addition of the fifth element, transformed this energy into Blue Spell as a form of release.

As White Forest faeries were dispersed, so their energy was cycled back to the next Elemental Faerie's life. But as the Ethereal energy was transformed through Blue Spell, it was scattered with each use. It did not cycle back. The Ancients had sacrificed their energies to appease the Dragon.

By keeping the White Forest safe, the Elemental Faeries had been destroying the Ancients.

Brigitta opened her eyes, dazed, but with a nagging sense of urgency, a sense that she was running out of time.

It also felt as if something were sniffing at her.

She sat up and wobbled. She was lying on the ground while hairy plant roots wriggled all around her like long worms. She screamed, and they zipped back underground.

How long had she been lying there? And where was there?

Oh, yes. She blinked at the giant flower in front of her. It wasn't as pretty as her vague memory of it was. As a matter of fact, it was looking less and less like a flower and more and more like an enormous stomach with tentacles.

"Lalam?" she called as she stood up, holding out her arms and flitting her wings for balance. "Glennis?"

She searched through the petals, which were definitely more like wide slick arms, until she came across Glennis, who was curled up inside one, the edges neatly folded around her.

"Get up!" she called in Glennis's ear and then shook her.

The young faerie open her eyes, yawned, and stretched. "Good morning, Brigitta."

"It's not a good morning. It's not morning at all. We need to find Lalam and get out of here."

"What's the hurry?" asked Glennis, sleepy-eyed. She yawned again and smacked her lips. "You said I could slide down the petals."

"You've already slid down a dozen times. Now, come on!" Brigitta peeled the slick "petal" away and helped Glennis step out. She wiped off her slimy hands on Glennis's tunic.

"I did?"

She leaned in closer to Glennis. "SNAP OUT OF IT!" she screamed.

Glennis shrieked and then laughed. Brigitta pulled her by the hand around to the other side of the stomach plant's gelatinous body.

"Oh, no," she cried, dropping Glennis's hand. Lalam was suspended upside down by two tentacles.

"Silly Lalam." Glennis pointed at the older Wising and laughed.

"Yeah, silly Lalam," said Brigitta. "I need to get him down. Stay there!"

She took a step toward him and the enormous stomach

burbled. Underneath its bulgy center, a long mouth, if she could call it that, opened up, stretching the length of the beast. A dozen purplish tongues flicked in and out.

"Bog buggers," hissed Brigitta and screwed her eyes closed.

Transformation, transformation, she tried to concentrate, but it was no use. She couldn't even pull up the Ten-Go-Ten playing grid in her mind, let alone any rootings.

She opened her eyes just as the mouth exhaled a gust of rancid breath.

"Whew!" Glennis waved her hand in front of her nose.

"Get back," said Brigitta, pulling Jarlath's frore dagger out.

"Are you going to carve something?"

"Not exactly." Brigitta lifted it up over her head. "Glennis, listen carefully. When I say fly, you grab one side of Lalam and fly! Understand?"

"Gotcha."

"I'm serious."

"Seriously gotcha."

"I hope so." Brigitta plunged the knife forward, slashing through the tentacle. Lalam dropped to the ground with a thud, the end of the tendril writhing around on the ground next to him.

"OOOOOWWWWWWRRRRRRRRRRRRRR!" roared the mouth, tongues flicking violently in and out, roots ripping from the ground.

"Fly!" screamed Brigitta, grabbing Lalam's right arm and kicking the end of the tentacle away.

But Glennis just stood there staring at the stomach beast and scratching her head. "Have you ever seen anything like it?" she asked.

The beast suddenly stopped roaring and searched the ground with its remaining tentacles until it found its missing piece.

"Glennis!"

"What?" asked Glennis, turning to face Brigitta and Lalam. She put her hands on her hips. "What's wrong with him?"

The beast popped the piece into its mouth and then pressed its remaining tentacles against the ground. There was a terrible ripping sound as it pulled itself out of the earth. Glennis wobbled for a moment, then shook her head as if her ears were water-logged. She turned back around to see the tentacled stomach-mouth before them.

And she screamed.

"Fly!" Glennis shot toward Lalam and grabbed his left arm.

She and Brigitta flew into the air, dodging brambly branches, up and up until they were far out of tentacle reach. They dropped onto a thick limb and set Lalam down so they could catch their breaths.

"He's – heavier – than – he – looks," panted Glennis.

"I – know," panted Brigitta as she handed Glennis the knife. Glennis held onto it as Brigitta slapped Lalam lightly on the cheek. "We gotta wake him up."

"Uh, Brigitta," Glennis poked at her arm. "What's that thing doing?"

The stomach beast had turned over so that it now lay on its bulgy center with the mouth on top, and its tentacles waving in the air. It reminded Brigitta of when Himalette used to lie face down on one of her beany mushroom bags, her arms and legs not long enough to reach the ground.

"Looka my big stomach," she would laugh and pat the

beany bag. "My stomach is so big I can't reach the floor."

"I have no idea," Brigitta said to Glennis, shaking away the memory.

Lalam mumbled and they returned their attention to him, now nearly awake, and puzzled by his surroundings. Before they could explain, there was a loud popping from below. The stomach creature was growing itself a new tentacle, each extension of flesh popping itself into place.

"Now that would be a useful skill," said Brigitta as the beast repaired its sliced appendage.

Once the tentacle was fully regrown, the stomach beast stretched all its limbs in turn. Then, it pulled back two tentacles, extending them through the trees behind it until Brigitta thought they would surely snap off. The bizarre beast had more stretch than festival taffy.

Finally, it let its tentacles go and they sprung forward, wrapping themselves around two tree branches, and using the momentum to propel itself forward.

"It's going to smash into the trees!" shouted Glennis as the stomach beast shot toward them.

It did not smash into the trees, however. Instead, it slipped impossibly through the branches and thorns and ivies, finding the exact shape to fit through every space, elongating itself and shrinking other parts. With its sheer enormousness, it should not have been able to do what it was doing. But there was no time to contemplate the logic of it.

"Fly!" they all called out and fled the tree.

Brigitta could feel the swoosh of air as one of the beast's tentacles flew by, wrapping itself around a tree in front of her, flinging itself in her direction.

"What is it?!" cried Glennis from below her.

Even if they had known, Lalam and Brigitta didn't have the breath to answer.

"Higher!" was all Lalam managed as he struggled to fit through the hanging foliage.

Something snagged Brigitta's ankle and pulled. She snatched onto a vine and pounded her wings, but couldn't free her leg. A quick glance told her it was being gripped by one of the mouth's long purple tongues.

"No!" Glennis cried and threw the frore dagger at it, slicing the tongue away.

Released from its grip, Brigitta sped through the air and grabbed Glennis's hand, pulling her after Lalam through the trees.

"Nice shot," she said, glancing back after Jarlath's knife as it disappeared. No going back for it now.

They flew without direction, merely following the natural space of the forest. They flew with every ounce of energy, and the creature followed. It would fall behind, then disappear, and they would think that they had lost it, only for it to come flinging itself forward again.

Scratched and bruised, they continued, Lalam and Brigitta taking turns leading the way and assisting Glennis, who was all but spent. Eventually, Brigitta looked back to find her fluttering to the ground. "I just can't—" Glennis cried.

"Lalam," Brigitta called, gesturing him back.

"Scout ahead," he said, already descending. "I'll bring her along lower to the ground."

Brigitta hesitated, hovering and listening. "I think we may have lost it this time."

She closed her eyes and tried to calm her heart, but it was overloaded. There was no way she had the focus to mist her mind out in front of them. And yet, she could detect something different in the air ahead. Something in the sound of it.

Below her, Lalam was giving Glennis a drink from his canteen.

"I'll be right back," she told them.

She flew carefully through the trees, glancing down at her bug-stained and web-covered tunic. At least they had been flying too fast to get stung or bitten by anything.

The air was definitely changing. Getting bigger was the only way she could describe it. She could sense the space of it. She could sense where the density of the forest changed and the space of air began . . .

That was it! Feeling the space of air on such a grand scale, she suddenly understood what Lalam had attempted to explain to her about transformation on the Ten-Go-Ten grid. She could feel those spaces now. Large and small. In everything around her.

Transformation was all about space! And to Brigitta, that meant focusing on Air energy. For Lalam, it was about focusing on Earth energy. She felt the space in order to find the "not space," while Lalam had used rooting to feel the "not space" in order to find the space.

She closed her eyes and flew, laughing. She could feel all the space, and not space, around her. She could fly with her eyes closed knowing this. Trusting this space and not space. She could trust her Air energy; she knew what relaxing into trust felt like thanks to Ondelle. She couldn't wait to tell Lalam! Couldn't wait to—

Suddenly, there was no more not-space stretched before her. Only space.

And she opened her eyes.

Brigitta had never seen such an expanse of land before in her life. Not even The Shift was as vast as this. She hovered in the air at the very edge of a cliff on the eastern border of the Dark Forest. Stretching out for what looked like hundreds of moonbeats below her were a series of low dark hills to the north and south. To the east, the hills rolled like waves toward a steep mammoth mountain that twisted so high it disappeared into the clouds.

It was a bit windy, but nothing she couldn't navigate. Still, she secured herself between two rocks before peering over the side of the cliff, which dropped straight down. It was enough to make even the strongest flyer dizzy.

A scream sounded from the forest.

"Lalam! Glennis!" she called, cursing herself for getting distracted. "This way!"

A moment later and she could see them speeding toward her, the ridiculously persistent stomach beast flinging itself through the trees after them. She could see the panic in both of their faces as they realized the forest ended and the world was about to drop out from under them.

"Go up!" she hollered, and they obeyed.

Before the creature could follow Lalam and Glennis up into the trees, Brigitta called to it. "Right here, you big blob!" She waved her arms and whistled. "Yeah, I'm talking to you!"

As the beast threw its tentacles out, grabbing two of the final forest trees, Brigitta dropped down the other side of the cliff. The creature flung itself forward, stretching past Brigitta, before realizing it had run out of forest. One of its tentacles slipped from the trunk, flailing through the air, but the other tentacle held, and the creature began to spring back.

"Oh, no you don't!" called Brigitta, peering up over the cliff. She focused on the space around the tree where the creature had taken hold. Then she felt for the space inside the tree itself, the minuscule pockets of emptiness there. Calling on all moisture in the surrounding air, Brigitta attempted to replace all the tree space with water, and disappear the tree's not-space into it.

But she couldn't do it, it wasn't transforming, and the beast retracted back toward her. She leapt out of the way as the creature slammed against the side of the cliff and dangled there by its one tentacle. It released a thunderous roar and began pulling itself up the cliff face.

Brigitta frantically tried to reconnect to the tree space, but couldn't find it in her panic. Above her, Lalam called out, and Brigitta felt his rooting through the not-space of treeness until it broke apart. A blink later and he had transformed the chunk of tree held onto by the beast, and it dissolved to dust and scattered to the winds. The top of the tree fell away, the beast's tentacle slipped, and the creature tumbled down through the air to the foothills below.

Brigitta didn't watch it land.

Lalam and Glennis glided down to meet her.

"Is it gone?" Glennis asked, face stained with tears and dirt. She had a nasty gash on her forehead, another on her upper arm, and blood dotted her ripped tunic.

Brigitta nodded and collapsed to her knees.

"I couldn't do it." She looked up at Lalam. "How in the world am I going to transform anything to save Jarlath if I can't even turn something as easy as a tree into water?"

"You'll get it," he said, flitting to the edge of the cliff and peering down.

Glennis followed along and he held up his hand. "You might not want to see this. I can vouch that that thing isn't coming after us again."

They made camp just inside the trees and considered their journey to Sage Mountain. Over a modest fire, they fried some meaty mushrooms and it reminded Brigitta of the night she had met the Nhords. How she had immediately trusted them, as she had immediately trusted Narru.

Were their counterparts waiting for her over on Storlglenn and Carraiglenn? She pictured the images in the room above the dome at Croilus where they had found the Purview. One representative from each continent had surrounded the empty chair where the High Sage should have been.

Glennis popped a hot mushroom into her mouth and sucked her breath in to cool it off. "Why not just go right over the hills?" she asked after chewing and swallowing. "They looked deserted to me."

"Don't let that fool you," Brigitta said, squinting into the darkness. There was no moonslight due to the cloud covering, so she couldn't even see the hills below. It appeared as if they were sitting at the end of the world.

And then, something shimmered in the distance, lighting up one of the hills. They all perked up as a swarm of something fluttered around and over the hills, silently skimming the surface.

"What is it?" asked Glennis.

"Dunno," said Brigitta wistfully, "but it's beautiful."

"Don't let that fool you," joked Glennis nervously.

Entranced by the movement, they all stared as the lights skimmed and turned, fluttered and dove. The flock disappeared from view, and the faeries held their breaths, not sure what to do. Suddenly, the lights shot up over the cliff and descended on them. Brigitta, Lalam, and Glennis leapt up as the swarm of lights buzzed around, moving as a single force, and then landed in a tree, covering each branch so that the tree lit up like a star.

Brigitta stepped a little closer and examined the lights. Tiny, winged, silver and white striped beasts no bigger than her thumbnail fluttered there, causing the tree to vibrate and hum. She let out her breath and they scattered, splitting their little tribe in two before swerving back together again and dropping over the side of the cliff.

Spellbound into silence, Brigitta stared after the little beasts until her heart stopped pounding, and then turned back to the others. Each had shimmering tears streaming down their cheeks, liquid silver. She touched her own wet cheeks, pulling away dabs of lustrous tears. In spite of them, they all smiled and quietly got ready for bed.

They tucked themselves in for the night with an unspoken agreement that they would figure everything out in the morning. She could sense the other two lying on their backs, as she was, eyes open, gazing into the trees, wishing that the fluttering lights would return. Even if it were only in their dreams.

A thought struck Brigitta. If she and Lalam and Glennis could be exiled from their forest, so could other beasts. Maybe that brilliant flock was also trying to find its way back home.

"One day we will have to tell this story," she said. "The White Forest Chroniclers will want to record the great tale of the faeries who saved Faweh."

Lalam and Glennis laughed.

"I'm not so good at writing things down, or telling stories," said Brigitta, turning onto her side. "Glennis, I hereby dub you the Chronicler of Our Journey."

"What do I have to do?" she asked, twisting around to face Brigitta, eyes eager.

"Well, first thing is you have to name those beautiful lost lights."

"That's easy," she said. "They're called illuminoops."

"Illuminoops," Brigitta repeated.

"Illuminoops," Lalam agreed.

The night grew quiet around them but for the occasional grunt, howl, or croak. As the other two fell into a rhythmic breathing, Brigitta concentrated on connecting with her Narine energy, collapsing it inward as Ondelle had done to find her.

She just wanted to see that Jarlath was all right. That he was still alive even if there was no way to get a message to him. She thought about the illuminoops, how they appeared so spontaneous, yet connected. A thousand individuals making one remarkable whole. More than anything right then, she wanted Jarlath to see them. To see that there was still beauty left in the world.

Inward she went, sinking deeper and deeper. And just before falling asleep, Brigitta began to sense subtle movements around her. She was suddenly surrounded by hundreds of Ancients lying inside a large cavern with a clear, pointed ceiling out through which she could see the stars.

Chapter Thirteen

Lalam closed the door to Ondelle's personal spell chamber. He placed a tray bearing a teapot and two small cups in front of her on her work desk, stepped back, and waited for further instruction. The tea was Ondelle's personal recipe, a combination of lyllium, ceunias, and sharmock with a hint of firepepper to keep it warm, though not enough to burn.

She was fond of Lalam. If she had borne children, she would have been proud to call someone like him her own. He was loyal, discreet, respectful, and willing. And, most fortunately, he was bound to Earth, the final element left for Narine to gift, and the one with which she had the least experience.

She set aside the map of Foraglenn she had been studying and poured tea for them both. When the cups were filled, she stood from her chair, gesturing for him to pick up his cup. They began their private ritual at once, locking eyes, inhaling and exhaling from their cores, then taking sips of tea. The comfort and warmth of it flooded her bloodstream. A perfect brew; Lalam was a good student.

They set down their cups and Ondelle moved closer, placing her hands on either side of his face. He stared back, impassive, clearing his mind of all thought.

"Ready?" she asked.

He nodded.

They relaxed and fell deeper into each other's eyes as she misted out to him, the minuscule spaces of his body now familiar to her. She could occupy them without much effort, distributing the infinitesimal pieces of herself into the spaces of his being.

With each breath, she found her way further inside, and when she felt completely connected, in that same way she had been drawn into the Dragon's eyes, she breathed her Air energy into those spaces, so that his Earth and her Air were counterparts.

It was agonizing; it felt as if she were wrenching her very essence away. But she had learned to bear the ache.

She breathed again, closer and closer to losing her energy entirely to him, unsure if she could get it back if she did. And just as the last bit of Air was released, she immediately drew it all back, rehousing the energy within her own body and sealing it within.

They both staggered back, breaking their connection. He put a hand to his head, gasping.

"Well done," she murmured, picking up her cup of tea, hands trembling.

He steadied himself, stepped up to her desk for his own cup, and nodded. He sipped as she sipped, breathed as she breathed, until they were both calm again.

"How do you feel?" she asked.

"Tired," he said, "but less disoriented than before."

They finished their tea in silence and placed the cups back on the tray, which he picked up as he steeled himself to leave. When he reached for the door handle, he turned around.

"May I ask a question?"

She gestured for him to do so.

"After our sessions, I experience feelings that aren't my own,'" he confided. "Feelings that disappear with a night's sleep. Sometimes feelings for people I don't really know."

"That makes sense," replied Ondelle.

"Is there anything I should do about this?" he asked.

"Do what you are called to do," she said, turning back to the map on her desk. "Thank you, Lalam; you should rest now."

He left the room with the tray. Left Ondelle to contemplate her impending transformation. She had to get this right, she thought. Her plan had to be perfect. If Narine's four energies were not reunited with the last of the Ethereal energy, there would be no more Blue Spell. Ever.

The air was growing thinner the farther they flew across the foothills, which they had discovered, upon trying to land on one, were actually deep sand dunes. It was unbearably hot, and before mid-morning, they were drenched in sweat and flying at half speed in order to keep up their strength. There was nowhere to land in the sands, no water or shade for protection, so they kept moving, limiting their speech.

Each in deep concentration, they made good time despite the lack of air, until at the final hill before the great mountain, the air disappeared altogether.

Brigitta was in front when it happened. The temperature dropped, and she plummeted to the sand, sinking to her elbows and knees. She tried to take a breath, but there was nothing to breathe.

Lalam started to ask what was wrong, when he hit the pocket of deadness and fell. He gestured for Glennis to stop where she was, grabbed Brigitta's arm, and dragged her back toward where Glennis hovered, gasping at the thin air.

They crawled, hands and legs sinking into the sand, which threatened to pull them under if they did not keep moving. Unable to breathe, Brigitta's heart pounded, and her eyes stung, as she struggled to get back.

When they hit air again, a relief even as thin as it was, Glennis held out her hands and helped them to steady themselves enough to flutter back up.

After her wings were steady, Brigitta inhaled enough to speak. "Croilus got across." She inhaled again. "So can we."

Lalam inhaled. "There's nothing . . . to breathe." He looked worriedly at Glennis. If she collapsed from lack of air, there was no way either of them could carry her.

"He got across," Brigitta said.

She took a gulp from her canteen and then rummaged through her pack. She removed an extra tunic, one of her blankets, and a serving bowl and dropped them into the sand, where they immediately began to sink. Lalam followed suit, dropping a tunic, a bowl, and a firestone. Glennis pulled out a blanket, her bowl, and her ceremonial drum. She paused before dropping the drum.

"I'll make you a new one," said Lalam.

Glennis nodded and dropped it among their other possessions. Brigitta's load felt minimally lighter, but perhaps it was enough to get her across.

"I'll go first," she said. "I know air."

Before they could argue with her, she took the deepest breath she could manage and struck out across the no-air, allowing her breath to fill every part of her body, and releasing it in a slow and steady stream. Focus was key, she told herself as she trudged through the sand. She mind-misted out a wingslength in front of her, no more than that for fear of using her energy up, and tested the space. Nothing, nothing, nothing. Eventually, she was going to need to inhale again.

Her heart began to pound in her chest.

You're not going to make it.

Glennis certainly won't make this.

Turn around!

He was there, she reminded herself. Croilus was there on the mountain with the Ancients; she had seen it the night before. If he had gotten across, so could she.

Just when she thought her lungs would burst for lack of breath, she felt it. Her mind mist detected the other side of the nothing and she stretched out, falling forward into the sand. Mouth full of grit, she had no breath to spit it out, so she ignored the sand on her tongue and crept on. At least she could breathe again.

Then, there was solid ground beneath her hands.

She spat and wiped her mouth. It felt so good she laughed out loud. There was grass, too, she realized as she stood up and waved back at Lalam and Glennis.

They had made it to Sage Mountain.

Lalam sent Glennis along first, and through Brigitta's encouraging she managed to get most of the way across before Brigitta had to venture back into the no-air and haul her forward. Lalam made it the fastest, and after he arrived, the three of them smiled relief. They could do this. They looked up the steep mountain, so tall it cut through the clouds.

"We need to get above them," Brigitta said, pointing up. "That's where he'll be."

As the day passed into night they took shelter under some fallen boulders that reminded Brigitta of the rebels' Gathering Place in Noe. *Secret Palace,* Brigitta imagined Thistle whispering, and she smiled.

"Glennis," she called as she held the dustmist in place for Lalam to spread the firepepper protection, "what shall we name those despicable sand hills?"

"How about the 'Despicable Sand Hills'?" said Glennis, and Lalam laughed.

They finished their task and settled on a cold meal rather than risk a fire in case Croilus had a lookout. Still, it was chilly, so Lalam and Brigitta set to warming the remaining firestone and it created a small amount of heat around which they gathered. With their combined energies and talents, their spells were getting almost routine.

Or was it that she felt more connected to him since remembering his and Ondelle's private transformation practice? His hazel eyes gazed in question as she stared at him. She hadn't told him of the memory and was curious as to how much he knew. But she also felt it an invasion of privacy, and if there were anything he wanted her to know, he would tell her. It was enough that Ondelle had trusted him.

The anxiety of being so close to Croilus made for a fitful night, and morning found them approaching the climb silently, saving their strength for what lay ahead. The air was still too thin to fly well, but breathable, and the sun glared down on them as they made their way up the mountain. But the higher they climbed, the cooler it became, until the discomfort of the chill replaced the discomfort of the heat. Brigitta wasn't sure which she disliked more.

She was about to break the monotony of the climb with this pronouncement when she saw the first white flake. As they progressed, more and more white flakes fluttered about.

"It's called cloud ice," said Lalam, holding out his hand. A flake landed there and melted into his palm. "I've been told each piece is unique."

Brigitta tilted her head up to let some land on her face. Dancing flakes of frozen water. Miniature worlds.

"I like it," she said.

"It's going to get cold," Lalam responded. "Everyone bundle up."

Wrapping their treated blankets around themselves, they flew and climbed some more. The cloud ice turned dense and then disappeared into a fog so thick the faeries had to hold hands to keep track of each other. Their wings grew heavier and heavier until they could no longer use them at all. Clinging to the side of the mountain, they found a trail leading across and up. With no choice but to proceed, they continued, placing one foot in front of the other, Lalam in the lead.

A strange windy echo sounded through the fog, and Lalam stopped, holding Brigitta back with his hands. He scooted forward, and she and Glennis followed, until they could see movement within the fog. When they got a bit closer, the fog in front of them was sucked away, as if inhaled through a giant mouth.

"Rock dragons!" Brigitta called, slipping on the path beneath her and stumbling backward into Glennis.

Lalam pushed them both into the face of the mountain and they all froze, waiting.

The fog breathed back out again. And in again. And out again.

"I don't think it's any kind of dragon," said Lalam. "I think it's the mountain itself."

As they moved closer they discovered he was right. The path they were on led straight into a cave in the side of the mountain, which continued to breathe in and out, whirling the fog on its breath.

"This is it," said Brigitta.

She turned to look at her companions, fog breathing in and out around them. Lalam, sun-burned and sand-blown. Glennis, dirt-smudged and skin-scraped.

"Hey, listen," she began, putting on a brave face. "You don't have to come any farther. I'm the one responsible for this."

"What do you mean?" asked Lalam.

"What do you mean, what do I mean?"

"I mean why do you think you are personally responsible for any of this?" he asked. "Destiny was set in motion the moment the Ancients initiated their plan."

Brigitta chewed on this. Why did she feel responsible? Why did she feel guilty for Lalam and Glennis deciding to come along? She thought of how Lalam had allowed her to take the scepter the night of the Masquerade, and how Glennis had thrown herself through the protective field as the Impenetrable Spell was cast.

"What he's saying," said Glennis, interrupting her thoughts, "is that this is bigger than you and you're being selfish hogging all the glory."

"Well, that's another way of putting it," said Lalam with a smirk.

"It's our destiny, too," said Glennis, placing a hand on Brigitta's shoulder.

Brigitta stared into the mountain's mouth, inhaling and exhaling its fog as it had probably done for thousands of seasons.

"Yes," she finally said, "you're right."

Lalam lit a globelight and they stepped inside.

After they moved away from the mouth of the cave, the passageway curved up and around, spiraling like the Hive. It was dark at first, but then it grew lighter and lighter until they didn't need the globelight any longer.

Windows of ice appeared in the cavern through which they could view the outside world. The faeries curved one way and saw the vast ocean to the east. They curved the other way and all was whirling white below. After a while, instead of forming frozen windows, the ice held things trapped inside. Once-living things. Flowers and beasts of all shapes and sizes, preserved in the walls of the mountain.

They slowed to examine each one: an immense purple-lipped, white-petaled flower, something that looked like a miniature warwump, a flock of illuminoops—all frozen in place.

When they rounded the next curve, a large golden-maned creature stood in front of them on hooved feet. He was dressed in a black robe and had a wispy golden beard and piercing yellow eyes. Close to him stood a large white bird, tall as his shoulder, with the same piercing yellow eyes.

"Chakau'un," said Brigitta, recognizing the hooved

beast from the illustrations on the wall of the Purview room in Noe. "I remember . . . Ondelle's knowing . . ." She could see the Chakau'un relaxing around the Standing Stones with the Nhords and Ancients. They had been friends.

She placed her hand up against his cold prison. "He's from one of the five civilizations. Carraiglenn."

"When we arrive there," said Lalam, "we will let them know of this one."

Brigitta nodded, then shivered. "Let's keep moving."

The frozen creatures eventually disappeared, as did the icy windows to the world. They had to rely, once again, on the light from their globes. They resumed a steady, rhythmic pace as they climbed, silently, higher and higher, until Brigitta got the sensation that she had been climbing inside the mountain forever.

When an unmistakable voice shattered the silence, her blood turned colder than the air around her. She stopped dead in her tracks and looked intently at her companions.

Croilus, she mouthed, and their eyes widened.

All this time, all this way, all this imagining of how this encounter would go, and here it was in front of her. With every bit of energy she had, she slowed down her heart and mind. This was a place of clarity. She would find that clarity now.

She signaled to Lalam and pointed to her temple, holding his gaze and hoping he would understand. As she fell into his eyes, she summoned the connection Ondelle and he had shared, and she misted out to him, searching for those minuscule spaces the High Priestess had sought. His mind felt familiar. And comforting.

Can you hear me? she asked.

He smiled and nodded.

Glennis's lips trembled as she shifted her gaze back and forth between them. There was no way to explain to her what they had done, so she simply signaled for Glennis to stay behind them.

Slipping quietly up the passage, Brigitta in the lead, they curved one final time before the mountain opened up. She held out her arms and gestured not to make a sound.

The massive cavern before them grew narrower and narrower as it stretched up and up, the cap of it a coating of ice so sheer they could see the blue beyond it. At the very peak, the ice reversed direction and funneled all the way back down to the cavern floor. Drops of water slid down the stalactite, dripping off its point into a hole in the floor and disappearing without a sound.

Hundreds of Ancients huddled around the edges of the enormous space, Jarlath a spark of color among them, and Croilus circled the icicle, hand rubbing at his chin. He looked too sure of himself, Brigitta thought as he smiled. They were too late. But a moment later, he cringed and held his temples.

The knowing, it's not settled yet, Brigitta thought to Lalam in their mind-mist connection. *But what's he doing?*

Croilus kept circling the icy formation as he rubbed his temples. Whatever magic the stalactite held, whatever clarity he was searching for, he was obviously having difficulty making sense of it. It was not too late to stop him.

I'm not sure he even knows, Lalam thought back to Brigitta.

Glennis looked helplessly at the two of them, and

Brigitta felt sorry about her lack of mind-mist training, but there was nothing to be done about it now. Maybe they should just send Glennis back to the tunnel entrance before she got hurt.

Brigitta was about to ask Lalam what he thought about this when a pressure formed in her gut. Something was pulling at her insides. Something wanted her to move into the open cavern, and she was having trouble resisting the urge.

Oh, no . . . the dry coldness pricked at her skin. *What have I done?*

Lalam spun to face her, and she grabbed his arm, yanking him back into the tunnel. As they reached Glennis, Croilus let out an amused laugh, its echo bouncing off the cavern walls. They turned to run, but a host of Ancients blocked their path to the tunnel. All eyes were upon them, but the Ancients didn't make a move.

"You may as well show yourself, Brigitta of the White Forest," he shouted. "You've come this far."

The three faeries looked to each other in silent question.

"We are three to his one," Lalam whispered. "And his mind is not well."

"What other choice do we have?" whispered Brigitta.

They took a collective breath and moved into the room, spreading themselves out a bit to cover more space. Brigitta eased her way toward Jarlath.

Croilus's head spasmed as he opened his arms wide. "Welcome to my new palace. I am renaming it Croilus Peak. What do you think?"

"It's a bit cold," said Brigitta, eyeing the Ancients. They didn't appear to be doing much of anything, let alone following any sort of orders from Croilus.

Croilus held up his scepter with one hand and leaned over to touch the stalactite with the other, rubbing his palm across its slick surface. The icy windows above them vibrated with a low harmonious hum.

"Didn't you think I could see through you as you see through me?" laughed Croilus, removing his hand. "Narine's energy binds us together."

She had no answer for him and cursed her over-confidence. It was an obvious conclusion that no one, not even High Priest Fozk, had come to.

"I didn't realize you were that stupid," Croilus said with a snort. "I've seen it all, you know. Your Elders, your friends, your family. Your *forest*."

"Yeah?" she asked, trying to contain the tremor in her voice. "Too bad you can't get inside."

"Who says I can't?"

Croilus wrapped his hand around the end of the stalactite, and the icy windows above them shook once more. The sound of it vibrated deep inside her; it touched her core. It was something beyond any magic she had ever experienced. Something so ancient she didn't even know its name.

She really was an idiot. She had no idea how the magic of Sage Peak functioned, only that it was beyond her grasp. Perhaps Croilus could harness it to enter the White Forest or even break the Impenetrable Spell. He held up the scepter and Brigitta could both feel and see the energy of the stalactite channel through his hand, across his body, down his other arm, and into the scepter where it burst forth into the room.

The Ancients jerked alert, honing in on Brigitta, Lalam, and Glennis. The three faeries backed up and turned to flee, but it was too late, they were surrounded. Brigitta tried to mind-mist, empath, anything to see if she could connect with them using Narine's energy, but it was no use. The three of them were yanked away from each other and held apart.

Croilus faltered once again, pulling his hand away from the stalactite to his head, and the Ancients faltered, too. But he recovered quickly, too quickly for them to escape. With a sneer, he pointed the scepter at Brigitta, and Jarlath sprung forward. He landed in front of her, all trace of the old Jarlath gone, and held a sharp stone to her throat.

"Oh, I love it when friends become enemies," sang Croilus. "It reminds me of my own departure from Mabbe."

"Please, Jarlath," said Brigitta, looking as deeply into him as she could. "Please. You know me."

Focus on Croilus, she heard Lalam in her mind. *Keep him unsettled; he controls the rest.*

She turned toward Croilus as he approached. "I will enjoy ripping those Air and Water energies from you," he said.

"You mean Narine's Air and Water?"

His eyes flickered. "They are no longer hers!" he shouted, heading back for the stalactite.

He can't do it on his own, thought Brigitta to Lalam. *He needs the clarity from Sage Peak.*

Croilus hissed and Jarlath grabbed Brigitta by the shoulders.

"You can take them from me," said Brigitta as matter-of-factly as she could, "but it won't make any difference. It's too late."

The Ancients fumbled around her, and Jarlath loosened his grip. She strode toward Croilus as if she already had the upper hand.

"What do you mean?" demanded Croilus, removing his hand from the stalactite.

"Her Fire energy is gone. You can't generate any more Blue Spell."

"You lie! And after I take yours, I will find it." He pointed the scepter at her. "Imagine, with my Ancient warriors, I will be the most powerful faerie who has ever lived!"

"Ondelle destroyed Narine's Fire Energy when she died." She knocked his scepter out of her way. "Once you use your Blue Spell up, it's gone forever."

The Ancients stood down; Glennis and Lalam were released.

It's working, Lalam assured her from across the room. *He's losing his confidence.*

"No!" Croilus spun around, addressing the Ancients.

"They can't help you," Brigitta said. "They already gave their energies up to protect the White Forest."

He looked up at the stalactite in desperation.

"Good luck ruling Faweh from in here," she said sweetly, stepping closer.

His eyes bugged for a moment, then he grabbed his temples and released an anguished cry. While he was impaired, Brigitta reached for the stalactite. An icy shock shot from her hand to her heart, and she doubled over. Gritting her teeth, she looked up into the stalactite as if it were a living being. She imagined its spaces widening and its not-spaces melting into them. With a quick twist of her wrist, she broke off its tip.

The ceiling of ice cracked and rumbled above them.

"What have you done!" cried Croilus.

Before she could answer, pieces of ice started collapsing around them. With a roar, Croilus launched himself at Brigitta, struggling to get the stalactite tip back from her. She held it away from him as Lalam and Glennis pushed their way through the Ancients.

With a hand on his chest, she held him back while she gripped the icy staff, her warm fingers melting into it. But he was stronger than she. He reached past her and took hold of it, grinning his sickly grin. Brigitta grew weak and dizzy, her energies pulling at her insides from where her fingers gripped the ice below his.

Somehow, she realized, Croilus was using his own Narine energy to draw hers into the stalactite. Even that mere tip harnessed enough power from Sage Peak.

And she was holding it, too.

With a burst of clarity, she gripped the ice harder and locked eyes with Croilus. "Two can play that game," she growled, and dove into herself like plummeting off of Precipice Falls.

She retreated so far it felt like she had left the world. Then she was inside of the stalactite tip, swimming in the spaces between the not-spaces. Feeling, as Ondelle had, her own self divided up, distributing the infinitesimal pieces of herself within the ice.

And once she was there, she called to Narine's Earth energy to occupy the spaces with her.

To transform them.

Come with us, Brigitta said to it. *Come.*

And it did.

As Narine's Earth energy filled the spaces, Croilus's

grip loosened, and Brigitta slipped back into her own skin, sealing the Earth energy into the stalactite tip.

Croilus screamed in anguish as he lost his grip. The Ancients dropped to the ground around Glennis and Lalam, and Brigitta pushed Croilus out of the way.

The ceiling shuddered and a block of ice fell to the floor, cutting Brigitta off from the entrance to the cavern.

"Go on!" she shouted and waved for Lalam and Glennis to escape. She turned to find another way out, perhaps up. But as she was searching, Jarlath tackled her from the side. She screamed at him as they struggled. "Jarlath, it's me!"

A chunk fell from the ceiling onto Brigitta's head, knocking her down. Jarlath seized the opportunity to leap on top of her and get his hands around her neck.

She gripped the icicle as her breath was squeezed from her. She kicked and bucked, trying to get Jarlath off of her. With the last of her strength, she thrust the icicle into Jarlath's neck and held it there as he howled in pain.

Dizzy and gasping for air, she tried to conjure the transformation spell, feeling the empty spaces within Jarlath, and the not-spaces of Narine's energy. As she felt the space and not-space, Jarlath's emptiness began to fill.

But it was all too much. She couldn't maintain her concentration; she had so little strength left. She lost her grip on the stalactite tip and her hand fell to the ground. The last thing she saw before she blacked out was Jarlath's distressed expression as blood-stained water seeped from the icicle's wound in his neck.

Chapter Fourteen

Ondelle was weak. She had never felt so weak in all her life. Weak and half missing. What was happening?

Oh, yes, she was dying.

She opened her eyelids, heavy as they were. Gola, the old Drutan, her trusted friend, stood in front of her with a pair of tired Eyes perched on her shoulder.

Ondelle placed a hand on her barky arm. "We are near our departure."

"Yes."

She summoned what was left of her energy and gripped her friend. "I need you to do something as I go," she whispered hoarsely. "It will be our final task."

Ondelle paused to cough and Gola waited until she could breathe again. She motioned for something to drink and the Drutan placed her knotty hand behind Ondelle's neck, lifted her forward, and put a leafed cup to her mouth.

"My Fire," she said after her parchedness had subsided. "Narine's Fire," she continued as Gola eased her back down to the pillow. "You must keep it safe."

Without question, the old Drutan nodded. "How shall I keep it?"

Ondelle closed her eyes again. "I need something non-living. Porous. Not a spell seed."

Immediately, Gola lifted her moonstones from beneath

her tunic and gazed upon them through the Eyes. "One last service to the faeries?" she asked them.

She lifted the cord upon which they hung over her head and untied the knot, slipping the end moonstone from the strap and placing it on the bedside table. She hung the four remaining moonstones on her mantel.

Ondelle opened her eyes, heaved herself onto her side, and managed the smallest of smiles.

"Of course," she said as Gola returned to her bedside and held up the stone.

Ondelle gazed at it, preparing it as she prepared herself. She dove inside it and discovered its spaces so welcoming it was tempting to release her Fire into it right then and there. But there were good-byes to make, and she did not want to leave her journey incomplete. Instead, she focused on burnishing its pores with gentle tongues of Fire energy. The stone slowly transformed, as if taking a long breath, opening itself up to receive.

A knock at the door pulled her from her trance, and she fell back onto the pillow.

"May we come in?" called Dervia from outside.

"After it is done, hide it within you," Ondelle whispered as Gola pocketed the stone. "No one must know. For Brigitta's protection. She and it will find each other when they are ready."

"Brigitta!" Lalam cried, startling her awake. Chunks of ice surrounded them and more plummeted from the walls of the cavern.

"Jarlath!" she cried, sitting up, dizzy and sore, her wing

paining.

"We've got him." Lalam helped her to her feet. "Come on."

They stumbled over and around the fallen sheets of ice as the cavern continued to shake. Ahead of them, just inside the mouth of the tunnel, Glennis dragged Jarlath on a blanket. She stopped, her face pooled in sweat.

Brigitta dropped to her knees in front of Jarlath and placed her hand against his cheek. Narine's energy was there; she could feel it coursing through him. Her body began to heave, sobs of joy.

"We left the icicle tip in his neck," said Lalam, pointing to the thick bandage around it. "We didn't know what would happen if we removed it."

"What of Croilus?" asked Brigitta, looking around. "And all the Ancients?"

"They disappeared," said Lalam, picking up the other side of the blanket.

"Disappeared?" asked Brigitta as she stood up again.

"Through the space under the stalactite."

"And Lalam held your spell in place!" added Glennis as they sped through the passageway.

"You made it so easy," he said, smiling down at her. "Ondelle would be proud."

Although Brigitta was relieved they had retaken Narine's Earth energy, it left her no way to find Croilus, she thought as they descended the mountain. She wondered what would befall the Watcher. He couldn't control the Ancients forever with what was left of the scepter's Blue

Spell. And without Narine's energies, he couldn't generate any more.

Narine's energies.

All that remained was her Fire. And thanks to Gola and Ondelle, the wisest beings Brigitta had ever known, it was now safely hidden inside the Impenetrable Spell. Ondelle had been right to keep it safe until it was time. Until Brigitta, and the rest of Faweh, was ready.

Perhaps all there was to do then was to ignite the remaining Purviews.

The Purviews. She looked at her companions as they dragged Jarlath along the path and thought about the four rings in the pouch around her belt. She had not recovered the scepter. She did not have enough rings to get everyone through.

First things first. She looked down on Jarlath's pale face. One thing at a time.

After a night at the base of the northern side of Sage Peak, Narine's Earth energy had still not settled in Jarlath. It exhausted Brigitta with its restlessness. In such proximity, she was constantly drawn to the energy, a missing piece of herself. But it also felt like an invasion of Jarlath's privacy when she allowed herself to be drawn in.

Instead, she concentrated on simply keeping him alive. The cold and the loss of blood were making it difficult for him to heal. The lack of food and water didn't help, and who knew if Croilus's spells would have a lasting effect on him. Brigitta dripped water on his lips and rubbed his throat, hoping she could coax him into drinking it. Food was out of the question.

They traveled slowly over the course of the next sun, northeast toward Icecap Forest, with Jarlath wrapped in blankets held between two of them at a time. The sand hills were petrified on this side of the mountain, and the group traveled cautiously over the coarse ground. They carried Jarlath in short shifts, took a little food and drink, and numbed their minds to anything beyond their immediate task.

That night, by the fire in a cave, Brigitta confessed her fears to Glennis and Lalam. "If he dies, it's my fault." She hadn't cried in many moonbeats. She was beyond tears.

"If he dies," said Lalam, "it is Croilus's doing."

"It was my idea to steal Fozk's scepter and leave the White Forest."

"And where would he be now if you had left him in Noe?"

Brigitta put her head in her hands.

"There is no moving backward."

"Ondelle used to say something similar," said Brigitta.

Glennis moved beside her and put her arm around her. "He won't die," she said.

Brigitta looked into Glennis's gold-flecked eyes and realized it had been a long time since she had been annoyed with her.

"I'm sorry about the mosspatch," said Brigitta.

Glennis shrugged. "I deserved it. I would have mosspatched me, too."

That night, Brigitta dreamt of the illuminoops. She dreamt she was with Jarlath in the lyllium field as the bright little flock flew back and forth, circling the two moons.

He turned to Brigitta. "Thank you."

"For what?" she asked, but he just smiled and turned back to the tiny silver and white striped lights.

She moved closer to him, taking his arm in hers, and together they followed the illuminoops as they danced across the sky.

"Brigitta," said Jarlath hoarsely.

As she turned to face him, the world was swept away. She woke up to the sound of him coughing.

"Jarlath!" she whispered fiercely, tumbling from her blanket and rushing to his side. She fell into him and held him tightly, crying and crying until she realized he was convulsing. "Oh, Great Moon, I'm so sorry."

She pulled away, and he coughed a few more times and then grinned. "Always trying to kill me, aren't you?"

She fetched a cup of water and handed it to him, but he was too weak to hold himself up and drink, so she propped her pack behind him and led the cup to his lips. He grabbed her by the wrist and looked intently at her, the deep, deep blue of his eyes calling. Narine's energy was strong between them. He felt it, too, she could tell.

"Thank you," he said, just like in her dream.

The energy continued to flow between them. It was almost like looking into herself.

"Uh, Brigitta," said Jarlath, "this is kind of weird."

"Yeah."

He let go of her wrist and they both laughed nervously.

"You'll get used to it," she said, busying herself finding him something to eat. "Having an energy bound to you, I mean."

He held up his hands and examined them, as if they would look different somehow.

She fed him and told him of their adventures, he doubting some of the heroics, until the morning light came and Lalam and Glennis awoke. Breakfast was a celebration.

They could move faster across the foothills, but Jarlath still required many breaks. He would also stop for no reason at all, it seemed, as he searched for something inside himself that he wasn't ready to share. Brigitta did her best to be patient with him. After all, he had been more than patient with her over the past season.

She hung back, not just to give him his space, but because the closeness of the energy was too much for her. She also knew that the Earth energy Jarlath had been given was not exactly the long-lost kin he had been waiting for but didn't know it. It was probably more like a brother he never knew he had and didn't quite trust.

It was odd that Brigitta never would have pegged Jarlath for an Earth Faerie, but there was a certain suitedness about it. He was more contemplative than she remembered, his body more solid. And, now that she thought about it, he had spent countless quiet hours with Gola studying herbal arts.

Lalam started teaching him what it meant to be an Earth Faerie, but also said it would be for Jarlath to figure out. There was no way to explain how each energy was bound to any other faerie.

"It would be like you trying to experience what it's like to be me," he said. "Or I you."

After one particularly long break, Jarlath returned from a meditation with a smile on his face. "I feel stronger today," he said. "More settled."

He still wore the bloody bandage on his neck, but he didn't seem to be in any pain. The color had certainly returned to his skin, and his eyes sparkled as he took in the view. The solid dunes had broken up into a chunky scree that led all the way down to the forest below.

"This reminds me of the petrified bowl in Noe," said Brigitta as she kicked at the ground, "this rocky stuff."

"Yeah," Jarlath said, then got that contemplative look on his face again. "But I can also remember it differently."

"What do you mean?" asked Glennis as she dug out some cookware and herbs.

"I mean," he said, "I can remember it as Narine remembered it."

"What?" Brigitta exclaimed, grabbing his arm, ignoring the pulse of energy between them. "How?"

"Narine's energy, I guess," he said. "Pieces of her memories are landing."

"Wait, do you think you received any of her knowing through the transformation?" Brigitta asked.

"Maybe," said Jarlath. "It was all mixed up inside of Croilus, her energy and her knowing." Jarlath turned to them and pulled the bandage from his neck. He wet the injury with his canteen water and wiped the dried blood away. Underneath was a star-shaped scar.

Brigitta reached up and touched the scar in awe, and Jarlath shivered. "The icicle worked kind of like a frore dagger," she said. "Only . . . prettier."

"I don't know how much of her memories I've got," he said, fingering the mark himself, "but they're filling me up."

"That will come in handy," said Lalam. He glanced across the scree to the horizon, and the ocean that waited for them there. "We're going to need all the help we can get."

Brigitta let go of Jarlath's arm. If he had enough of Narine's memories inside of him, surely they could figure out how to get through the Purviews, balance Faweh, and get home. Everyone must have been thinking the same thing, as they all suddenly smiled and a lightness of spirit settled on the group.

Jarlath's eyes twinkled even more and the familiar smirk returned to his lips. "And, boy, have I got things to tell you."

Lalam started a fire, and they huddled close as the sun descended and the two moons perched themselves above the forest. After they had eaten, and the gundlebean stew had begun to digest, Brigitta, Lalam, and Glennis sat expectantly, all eyes on Jarlath.

"It might take a while," he warned, poking at the fire with a stick.

"We've got time," Brigitta replied, pulling a blanket around her shoulders, and settling in for the night.

Lexicon

Blood Seed

The narratives around the Blood Seed are as old as the **Saari** civilization. They believe it is the heart of their land, and that it pumps energy through its roots. It was a very big deal when, thousands of seasons ago, they decided to place the Purview, a gift from the Ancient Faeries of Noe, on their sacred Blood Seed mound, a fertile hill made almost entirely of roots. They thought the Blood Seed energy would both feed the Purview and prevent anything harmful from coming through.

Over the seasons, the stories have reshaped themselves to incorporate the Purview as part of the Seed. It is said the heart has been sick ever since the Great World Cry. To honor the mother Blood Seed, each floating island of the new civilization carries a small red stone buried in its center. It is believed when Faweh is balanced again, these stones will grow roots and anchor the islands. (see also **Pariglenn** and **Flota of the Saari**)

blossom bells

Hanging chimes, shaped like flower buds, that can either be struck lightly for a quick, clear note or rubbed with a finger for a longer, deeper one. Striking different parts of the "bud" elicits a different sound, so there are many combinations of notes that can be played even on a small set of blossom bells.

Brigitta "of the White Forest" / "of Tiragarrow"

Faeries are generally called by their given name and village-nest of birth. Sometimes faeries change this reference if they have lived in a different village-nest for a long time, or even if they simply feel a kinship to an area. If they are referred to as "of the White Forest," as an Elder might be, it is to indicate they are in service to the whole forest. When Brigitta was called "Brigitta of the White Forest" by Fozk of Fhorsa, it was his way of showing respect and acknowledging her as part of the Center Realm community.

broodnut
Its "shell" is soft and thin, so that when carved into, the red meat of it is exposed. Named "broodnut" because love-sick faeries use it to carve messages to their heartthrobs. Also sometimes used in faerie games because it is light and soft. The meat of it is plain, but when cooked and spiced makes a great party snack. Broodnut trees grow best in the forest between the Earth and Water Realms near Green Lake.

bubblebug
Entertaining little winged bugs that skitter themselves across the top of still water and call to each other by popping the bubbles they create. They blow into the wetness with their long noses, gather up a stock of bubbles, dance around them with their tiny legs, popping as they go. Kids love to watch them and listen to them, but they are generally too fast to catch.

cloud ice
What we call snowflakes.

dusk owl
The largest bird in the White Forest, although there are only a few dozen in existence. Its coloring is so like the light at dusk, that no matter what the season, for a brief moment in time each day, the owl is completely camouflaged to the world. Its cry is a high-pitched breathy hoot. The White Forest sprites have been known to fly with the dusk owls that frequent their uul tree.

dustmist

A diverse and useful tool (created most often by a talented Air Faerie) used to spread spells, aromas, sounds, or any other light item through the air or to make it stick or stay in one place. Can also be used to conceal things. With a great deal of practice, one can learn to send messages using dustmist. Mothers can use it leave lullabies in the air above their babies. Festival grounds can be sprinkled with dustmist to keep sparkles or musical notes in the air.

Eternal Dragon (Tzajeek)

Most faeries in the White Forest only think of Tzajeek as a mythical creature from ancient times. In reality, the **Eternal Dragon** is as old as Faweh itself. A winged sea-serpent with the ability to absorb, transform, and redistribute elements, Tzajeek is the only one of its kind. Its origin is unknown.

Tzajeek is neither good nor evil; It simply is. It originally fed on and redistributed the fifth element (as Blue Spell), visiting the Ancients through Lake Indago each season. After the Great World Cry, when the Lake disappeared and the Dragon's cycle disturbed, the Ancients sacrificed their basic elements to the lesser faeries and their fifth elements to the Dragon, which became a vessel to deliver Blue Spell to the White Forest faeries. It was a way to satiate the Dragon as well as distribute such power slowly and methodically over time. Eventually, the fifth element, and therefore Blue Spell, was bound to run out. The Ancients trusted the world would be rebalanced by then, and they would be properly dispersed.

firepepper

A Fire Faerie specialty. Fine, treated granules used to make something hot to touch. Firepepper can really burn, so it's not often used full-strength. More generally it is diluted and used in anything you'd want warm, like a compress, blanket, or water to bathe in. Some Master Gardeners use it to keep little beasties from getting into their gardens. Could be used to play practical jokes, but that would be mean.

'Flota of the Saari

After the Great World Cry wreaked elemental chaos all over Faweh, the **Saari** of **Pariglenn** were forced to relocate to the water due to the land's over-fertility. They constructed island villages out of "planxis" (a combination of seaweed, earth, and salts), ever-changing with the tides, in order to avoid the strangling overgrowth. **(See also Saari)**

founding / ersafounding / erdafounding

Foundings are what the Saari call their parents, and ersafoundings and erdafoundings are what they call their foundings' foundings, meaning their grandmothers and grandfathers. The term "founding" is used because the Saari females all give birth at the same time annually in communal ponds to tadpole-like beings. When the babies are ready for the world, they simply crawl out of the pond and "find" an adult Saarin to care for them. There is no way to tell if the Saarin they find is actually a biological parent, but that doesn't seem to matter to them.

frore dagger

An ice-cold dagger that immediately heals the cut it makes. Originally used by the Ancients on anything that needed to be trimmed. For instance, if a tree had a sick limb, it could be cut off with a frore dagger and not leave a wound. A frore dagger can still be fatal if it strikes the right organs, as when Queen Mabbe used one on High Priestess Ondelle in Noe.

hands (as in "12 hands deep")

Faeries literally use the width of their hands to measure things, though the proper measurement of a "hand" is about two ½ inches. If you wanted to call someone small you might say, "You couldn't even measure with her!"

illuminoops

When Glennis named the fluttery flock of bright little silver and white creatures, she wasn't too far off. To the Ancient faeries, they were known as *luminamins*, but that name is long forgotten. They only live on Foraglenn, but their habitat was destroyed in the Great World Cry. The flock Brigitta and her friends witness is a collection of lost luminamins, continually searching for others like themselves to lead them home. Their deep longing for a place to call home can bring even the grouchiest of beasts to silver-hued tears.

lingomana

One of the many fantastic fruits available on Pariglenn, with a crisp, tangy outer peel and a sweet pulpy inside. Fruits and tubers are the only things the Saari eat from the mainland, because they are easily accessible from the shore. They simply swim up and harvest them. Their floating islands aren't very fertile, but the Saari are able to gather sea plants, extract salt from the water, and collect spices from the sea life. The Saari are vegetarians.

Lodge of Eastern Months

Like the faeries have their "season cycles" and the Nhords have their "sand cycles," the Saari have their directional cycle: Northern, Southern, Western, and Eastern. They are tremendous gatherers. Of all the old civilizations, they were the first to explore the other continents because of this gathering instinct. They would make great pilgrimages to the other continents for seasonal items, often trading with the inhabitants. When they traveled east, they took lodging on Foraglenn at Icecap Forest. When they went west, they might stay on Storlglenn or Carraiglenn. North was Araglenn and south was the Valley of Noe. After the Great World Cry, the ocean was far too rough for travel, and the sea life too vicious, so the lodges were abandoned.

Masquerade / Festival of the Moons

The Masquerade, which takes place during the Festival of Moons, is exactly that, a costumed dance. But as Brigitta said, historically there's more to it. When the faeries originally came to the White Forest, all of their celebrations held more symbolism, because they were celebrating in gratitude for the generosity of the Ancients, for the protection of the forest, and for having each other when the rest of the world had lost so many. The fact that they had reasonable seasons that transitioned into each other because of the protection of the forest, was indeed something to celebrate. But as with the rest of the holidays, the celebration continues out of habit, even if the original meaning behind it has been forgotten.

moonbeat moths

An invention of Brigitta's Poppa. The moths glow and change color every moonbeat (which is about 15 minutes), so not only are they pretty, you can keep track of time with them. At night, at least. They don't glow in the daytime.

"mind body" speaking

What the Saari have developed over time is similar to faerie empathing. The Saari didn't always communicate this way, although they have always had some empathic abilities, which were mostly used for foundings to keep track of their young. After the Great World Cry, every beast had to adapt to new environments. The Saari grew ever more suited to life in the ocean, and "mind body" speaking is part of this evolution.

Moonsrise Ridge

Located in the northwestern part of the White Forest, Moonsrise Ridge is the highest land form in the faerie realm. It is a crescent-shaped ridge, rising like a scree-filled wave from the west and dropping into a sheer cliff face. The ends of the crescent rise from the forest floor so gradually one could easily walk up the ridge.

mossleaf patch
Basically a faerie bandage. The size of the leaf is the size of the bandage. One side has a treated moss that not only makes it stick to the skin, but speeds the healing as well. The treatment is harmless when placed on non-wounded skin.

oddtwins
These creatures, who are a phenomenon of the elemental chaos, did not exist before the Great World Cry. Brigitta is the first one to encounter them who actually has the ability to name them, so we'll call them oddtwins. They are not exactly real, but not exactly imaginary either. They are manifestations of projected energy. This chaotic energy creates from any consciousness it comes in contact with. Brigitta uses this energy, without exactly knowing how, to create the wind-winder for her escape.

Pariglenn (and the continents of Faweh)
The Saari's floating islands are located in a large bay off the northeast coast of Pariglenn, west of **Foraglenn** (where Brigitta lives). Pariglenn is the smallest continent on Faweh. The Saari were its major civilization before the Great World Cry made the land too fertile for them to inhabit. If one could spend some time there without becoming rooted to it, they would discover a tremendous diversity of flora and quick moving fauna. Faweh's three remaining continents are **Araglenn** (where the Nhords are from), **Carraiglenn**, and **Storlglenn**.

pebblenotes (see also song flight)
Small stones that vibrate with sound. They can be used for all kinds of things, from scoring original music to teaching songs to young faeries. They are spellcast to ring with a note fed to it either via voice or instrument, then suspended in the

air and directed into song. (see also **song flight**)

poisondarters

Say you took an ant and multiplied its size several times. Then you added long, coarse, dark hairs and a pincher mouth that could slice through tree bark. Oh, and a deadly stinger on its rear end. That would be a poisondarter. Luckily, there are only a dozen or so nests of them on the entire continent of Foraglenn, as they too often fight amongst themselves and the fights result in less poisondarters. Also, they are not really hunters and do not stray far from their nests. They simply wait for other beasts to accidentally fly or crawl by. They also like to steal things from birds to line their own nests.

rainbow lizards

So called for their colorful stripes, which run in rings down the length of their body, including across their tongues. Faerie children love to catch them because when provoked they will spit different colors. Faerie parents hate them because the colored spit can stain. Artists have used rainbow lizard spittle for festive projects, though it's a tough material to work with. The colors don't mix well and it can be a bit sticky. Plus, who wants a breath lantern decorated with lizard spit?

rooting

As with mind-misting and empathing and transformation, there is a basic concept to rooting, but how it is applied is personal and each faerie finds his or her own rooting process. It's a technique used more often by Earth Faeries and involves stretching one's thoughts out and around matter like very thin roots (vein-like, really). From there, faeries can detect the attributes of the matter, its weak points, its density, how much water it could hold, etc. Rooting may also be used as the first step in transformation.

Sage Peak

As with most significant locales on Foraglenn (the Standing Stones, Dead Mountain, etc), before the Great World Cry, Sage Peak served a much different purpose. Its substantial height, funnel shape, and location near the heart of the continent produced a certain resonance found nowhere else in the world. Up there, the mind became so clear that a visitor could examine each of her thoughts like a physical entity, could even remove the thought from her head to contemplate it from all angles. But seeing one's own thoughts can be immensely disturbing, so only those who could deal with that sort of clarity would make the journey. In particular, new Sages to the World Council would visit before taking their posts.

The mountain rises steeply until it comes to a point and then turns in on itself to form an icy stalactite, which has been around for as long as the mountain. In the past, the rhythmic dripping was used for meditation. After the GWC, the clarity hid away in the stalactite, forming a very powerful magical hold on the peak itself.

Saari (singular Saarin)

The Saari of Pariglenn developed as one of the five major civilizations of Faweh, and they were the first to join the Ancients of Noe in creating the World Council of Sages. Next to the Ancient Faeries, they were the most industrious society at the time of the Great World Cry. Before the GWC, they even had several ships, being master navigators, gatherers, and traders (they preferred sailing the oceans to using the Purview).

After the disruption of the elements, however, when they were forced to move off the coast of Pariglenn to their mobile islands, they gave up world exploration. Over time, their physical features adjusted to ocean life: their fingers and toes grew webbed, their skin water-proof and luminescent, and their language transformed into telepathic "**mind body speaking**." **(See also Flota of the Saari)**

Singing Caves

There are plenty of interesting places to visit in the White Forest, and each elemental realm contains unique features. In the northeast corner of the Earth Realm, for instance, lies a particular patch of rocky land so perfectly suited to playing with the breezes that gaping holes in the earth can swallow the air and blow it back out, forming soft low notes. Each cavern emits a different sound, and it often seems like the caves actually know how to sing in harmony with each other. A lovely spot for a stroll at night.

song flight

A special kind of song that is directed while suspended in the air, usually using pebblenotes, but one could also use sound bubbles or marbles or any other kind of note that can be hung in the air. **(see also pebblenotes)**

smelting stones

Brigitta gets a few lessons in "smelting" by Hammus and brings a smelting stone with her on her journey to Sage Peak. Smelting is heating something up to extract parts of it that can be used in various capacities: healing potions, food preparation, clothing, arts and crafts, etc.

Standing Stones

As Brigitta pointed out to Ondelle while they were in Noe, the Ancients didn't have very creative names for places, and they tended to simply name things for what they were (their logic being that all beasts would then understand to what it was they were referring). So, the standing stones found by Brigitta and Jarlath were indeed called the Standing Stones. And they weren't so much a sacred place as a place of leisure. There were so many stones upon the plateau, each with slightly different characteristics, that one could find the perfect combination of sun, shadow, temperature, sound, or soundlessness to match one's mood. One could sunbathe, read, meditate, practice a song in a lovely echoing spot, or simply take a nap.

"stomach beast"
Just like the oddtwins, the strange stomach beast that Lalam, Brigitta, and Glennis encounter in the forest is simply an anomaly. No one will probably ever know how it came to be, other than a product of the Great World Cry's elemental chaos. It is one of a kind, eats pretty much anything, and has the ability to entice any living creature to come to it. It is also exceedingly elastic.

thought-looping
Definitely an advanced technique, as with anything that manipulates thoughts. Minds are messy places and no two are alike. Generally, you take something someone said or thought and loop it around in order to give them a singular focus. You can loop one or more being's thoughts, but the more minds involved, the harder it is to make it stick. If someone said, "Good-bye," and another someone said, "See you tomorrow," you could fix that loop because it's logical. Thought-loops eventually slip away as other thoughts sneak in. Manipulating thoughts so that someone actually performs an action is much more difficult, especially if that action is counter to their nature. As a meditative practice, one could loop her own thoughts.

whisper light (Narine's)
It is true that whisper lights in general are just playful (or pesky) little plants that grow in fields, like the one outside of Gola's tree-home in the Dark Forest, and whisper the nonsense of subconscious thoughts to anyone nearby. These

whisper lights were discovered by Gola and Narine when they were hiding out during the Great World Cry. Narine later made a pact with Gola, and hid "knowings" inside of whisper lights to be released to each continent when the time was right, so that the five civilizations would seek each other out through the Purviews.

wind-winder

Not all faeries are strong flyers. Air Faeries tend to be the fastest and most dynamic flyers, while Earth Faeries are slower, but steady. Wings can also be broken, torn, or injured and sometimes never completely repaired. The wind-winder was invented by an Air Faerie Inventor named Holt, and it took him a very long time to figure it out. The faerie using it must be adept at conjuring pockets of air in order to use it. Once each hole in the net-like structure is filled, the faerie is completely buoyant, growing less so as each air pocket ruptures. The better the faerie at conjuring the pockets of air, the more stable the wind-winder.

Coming Summer 2015
Faerie Tales from the White Forest
Book Four

The story that started it all . . .

Narine of Noe

While on a visit to Dragon Mountain, young Narine, daughter to the High Sage of Noe, witnesses the lonely miracle of a Drutan's birth. Called back home from her retreat due to political tensions in Noe, Narine spends her days distracted and haunted by her memory of the Drutan's cries.

Soon after her return home, though, Narine witnesses the four World Sages casting bad magic, and her father is caught in the crossfire. All of Faweh turns to elemental chaos, and the Ancients must decide quickly how to save their lesser faerie kin from a world gone mad.

An elaborate plan is hatched, and Narine's place in the plan is instrumental. But, she risks it all to travel back to Dragon Mountain in order to rescue the lonely newborn Drutan left to the elements that have grown unruly after this Great World Cry.

Award-winning author, spokenword artist, and educator Danika Dinsmore teaches creative writing and world building to writers of all ages. When not in British Columbia with her husband and their big-boned feline, Freddy Suave, she takes her Imaginary Worlds program on the road to schools, conferences, and festivals across North America.

Made in the USA
Charleston, SC
01 May 2016